These stories are note-perfect, pl
reverberates for days.
—Holly Walker, *Spinoff Book of th*

This is a stunning, feral, gut-pun
depicts a real New Zealand, an ign
from these stories, but that New Zealand would still be there. It's white,
working-class, bogan. The characters aren't ciphers or allegories about sex or
violence; they're real and unexpected. Sometimes, the stories hurt too much to
contemplate, but that's why we ignore them in real life, too.
—Charlotte Graham, *New Zealand Books*

The language sparked like a cut power line. I was shocked awake every time I
picked this book up . . . ended up wide-eyed, brain buzzing, unable to sleep. Go
and get it, and tell your all friends to do the same.
—Grant Smithies, *Sunday Star-Times*

Slaughter's cumulative descriptions are intoxicating. These stories are self-
assured, forceful and filled with close observation—and yes, they do often
punch you in the face.
—Nicholas Reid, *Listener*

Slaughter's sentences are resplendent with detail that punches out physical
settings and human descriptions that shine so bright it almost hurts. She writes
with the ear of a poet because each sentence is like a musical phrase in a sonata.
Few things make us feel life like this. Slaughter has delivered a masterpiece.
—Paula Green, *Sunday Star-Times*

Slaughter's short stories are vivid, truthful, and incisive. They're a feast for
the senses. Her syntax is a sword; her choice of words a magic wand. In sum,
Slaughter has rejuvenated the short story with poetic finesse.
—Azariah Alfante, *Booksellers New Zealand*

This is a remarkably assured book. Her language beguiles and delights.
This quality of writing is adventurous, challenging, not at all about passive
entertainment. Such fresh magic permeates every paragraph.
—Raewyn Alexander, *Landfall*

The intensity Slaughter achieves in her writing and the concentration of apt
description turns the prose at times in to poetry. Every word is weighed and
the balance comes out right.
—Peter Dornauf, *Nexus*

Taste and enjoy, despite being hungry for more because they are so gripping, so
good. They are gifts that keep giving! It is a remarkable book.
—Elizabeth Coleman, *Takahe*

deleted scenes for lovers

tracey slaughter

Victoria University Press

TE WHARE WĀNANGA O TE ŪPOKO O TE IKA A MĀUI

VICTORIA
UNIVERSITY OF WELLINGTON

VICTORIA UNIVERSITY PRESS
Victoria University of Wellington
PO Box 600 Wellington
vup.victoria.ac.nz

First published 2016
Reprinted 2016

National Library of New Zealand Cataloguing-in-Publication Data

Slaughter, Tracey.
Deleted scenes for lovers / Tracey Slaughter.
ISBN 978-1-77656-058-5
I. Title.
NZ823.3—dc 23

Published with the support of a grant from

creative
nz
ARTS COUNCIL OF NEW ZEALAND *TOI AOTEAROA*

Printed by Ligare, Auckland

for my family,
Paul,
Liam & Joel

&

with deepest thanks
to Catherine & Jack

contents

note left on a window

I had sex with the hitchhiker down on the beach, because I couldn't bear to take him into the caravan. By that stage I knew he wasn't the dangerous type, but I also knew a part of me had hoped that he was. He was just dirty in that arty way: I'd pulled up expecting something criminal, but I'd got a thinker, equally unclean but without the cruel streak. I should have guessed from the image of Che Guevara on his op-shop shirt, the sideways visionary stare unclouded by the grease. I might have wanted to take someone derelict, someone mean to the caravan, a guy who'd fill its room with smoke and the mechanical racket of a sudden hard fuck, someone prone to smashing up things that deserved it the way that caravan did. But I couldn't have stood gentleness there, or thought. What I had wanted was a kind of assault: what I got was method, tenderness. It was bad enough down on the beach, his stroking approach to the places I wanted cracked open, his fingers exploratory, creeping slowly in and out of me as if following some kind of protocol. I could hardly stand such an analytical fuck: under his ribs and hips the sadness almost rolled up from me, almost got loose from my eyelids. He murmured to me, proposals of touch, of entry: with knuckles and heels I clawed up and rammed him in. His hair fell forwards and picked up sand and weed in pods and husks and star shapes. I stared at that, and that was my mistake. His eyes were a forgery of Michael's, and so, I admit, for a while I clutched his face and the collarbone that spanned out into the angle of shadow that Michael's also sharpened to. The hitchhiker might as well have been Michael's twin.

The one good thing was his philosophy had the same effect as violence: he was too absorbed to pause and ask about a condom.

When I got inside the caravan, later, I remembered a movie where a suicide note was left on a window. Someone breathed all over the glass in the dead one's room and there it was; a reason, a clue. Perhaps I had even watched that movie with Michael's warm head dumped, dozing, on my legs, the shaved hardness of his skull bedded back on my stomach. But I couldn't be sure I had. And that thought—that I could not be certain of the place of his head, its dark mongrel cut, the dust that turned yellow and resinous along the curves of his ear, which I'd clean with my fingernail, poking him, teasing, *Scruffy bugger, for a spunky bastard you're a right grot*—the thought that I couldn't remember exactly where his body was when I watched that film, made me push round the caravan even more quickly, huffing on its windows until the whole metal hut sang and shivered on its chocks and I stood, clinging in the aisle in the middle, waiting for my ribs to remember the right way to breathe. I held on to the hooks on the row of skinny cupboards along the cabin and I thought of how he would've been too tall to stand up in here, thought of the black stubble over his skull pushed up against this squeaky ceiling, and slid my hands across it as if some grit might have stuck along there like braille. And I thought of the thumb-sized dent behind his ear where I'd once discovered he'd picked up headlice from his little brother, and thrown his head off me like a ball, and then, calmer in the bathroom later, I'd yanked it back and scrubbed it till it foamed, and traced all his hair (it was long then) for the dead gluey stars. I thought of that exact feeling, the delousing, his wet hair slipping up my fingerprints, the tiny hulls filtered down the length with my nails. It took so long to strain all of the eggs out that way: but I loved his hair, its wild, black rigging. And then he cut it, probably tired of my scratching. I thought of the pulse in his neck I could look down over, then, lazy, half-asleep myself, watching it flex in the haze from the fizzling television. But nothing I could remember was on the screen. Except the reflection of him.

Nothing was on the windows of the caravan, either. Webs, of course, a whole city of strings, triangular nests at the corners, sticky and dense, a complexity of clear lines trickling out. That was the film I watched while I stayed in the caravan the old lady had rented to me. It became so quiet I could hear the white scabs of fly bodies tapping on the windows. But I never saw a spider the whole time I was there.

The old lady's hair was the counterpart of the spiderwebs, just like the asterisks of grass that blew on their parched rays around the caravan were the counterpart of the stars that had long blurred spokes above it each night. Dusty wheels of grass; the stars hard as staples; the blues overlapping in Michael's iris like the stretched rings on his tie-dyed shirt: that's all my head let occur and recur as I spent my first days toking up in the caravan. I drank a bit, too, but not a lot. Mostly I crouched on the steps and the day patched into night, and I thought of the hub of diesel at the centre of Michael's eyes, the strokes of black that leached from it, warping the blueness. I smoked and looked outwards with my back to the room and sometimes it felt like Michael was in there behind me, his warm untidy body taking up the whole coop: *Gizza durry*, he would have mumbled, sticking out a toe to nudge my neck, and the splints at the corners of the wagon would have creaked with his clumsiness. *Fuck off and get your own*, I would have said, then maybe gone to kiss him, nuzzling his thick lower lip that felt like flax. I wouldn't have gone out, staggering over the grass and hurling onto the sand dunes, the kind of sick that flies out like a liquid scream. Or even if I had, Michael would have held back my hair and whispered to me as I jerked: I would have known that I was not stifled, I was not extinct, because I could hear those whispers. Michael would have dug me up out the sand and held me there kneeling, would have laughed and said, *I'm about to break the last commandment: never kiss a girl that's just puked.* Or maybe we would have brought his little brother with us, and we would try to stay mostly sober so somewhere in the night we could peel Smudge out of his sleeping bag and cart him to the long-drop so he didn't piss his bunk, or even if we missed it, we wouldn't have made him feel like a criminal, wouldn't have belted him for it. So when I woke up the caravan might have smelt like pyjamas gone fuzzy with piss, and we might have spent the semi-dawn groaning at his brother to stop scuffling round and singing those chewed-up little TV tunes, *Dinosaurs, of all fucking predatory things, singing about happy families.* But even groggy, sleepless, it would have been good: it could've been, if we had ever come.

Instead, I turned over somewhere about the fourth day and felt my brain in my head like a bruised fist. The caravan was not a little family cocoon. It was a crypt. And at the door stood the old woman who had rented it to me. Obviously disgusted.

The old woman's hair was spiderweb, watered and combed across a tiny skull. It was scraped into a bun no thicker than one of her knuckles and stabbed in place with a wheel of yellow pins. I had seen her, over the last few days, when I surfaced, banging stakes into her garden with the back of a tomahawk, climbing up a ladder to a tilted birdhouse, scraping at the pelt of a mangy cat she held pinned to the lawn with a small implacable hand. She was miniature and ruthless. Mostly she'd ignored me, not out of hostility, but industry. She was simply too busy to be bothered with a waster like me. But at the door of the caravan she fixed me with eyes whose colours seemed to have dissolved beneath the lens, almost as clear as blisters except for the pinprick at the centre. That black fleck of pupil was shrewd.

After she stared at me she looked out over the lawn beyond the caravan.

'About time for drying out, I should think.'

Of course, she could have been talking about the lengths of rain above the section, so thin they were almost invisible, and seemed to rise rather than drop. Even on the tin this rain was soundless, except for a sudden thicker slap. You could see a few of these darker patches twitching over the washline, a weak sun exposed through them.

'I don't care,' I said, looking out. Even that light made my eyeballs ferment. When I talked I felt fibres break, crackle. My throat felt like tape.

'You'll come to,' the old woman said. 'If it lasts. If it sets in you'll be crying out for a change.'

In her grip was a plastic plate with one of those paper doilies you never see now. Dinky sausage rolls, biscuits cut into stars, a lamington bleeding grease and syrup. Just looking at it I could taste crystals, coconut the shape of the skin you chew away from your nails. Pastry, clumped and humid, forming a dam of butter behind your front teeth. She passed it to me, the gladwrap blurred with icing sugar.

'From down at my cardiac club. I told them I would fetch some leftovers back here for you. I always say you may as well take what you need. While it's offered you. Waste not, want not.'

She trudged away across the lawn in her rubber ankle boots. Her dress was checked with a tea-towel pattern. Veins slithered through the tough skin of her calves. Before she turned at the brick verge of her house, she looked back once at me, a shaky rotation of her head. At that distance the discs of her eyes looked like liquid. I flattened myself against the door of the caravan. She would be kind but not lenient. Wondering what she guessed made me start to breathe badly.

It came to me, with a strange kind of longing, that there had been no one like her at Michael's funeral. There was no one catering, sorting, bustling, dishing round teas as if holding the cup straight was the first step in getting over a hard knock. As if survival was a process plodded towards through the small ordinary routines. If the old woman had been at Michael's funeral I could imagine her closing her ragged lids, her blue-brown head with its wrinkle of bun nodding slowly in recognition. Then putting on her apron with a grim flick, directing me, away from despair, around the kitchen. But there was no one old. No one bleakly cheery. No one to pat you with a hand crooked with know-how, to tell you, *Chin up, you got to keep on.*

I wondered if that was why Michael had chosen her.

There were two kinds of people at Michael's funeral. And there was me, who belonged to neither of them.

Mostly I stayed with the university group, the circle Michael and I had met in the few months we'd spent together on campus. They loitered, in the consciously deranged clothes they paid too much for in chic charity shops. Over their tight, ancient dresses the women wore men's jackets still dense with working-class smells: smoko, Brylcreem, betting stubs. The male heads either spilled coils of ratted hair, or shone gauntly through caps of stubble; their glasses were two revolutionary circles, earnest and clear. They discussed Michael's death with me, monotone voices assembling the facts, intellectualising them. Some of the women touched my arm, blinked heavily, clasped the bone-carvings at their necks. It was not that they did not care. But their mode of caring took place in their heads, in the effort to comprehend Michael's actions. Outside the church, a kind of impromptu tutorial was held, and Michael was material, a case study. I could see that here, as much as in their lectures, they were proud of their faculty for analysis, for stringent debate. I stood amongst their talk—Michael's *rationale*, his *choices*—and knew I would not be returning to any of my classes.

I'd thought Michael would last at university. It seemed he had found his element. I'd watched him, as he crouched in the quad, his elongated limbs curled around his satchel, squatting on the platforms to listen to a speaker, then straining forward in contention, illogical but charged. He had never had a chance like this in his life. His childhood had been too messy to achieve in; as an 'adult' student he closed everything out but books. All at once he read everything, stacks of scuffed Penguin classics kicking round, shucked pages highlighted and flapping from the fridge by magnets or pegged along the walls. But he read everything too late. The whole flat smelled like extinct theories, a nest of broken social contracts, disused principles. I took them all down after he died and dropped them in one swoop from the roof of the apartment block.

Outside the church on the day of his funeral one of the university women started to talk of her own attempt. She had been meticulous, she said, from her first experiments, slicing vertically just below her elbow; she had mapped and planned, made annotations, she had compiled a kind of dissertation on death. It had defined her, the deadline she had set for finally extinguishing herself. She had worked towards it as she did for an assignment's due date. There was an academic chill in her voice, as if she still believed a razor could be pulled across a wrist in a postmodern sense.

I thought of how, when I dropped Michael's pages, they rippled into factions, all the great thinkers, hung or plunged through the shadows, hissed across the concrete forms, disappeared into the city.

The only other people at the funeral were the men who had been, or still were, in the life of Michael's mother.

Michael's mother was a slut and a slave.

By the end of the day of his funeral I had told her that to her face. Perhaps it helped me to stand up through that day; it reinforced me, that hate. When she got up to read out a poem she had written for him, a current arced out from my spine, so strong I thought it might shatter some ribs. It was the rhyme, the *da-di-da* beat of what she was saying, the chattering fuzzy effect. It was the fact that she really believed in the healing cuteness of what she had written, thought she could simper through some cheap scribble and that would help Michael, help all of us, *rest*. She rhymed that with *best*. Her head bobbed sweetly on the final rhymes. Once, her fingers even tapped on the altar rail, *di-dum*. She sucked a lot of air as if her jingling voice was hindered by real grief. When she'd finished she staggered off delicately. I heard her graze her skinny arse past some man in the front row, notches of lace tugging open as she bent to coo her apology.

For the rest of the service I sat behind her and stared at her head, so tiny, so flat in its hood of hard gel. I stared at her ears. The two nodes where her long clips dangled, the gutter of skin up the back of them, a white seam through the bottled glitter of her tan. I thought about how Michael had not liked his head once he'd shaved it because it reminded him of his mother. I thought about being left with him for a while in the funeral home, climbing up to lever his head onto my lap, the vacant heavy orb of it, bristled and chill. I thought about the inquiring look on his face, the texture of his lower lip, mottled and dry, the scope of incoherent, soulful light that kept gathering and breaking on the lens of his eyes although no soul was under them. It was just the wavelengths of emptied fibre shimmering at me. Catching and deflecting all that useless radiance.

I thought about how, very soon, that shimmer was going to be replaced. By the shimmer of his ash. By his ashes as they lifted, released, dispersed into shade, as they spread across everything, just for an instant, coated trees, stones, water, clung in currents of air like the form of a ghost. Then I would close and open my eyes, and all that dust would be breathed away, invisible. The outline of everything I saw would look sharp, detailed again, but empty. Haloed by his nothingness.

Right then, I knew I couldn't leave him to his mother. She'd put the urn up somewhere gaudy, show it off for a few pissed days, she'd stroke it with her tacky hands, I could just hear her false nails clicking on it, the remains of her baby prickling at her touch. She'd stumble round the after-party with it, yelling stories, rocking it down by her pelvic bone. She'd give up the act when the drinks hit double figures or something stronger rushed her brains. If she didn't spill him, Michael would end up on the bench somewhere among all the empty vessels. So I planned it, right then, how I would take him myself, although I didn't know yet that I'd drive him straight back to the caravan.

She had done a surgical job on her make-up, his mother. I noticed that when I went over to her after the funeral. Strokes of pencil were oily in the sparse fluff of her brows. Her lids were lined with black wedges, and the sockets shone with blues. She thought she could talk to me, that I would stand and listen to her melodic blabbing, the cadence of a born slag. While she prattled I could see in her body she was aware of several men looking on. Her hips, working under the lace, her gaze, in its visor of sticky lashes, her talk, with its travesty of Michael-centred stories— highlights of his childhood that I knew were shit—everything about her was gauging the notice of men, as it always was. She was no more interested in me than she'd ever been in Michael. She would look you in the eye, but you could feel the pull of her attention, sleazy and lateral.

I told her what I thought of her. Michael wouldn't have liked me to be so cruel. He loved her the way a child loves a rodent or a bird, some mauled thing you retrieve from a pulpy nest to watch it die slowly in a shoebox. But I had outgrown the idea of rescue. I knew hers came at the cost of her kids. When she was nourished she fluttered away to bring the next predator into their life. How she tracked them I just don't know: she had radar. When she was smacked-up once again she crawled into the corner of the kids' room and expected to be pitied, although by the stage her beatings were dished out the boys had already lived through weeks of their own. I thought she should have been put out of her misery long ago.

The funeral director must have sized her up anyway. It didn't take too much convincing to get him to hand over Michael to me instead. I paid: Michael's mother had told the guy she'd need welfare assistance to cover it. He had a mass of forms filled out in glitter pen, her printing loopy and babyish with oooo's and aaaaa's. But I put it down in cash, everything we had saved. Sometimes when Michael and I got somewhere in our savings we'd talked of a kind of future, of things we could use the money to try to set right. Mostly we'd talk of taking Smudge from his mother, of trying to keep him safe. We had thought it probably wouldn't be hard to make her cave in and leave him for good; she wasn't much interested, except in the welfare, and sometimes we had Smudge camped out for weeks, while she was AWOL, toasted or 'in love'.

When I tipped the money onto the desk at the funeral home I thought about that. I thought maybe I should be using it to take home the living son, not the dead one.

It might have been the thought of that that made me so angry when I got Michael's canister that I kicked it under the back seat and just kept driving, shortcuts I'd never taken before but which I knew were headed somehow out through the hills to the caravan he'd killed himself in, and picking up a hitchhiker I was planning to fuck before I had even pulled into the gravel, because the simplest way to hurt Michael was to act like his mother, and show him that now he had done what he'd done I could easily settle into her life, sink into her dress, put on her red shoes and get myself a man who'd make my nose bleed, my hips black, my heart too blurred to see straight back into the past.

I swallowed some of the food the old lady had left me and lay in the caravan trying to come round, clean up. But I had trouble. That caravan was as good as a dark room. And the images were cleaner then, so distinct they moved along my skin and through my insides. There were images of Michael that would not leave me, unlike the real thing. He met me at a service station where I was pumping gas, and he had just pulled his wagon in from the nearby beach he'd been surfing at. He only had boardies on, crusted with sand, knotted with a shoelace where the hair spiralled down on his belly. He'd cut his leg on the fin of his board and it was bleeding. He limped off to wash it at the tap on the concrete blocks at the end of the pumps. But he turned to stare back at me while he did it, looking hard at me while blood diluted under the long rub of his hand, streaked down his foot and dripped from it, joining the slick of petrol that belched from his car when it reached full. I didn't know then how precious that was, that stare. I didn't know then how his usual look was past you, into the space beyond the left side of your head, as if your angel, your double, stood there, a trace of a past self that hung around or a future one, a shadow you hadn't quite stepped into. When he came closer, the day we met, I said, *I'm so sorry* for spilling the gas, and he looked right at me, right in the face for a while, before his gaze slid away to the side, where I would learn it would mostly stay in our years together, eerie, cute, off-putting. It was long enough for so much damage to be done: in a single look I'd already learned him, especially the eyes with their troubles and stains and translucence rippling ring through ring, the pillar of bone up the middle of his chest, the thinned blood still drizzling down his ankle, the bud of joint there very white amidst the dark hair wrinkled darker with water. *Forget it*: those were the first words he said to me. I kept saying *Sorry.*

No way, forget it, he kept repeating. He wore a necklace like a dog tag on his chest, and on its bright metal there was still a single suspended fleck of the sea. He went on saying *Hey, forget it*: I went on staring at that drop, that clarity. I should have known then that Michael had brought me a terrible gift, of images that wouldn't leave.

In the caravan I thought, if I choose to follow Michael, that fleck of salt water glinting from his necklace might be the last thing that I see.

But I also lay and thought about that water, that tiny circle shining and irrelevant . . . and thought I saw everything reflected in it. So much beauty left behind in something so useless. A nothingness and a shrine, at once, a waste and a universe. Like the cell he may have left behind in me.

I couldn't stay in the caravan thinking that. To think it was to watch all the questions, everything beginning with *if*, coming into focus like the ghost of Michael's fingers brushing words onto the glass for me. Waiting for my breath.

I crashed out the caravan so hard I startled the old woman who was in the garden. She was pushing a spinning blade on a stick along the concrete rim of the flower beds. It droned and squeaked, opened a dark scar of dirt. Her mouth opened in a smile as dark and dry.

I said nothing, because I couldn't. I walked straight ahead, through the weeds she had neatly stacked onto polythene, through loops of her washing, the wilted singlets as thin as webs strung across the light, not clothing but apparitions of thread. She clucked but she didn't bother staring at me. I heard the whining of her garden tool go on, the gritty sound of it chipping at the concrete.

I got to the beach and stayed there a long time. There weren't many people down there: a couple of grommets wagging school to surf, a few brisk, pastel-toned women in plastic sun-visors with handbag-sized dogs. A guy clicked by in jandals and a cap, a red-brown paunch jogging over his speedos and a cigarette pack tucked down above his arse. He stared at me through wraparound shades and slid his tongue in and out so I heard saliva jostling. But when I ignored him he just shrugged and squeaked past. Out to sea the light was so thick it looked like someone had spilled sand along the horizon, and a triangle of shimmers too painful to focus on poured down. The waves moved in like a diagram of themselves, measured and rustling. I thought about tipping Michael in with them, but every time I looked black tangles of debris were dragged to the same place in each wave, as if the sea kept spitting up the same junk, unable to leave it. So I lay down then and closed my eyes, and the sound of the waves became a dream, the sound of Michael trying to fix his secondhand finds, taping their pages at one place while their spines just cracked straight open at the next one, until he gave up and plucked them, pinned them up round the flat. And we'd lie there on the bed under those strings of thinking and watch them, flicking yellow kites, and I'd forget how flimsy, how limited those theories seemed mingling on our wall when Michael climbed onto me and peeled my pelvis and his out of the basics of underwear and joined us, gently and wetly, into the one glazed body we were meant to share.

When I woke I thought about fucking the hitchhiker there on the same stretch of beach. Stumbling the dunes the hitchhiker had tried to talk, to add a dimension to the screwing, but once we reached the hard sand I'd pulled up my skirt and taken his fingers and shoved them under fabric, wedged them as far as I could get them in one jolt into me. As earnest as he was, he had gasped and unbuttoned. But he wasn't happy without his ideals for long. When we were done he went on talking, about himself when he found he couldn't learn about me. He told me about his project back at art school, an installation, cross-referencing cyberspace and God, he said. He blended things like chat room threads with religious texts; he was going to call it Cannot Find Server. He was hitching this way to look through junk shops and dumps; he wanted old circuit boards, valves and cylinders, anything that looked mechanical yet obsolete. He was going for a look of intricate components, technological complexity, yet ultimate emptiness, a vast systemic void. He was planning to splice other objects in, odd defunct icons from routine existence, and an active current would run through to randomly light up words he had taken from the bible or the net: No New Messages, Unable to Establish a Connection, Click Here for a List of Errors. I told him I could give him a great piece; I told him to come back to the car with me. I still don't know if I would have gone through with it. I heard my voice talking as if it was a voice on tape. 'Put it under Deleted Items,' I said. I got as far as unlocking the car, brushing under the seat for the canister. It spun and slithered away from my hands, but I got a hold of it and turned and offered it to him. I wasn't sure if it was shame or pity in the hitchhiker's face, but it was not neutral. He twitched as he was talking, nothing but shocked platitudes. 'But I thought we were talking about the postmodern,' I said. I held Michael out. 'He didn't leave a reason. So it was like all of the things you just said, pointless, disconnected, drained of value, arbitrary. All of the fucking clever things you just said. An uncommitted suicide,' I said. 'Ha, an uncommitted suicide.'

When the hitchhiker left it was what I wanted. I let myself into the caravan alone. I still had Michael in my hands, and the residue of the hitchhiker trickling inside me. If and when I had to face the baby as definite at least I could pretend its source was unclear, and a child that potentially had nothing to do with Michael would be easier to dispose of. But, really, I knew that line of thought was irrelevant. I knew it all broke down to just us three: me in the caravan, Michael in his chrome, the possible baby cooped inside me. One dead, one alive, the third one somewhere in the middle, undecided.

Uncommitted. Perhaps Michael had not let himself know either, had not been certain, until the very end, which way his decision, or indecision, would go, where it would take him. Perhaps he had been keeping his secret the way I had been keeping mine, even from myself. Perhaps when he came here he did not drive the distance head on, fixed on his suicide, but only felt the suggestion of death wavering along the outskirts of the strange road, a wayside of hazy possibilities, hissing as lightly as the fenceline crosses or the ferns. Perhaps he could lie down in the caravan and trick himself, dozily, pill by sip. Perhaps no capsule or gulp seemed terminal, not even the small knife he steered down his forearm, docking it finally in the deep mess of his wrist. He only cut one—maybe he still was irresolute, playing at that slash, unfocused. Maybe he was fooling himself. The same way I could walk back there from the beach and trick myself that my body was empty, except for an accidental rivulet of no one special's sperm.

Any way you stared at it, that caravan looked like death's door. When I walked back towards it after my short crash on the beach, the sun was shooting off it in all directions. I suppose my eyes were done in with more than just glare, but at first I didn't see the old girl was still outside. Only then, as I got across the section, I spotted her and I could tell she wasn't herself, not picking or fussing or digging at anything, just kneeling, making little bursts of off-pitch, scrawny movement, trying to claw up, then swaying back as if the buffalo grass was too spongy for take-off.

We'd hardly spoken two words but the sight of her, withered like that, made me run.

Her breath was scratchy, so I made her sit back and stop clambering about for a moment. She was not an easy old bugger to boss, so I got down with her and propped her up from the back and told her off, gently. She snapped, *Leave off, will you*. But after another lurch or two, she came back against me. Fragile lengths of rib shimmered through her old frock as she wheezed, and I could feel her heartbeat, puckering oddly. I didn't have to bully her still anymore, so we just crouched, watching the caravan.

Finally, when her torso was steadier, she tampered with the fingers I was holding her with and said, 'Well, that was a bad business.'

'What? Did you fall?'

'No,' she said, gruffly. 'I meant what your fella did. That was a bad business. What he came here and went and done to himself.'

I owed her something in reply but the cold in my lungs was packed solid. No words were getting in or out.

She said, 'Thought you'd keep mum about it, did you? I spotted you right away. It's a giveaway, your face, did you know that, dearie? I was wondering when you were going to pipe up and say. Anyway, I don't get that much call for the caravan. I only pin up that little note to rent it at the dairy and it's not like we get lots of outsiders through here. And never back-to-back like the two of you've been. We're the black stump out here, love. God's last shovelful.'

She nodded at the caravan, light still sharp all over that hutch. It looked even more rancid, bent on its piles and the scruffy grass I'd flicked full of smoke butts.

'We lived in that, you know. Me and Bert, when we first came here. He built the house later. Every last brick, he did. His back was a swine of a thing ever since,' she chuckled. 'I've never let it get run down to this state. Not in a month of blessed Sundays. But since your young man put his lights out in there I've felt too funny to get in and do it. The young cop gave it the once-over for me, but you know young blokes. So I bring the bucket and things out to get stuck in and give it a real good going-over. But I come over all unnecessary, I don't mind saying. And that's not something I'm used to, my girl.'

'Not me,' she tutted on. 'Not ruddy likely. Tough as an old boot. Always have been. I tell myself, there's worse things happen to old birds like you stuck on their own. There was one not so long ago. Bludgeoned, she was, in her bed, and the fella they caught for it was only a mite. So I'm a darn sight luckier than that poor duck. Nothing to stop your young fella being one of those. And how would I've known.'

She shifted, creakily, fastening herself, tapping away at

sticking grasses. Her fingers we're fibrous, a pinched blue at the joints.

'I need to get into gear now,' she said.

I stayed behind her, levering. I didn't have to see her eyes from there. She took a few steps once we were upright, but they were curtailed, doddery. I told her I could taxi her to the doctors. Mad, her eyes were wide in their crinkle of skin and she looked like she fancied cuffing me.

'Not ruddy likely,' she said. 'I'll be right as rain. The way that doctor fluffs about gets me peeved. Good and proper.'

I hobbled her over to the house, her twitching me away, then relapsing, vexed, into my grip. In the long run she wasn't going to be thwarted. She waved me down a side of the house I hadn't been. Along the end wall was some kind of knocked-up cage or sun porch, just a frame stretched with tatters of black mesh.

I said, 'Michael had . . . a rotten time. When he was a kid.'

'Well,' she said. 'You hear a lot of that talk these days.'

'But Michael never would talk about it. He wouldn't tell me anything. Not any details. But once I had to drive his mother to the hospital and she jabbered out a whole load of stuff. I think she was sorry for a flash, but really only for herself. Anyway, she told me that once a guy she'd moved in with had lived at an old zoo park. He was closing it down, and he'd sold off most of the animals, and just had the leftover birds hanging round. He'd open the cages from time to time, but they couldn't get the picture. You know what they say, the cliché, too used to being locked up. So one night, when Michael does something, or nothing, like little kids do, to piss this guy off, he drags him out and chucks him into one of those cages. She said some of the birds went crazy, him being in there, screaming like you can imagine. But it was the dead ones that bothered him the most. There were some that were dying cos the guy couldn't be bothered feeding them.'

'Sounds like a nasty piece of work.'

'She had a stack of them. His mother.'

She said, 'Well, I expected something like that when I never heard from the family. You'd think that someone'd be out to ask me about it, if he'd come from a decent bunch.'

'He didn't.'

'As things go, dear, you seem decent enough.'

I watched her from a pace behind as she shuffled to the back door, holding back the streaks of vinyl that flagged away the flies. She jimmied off her boots and worked her feet into wizened velvet slippers. Holes were sawed into the tips to leave room for her corns.

She turned and said, 'If you ask me, mothers like that want being taken out and whipped. I can't fathom them. I would've gone to any length, for a kiddie. But Bert and me were never blessed. Not for want of trying, mind you. That's why Bert started work on the house, y'know, even though we only had the dough to get going slowly, to put it up brick by brick. He said it'd come to him that while we were stopping in the caravan a little soul would think we didn't have the room to take it in. It sounds like an odd idea for a man to get, but it turned out that it really worried him. He couldn't rest easy in the old crate fretting that our little chap might be out there, in the ether or I-don't-know-where, looking down on us but feeling we weren't making the space to squeeze it in.'

There was a silence.

'I'm sorry,' I said finally. 'About it all. You having to find him. I don't know what . . . else to tell you. Do you—you know—need me for anything?'

'I'll be right as rain. Like I said. You get used to being alone. I don't think I could stomach anyone now. Couldn't put up with it.'

I didn't think I should walk off but she clutched at the doorframe, wiry, not to be crossed.

As I moved back the cat sidled up to her, croaking. She nudged a saucer, speckled with congealed meat, towards it, talking back to it in coarse little yowls.

'Oh, and this is Widow,' she said across the lawn to me. 'When

I was telling one of my pals down at cardio club she thought I said Pussy Widow, not Pussy Willow, you see. Silly old duffer. Then Widow just stuck. Just thought I'd tell you in case she tries to take over that caravan.'

'Widow,' I repeated.

'Still, I don't suppose you'll be long in staying. I imagine you've got plenty of things to be getting on with. Being alone'll do me. But it's hardly the ticket for a girl like you.'

I thought about my plenty as I wandered back to the caravan, lay down in its hovel.

There had been a baby there on the day of Michael's funeral. Someone tacked on to the 'family' through one of his 'uncles' had come along with one, humping it late along the aisle against her leather skirt, smirched with reflux. She'd slumped down beside me, yanking an older child into the pew before her. The older girl came down clumsily—there was a hardbacked bible on the seat and she gripped her leg, tittering. All through the service I could hear mucus and misery squealing through the baby's tiny face. The mother stuck it out on one knee, shook it back and forth a while, making its whine come up in waves. When she tried to swing it to her other knee for a break it bucked and made a grab for her, catching the ring in her eyebrow. The ring unclipped and dangled from the socket, joined by a tiny dash of blood. Cursing, she shoved the baby sideways onto the girl's lap and stomped off down the carpet. But the girl only smiled, hauled the baby up by the armpits, and shimmied her ponytail down at it with jolts of her head. She nuzzled close, letting it suck on her hair. In its dirty stretch-and-grow the baby's legs hung like little pipes.

Later, in the toilets, I was in a stall when I heard the mother laying the baby down on the tiles. Its stench choked the cubicle and it shrilled louder as she pushed its limbs in and out through its clothes. When I came out she had pulled paper down from the dispenser and was scratching at the dirty skin. She stuck the fresh nappy on wildly, then knelt back and stared, blank, at the baby. It was still thrashing. She shot forward suddenly, dropping her face down right over the kid's. 'Am I pissing you off, am I? Well, now you fucking know how I feel,' she screamed at it.

'Go easy,' I said.

The mother looked at me. 'Oh yeah,' she said. 'Well, it's all yours if you want it.'

I said nothing.

'Nah, didn't fucking think so,' she said.

I walked away. Around the corner from the stalls was a long bright bench of mirrors. Standing there was Michael's mother, eyelid hooked down by a little finger, calmly tracing the pink band with a tube of silver grit.

If there was one word I'd have expected to find appearing under my breath it was his brother's name. But if the caravan was death's door, death's windows didn't have a mark on them. I don't know why I kept looking. I kidded myself there might be some science to it, some principle of friction, the moisture content of exhalation, the differing qualities of light. I had no shortage of dreams of Michael's fingerprints, traced on the window, on my face, or on the inside of his flask. But no good ever came of them. Except the surplus of shivers which made me grope for his container and hunch around it, or snarl at it and shake it.

When I left the caravan I'd really no idea what to do. The old girl just shrugged when I dropped her keys back, as if she wasn't much bothered. But then she rambled beside me, out to the car, sinewy in a fresh frock. The cat toddled behind her at first, then darted off, shifty and primitive, flicking through the toetoe. When we got to the car, the old woman looked at the canister I had cradled in a jersey on the seat.

'You mind?' she asked me. I reached in and passed him into her hands.

'Well,' she said. She rocked him in her grip for a bit, weighing him. I think she was testing herself. I heard him in there, gliding along the surface.

'I got my Bert back in a ruddy box,' she said. 'Fancy that. Cardboard. I suppose it was daylight robbery for this.'

Then she said, 'He was a handsome type, your lad. Strapping, you know. I would have said, robust. Not likely to go down without a fight. Still, it takes all sorts, I suppose.'

She bent down and tucked him into his nest in the car.

'Well,' she said. 'You want to come back for a spell, the caravan's there.'

I would have reached out and touched the ridges of her cheek or knuckles, the streaks of scalp that shone through her hair, but she was too spry.

'Off you get now,' she grumbled.

I obeyed and drove away, Michael taking the corners beside me.

From time to time as I drove I thought about making a switch, a trade, about driving straight to his mother's house and saying, Here, give me Smudge, I'll give you Michael. But I didn't feel like giving anything up.

On my last night in the caravan I had dreamt of upending his ash. But instead of his silt there was a rush of birds and pages, pulsing out into the dark, my breath pouring with them, a part of their luminous thrash. When I woke up I remembered the last message Michael had sent to me, a text before he left, just a dumb saying I thought he tapped out for a joke: WHT DSN'T KLL U MKS U STRNGR. Sometimes at the point that you get a message, it makes no sense. What it means might get clearer, later, or you just have to breathe the meaning in for yourself. So I drove back to the city, choosing a vowel.

deleted scenes for lovers

They are the lovers. You can't blame them. At night in your house you let them appear on your screen; you want them to do more damage. They are too good looking for the third-world streets they have driven to; you wish they didn't have to hide. He gets his fingers in under her clothes, midsection, and you find it hard to exhale. You know it's cheap; the rain on the passenger window beyond his head looks digitised. But you wind back, you lead their bodies through it frame by frame, to see how dark her eyes are with the tenement backdrop, how the thick base of his thumb is a brace for her throat. There is one shot, true, that is done so badly it distracts you: it's her (it is always her) spreading her fingers on the glass, sliding open in the mist, a dislocating squeal too loud as they slip upwards. Like the sound some woman in an advert would make, demonstrating window cleaner, smiling as she bleaches everything. But you have control; you can edit. Hit >>X2 X2. You can set them up, there, in the shot in the alley where it looks like shrapnel is bedded in the door he steers her through, staggering, where her hairline looks jagged and perfectly white shot down from the slant stairs above, like her scalp is struck with fate. You want to see her pinned, a star on the derelict wall, where her shadow spills over. You want to see her shiver, open-legged. You do it, and do it again, let them break worlds open, alter lives. You push. You push the lovers. You feel you have to. It's so sad, the odds against them.

*

He calls her. He says he's wagging his conference. He should be in a session room right now, but he's missing it. Missing what, she says. What are you missing. He tells her, Taking a personality test. You should, she says. You should be. He says he walked out, he tried to listen, but he couldn't think straight. She asks, Did you do any of the test. He says, Yes. She says, What did it tell you. He says, That it's too late. Why, she says. Because I'm already too deep. You, she says. *You're* not *deep.* She tries laughing. But he says, I'm deep in this. In what, she says. In this thing, with you. Don't say, she starts. He cuts her off. He says, But you know what it is.

She ends the call. She drops her hand and looks down into the phone as if she's heard news of an accident. But as long as she goes straight home now, she can stop some crash occurring in advance. She goes home, and her routines are all waiting for her, the shake in her hands doesn't change any of them. She toughens the way her teeth dig into her lip, and her husband sees new muscle in her cheekbone, vertical. He thinks she's getting older. They run water, they wipe surfaces. They sip wine, they pay bills, waiting for the kids' sleep to kick in. They feel all right, on the usual set of evening, moving in its dull patterns, its homely lull of joint need.

The children have beautiful torsos, pearly blue in the last hour of moon when she checks them. They have fistfuls of blanket in the silk of their grip and the rooms smell sour, angelic with the murk of their skin. She sits on their beds and thinks for a while she might go out and talk to her husband. But then a child wakes in a ripple of nightmare that only she can guard against. She sings, a shield against the side of his wet head, a lonely song that comes in small doses.

*

You don't like the next episode. They have him in a high-rise and there's too much light at the apex. He is deciphering things on file. There is too much paper and artificial light. He looks like a man in an office chair. He sounds like a man in an office chair. You don't like the way he says *break even*. You don't like the way he says someone will *take the bullet*. You don't know who had the shooting script. Sometimes, you know, they switch directors. Which can make even the actors' faces look wrong. You make a note to watch for that in the credits. But for now, you watch on. It doesn't improve. The light does not get the job of hero done. It is fake and sharp and blocks you believing, even in the soundtrack, even in the mingle of bass and descending major chords that mark him tracking her movements down the central glass hallway, his iris targeting her, while he's still on the call, while he's closing the deal in a kind of vertically blinded light that looks cut-throat. The scale is off, like soundtrack stock they spliced in from metal leftovers on the cutting-room floor.

The light is even on the sex later, when they get to it. It is poured down, air-conditioned. It is harsh, on tap, a kind of burden on your gaze. Their bodies look caustic, and the grip they get into is upright, gaunt and catalogue. You don't know what it is. Yes, you do. It's the music, the formulaic scales and the light. It's synthesised. It's the apartment. They don't look tragic in this setting. It makes them look like people with options, with plenty. Like they had plastic-coated choices. Everything they do, even their kiss, looks coded, somehow backspaced. Their fuck looks kitset, like the furniture.

*

She is in the kitchen. The children are staring at the things on their plates they don't want to eat. She is cutting open the clear plastic circles on the six-pack ring off the top of the cans. She has heard that they drift out to sea and act like nooses. Sometimes she feels sick of recycling. The children are whining about things they won't chew. She stands in the kitchen and looks at the tins she must rinse, the plastics she must check for numbers and crush. She feels tired of it. A tired that rises in her like a hum. So, she makes herself think of the birds. She closes her eyes and sees them, hanging at the surface, oily and limp, in a fine transparent snare set by her torpor.

Her husband is on the deck, fixing the chain on one of the children's bikes. He can't hear the TV, so he yells at her to crank the sound up. He uses that word, *crank* it. She doesn't. He yells again, You're *closest*. She does. There is a couple on the screen, taking part in a game show. They have come to the place where they have to decide to take the deal, or gamble on the secret prize that could wait in the woman's briefcase. The briefcase is silver. There is only so much it can hide. The audience chants at them to take the risk. It is what the audience always does. *Take the risk.* The wife wants to play on. The studio can see it in the way she's jigging on her heels, the way she tips her hair over her shoulder with one bold punt. It is not beautiful hair, but there is a gloss to how she throws it, a lack of caution. It almost makes her glint. The host turns to her husband, grinning. The husband does not like the spotlight. He pauses for a long time. Then he blurts, But she's just not *lucky,* Geoff. She's just *not.*

The children roll their food around their plates in cold grizzly circuits. She goes outside with the cans piled on the plastic, makes a ceremony of mangling all of it down into the bin. She can hear her husband still laughing from the deck. He's hooting the words themselves, She's just not *lucky.* She's just *not.*

She will have to spray his clothes with extra cleaner after he's handled the chain. He will end up with the imprint of black teeth tracking his clothes. She will have to. She will just have to.

*

He calls her. He says, What are you doing. She says, I'm in the Salvation Army. He laughs at her, You're what. Are you trying to get saved. She says, No, I'm saving something. What are you saving, he asks. She says, Well, at the moment, I'm thinking of whether to save this figure of a woman. He says, A what. She says, It's a figurine, they have a red sticker on it that actually reads *statuette*. He says, Oh yeah, do they. And how much are you saving her for then. Five dollars, her salvation is costing me. Big money. I think she's worth it. She's beautiful, she's china, I think, and there's not a crack in her, or none that I can see. There's a crack in everything. Don't, she says. Don't quote that song. I love that song. Well don't love that song, we can't love the same things. You can't stop me. No, but. I was telling you about her. She's very white. Oh yeah, he says. So—what's she wearing. Not much. Go on. Tell me. There's not much to tell. Go on then. On her lower half, she's wearing a sheet, or sort of, draped round, you know. And on top. She's wearing her hair in a bun. Ha ha, what's in between? What's in between? That's right. She's hollow in between. She's hollow so you can turn her over and breathe right up the middle. And she makes a sound. He makes a sound. He says, More. Tell me more. How about up top. Where. Tell me about her, mmmm, shoulders. She's not wearing anything. Nothing. No. No. She's not. And you'd have to dress her. Why. Well, because. She's Venus. She can't help herself. She's not even wearing arms.

She starts to laugh into the phone. Then stops. She buys Venus and takes her outside to the Salvation Army carpark. The carpark has constellations of birdshit and chewing gum everywhere. It is empty and hot. Venus has not been wrapped and it would be so easy to drop her.

*

This is better. There's a shot of her bare feet stretching down to meet the floorboards. It's a morning shade of floor. The contact is slow so you can feel the cold her skin would be stepping into. Her toenails are unpainted. This feels right to you. This says *history*. The bed is red too, the old red that is rich and heavy with heritage. The mess of it is sculptural. Her steps are smooth and you can hear her skin, lifting away with soft baroque whispers from the ridged surface of the boards. You like the knots, deep and coarse, coiled and secret as a series of muscles. The camera rests a long time, among those knots. She does not cast her hand around for her clothes; you may be able to say *garments*, but you're not sure yet. They are ornate. She does not need them. In this shot she will walk naked to the window and be herself and glory in it. There are tall amber bottles on a table, there's a quill, there may even be rosary beads. It is natural light. It is beautiful and distant. You think, *Tower*. You think, *Hooves*. The theme could be vampiric. You can feel how everyone is sleeping. Except the man whose eyes are just beginning to open, in close-up, lash by lash. You can smell his skin, waking up, medieval, in the room.

*

She sees a man walking through her back garden. Her spine feels very tight at the stem of her neck. Two areas of buzzing start just behind her ears. The pitch is off-key. What is he doing here. It is summer in the room she watches from, high and airless. She is freezing.

It is only a repairman. She goes out through the slider and he doesn't seem to be bothered. He's been dealing with her husband. It's sorted. It's the tank, he says, when she insists. The tank is leaking, into next door.

Her husband has not told her anything.

The workman shrugs. Your old man said you're hardly home. It can't be left, it's leaking into the next house.

He goes on driving a stake into her dark grass.

*

She says, Why are you calling now. He says, It's at the point where I can't stop myself. But just this second, she says, I can't believe you'd call now. Why, he asks her. Because—I'm at my desk, I'm trying to work and I just went to type the word 'him'. But my fingers must have been at the wrong place on the keyboard, so instead I wrote 'gun'. Why have I never seen that. They're exactly the same pattern on the keyboard. Your hand just has to be off, just wrong by one space. He says, Well, you know what they say if there's a gun in the story. She says, But this is life. Do you think this is a *story*. She pushes the button three times, like she could dial their talk backwards, hit blank, delete.

*

Tonight, there is going to be a war. But you don't mind. You know the lovers do well in these conditions. The camera will be aerial, gliding. They will run to each other while the freeze-frames of dirt blast up. The fallout of history will shower down around them, but they will struggle to each other, in strangely clean clothes, amidst the shocks. High-definition haloes of soil will ignite from their footsteps but they will still kiss. The buildings are blistered, the faces of an unnamed cast are fragmented and buried in a gush. But it's the kiss you watch. The violins will sing above the slow-motion minefield—of everything love conquers.

*

He says, Do you dream of me. She says, No, I'm too tired out by this to dream. She says, I close my eyes and the only things left of my body are the last places you have been. He breathes on her belly, a line of proud graffiti, hooks the leap of her rib with his tongue.

When she gets home her husband is hanging a mobile up in their little girl's room. It's a silver hoop with strings of mermaids attached. She's been asking him to nail it up for weeks. But now it's done, drifting, she stands in the doorway and doesn't like the swim of them. Their sheen hovers in the closed room. The walls go under in the sway of their scaly shadows. She says, Take it, take it back down. Her husband is aggravated. He says, Why the fuck. She can't say, Because it makes her feel *slippery*. She says, It'll keep her awake. But he won't remove it. She stands and argues with him until she feels a channel of her lover's fluid slip like a thumbprint out between her lips. No one has noticed her dress is off its axis, no one knows she's wet beneath, clumsy with the aftershock of coming, inside studded with another man's come. She stares at the suspended women and wishes they would all drown from their leashes.

She doesn't tell her lover, when he rings, that she dreamed last night. She was packing her children's lunchboxes. Tipping in layer after layer of slick dead birds. Pushing down the beaks, compressing the slimy fan of feathers, snap after tiny snap.

*

You don't like where they're taking the lovers. They are handheld now. It's unsettling. It makes them hard to follow. There is nowhere to rest in the close-ups. The skin spills sideways. Your sense of the room gets lost to each blink. The shake of the film tips you up, internalises everything; you watch them and feel cornered in your own pulse. There are sequences of doorways and fingertips and streetlights and everything jerks on the diagonal, rapid and silver on the screen, like mercury splashed from a thermometer so you can no longer get a reading of the heat. Nothing is accurate. There is a shot of a cobweb, a child's blue sketch in crayon, strands on the dial of a machine. It could be an amplifier, but there is no soundtrack. Only footsteps, calling the unseen distance into place with their retreat. There's a line of dialogue: he says his hands are just hardwired to touch her. But in the next frame his wife is mounted on him, and he is saying her name, and it's the right name but he has to concentrate to say it, and you can see in the wife's spine that she can hear that, the pressure it takes for him to focus his mouth on the syllables of her name. And so her orgasm looks lonely, looks solo. The ridges of the sadness she's learnt in that moment run through the muscles of her back like breaking wings. The camera stares at her. And then the camera is on the floor, and figures pace in and out of its ankle-deep horizon. Until someone runs at it, and the soundtrack clatters, the film still spirals, the room the story is coming apart in swings, kicked across the surface of more than two lives.

Everything is overexposed. Fruit is shrinking on a chrome plate. Someone packs a yellow suitcase with clothes. The child's blue sketch has pain in the strokes of the crayon and is shown pinned. Something cowardly and handwritten flutters from a fridge.

*

He takes her out. It is like a date. He arranges someone to look after the children. So the *he* in this sentence is her husband: it's also a hard change for her to make. It is not her husband whose face she sees, whose skin she tastes, when her body thinks the word *him*.

But he does the driving. They drive to the ocean. The roads here bend and are narrow. They turn dark and loose with stones.

The towns are all closed-up sheds with signs that read *Library* and *Homekill Butcher.* The houses are alone and leaning in the fields, flaking two-room shells with too many summers in the walls. She turns the dial to find something she can sing to, but her voice won't fit, so they listen to AM, men agreeing with other men who call in middle-aged tones to tolerate nothing. He drives, and she knows something is off when he agrees to pull over at a roadside gallery. Her husband always likes to drive straight, unbroken, from beginning to end. He waits in the car while she walks round the weathered barn and stares at a recycled cathedral window. It has a tall, sharp arch she has to drop her head back to see. It is luminous and dizzying. She feels it split her face into unholy stains.

The end of the coast road has a sign. It outlines rules for leaving the shore, so they don't read it. They use it to hold their towels and tuck their shoes in its shade. They walk and feel the chill collapse of the beach, the slippage of unseen sticks and stones. It's a short walk, but it punctures their feet. They don't need to go any further.

He says nothing until they are sitting in a small, rough café. He has not bought them much, because they don't like what's waiting under muslin in the plastic cabinet. Everything looks dried at the seams. Even the meat and the cream are dark along the rim and curled. So they don't eat. But he pauses over coffee and says the words: I am your husband. And she knows everything that's wrong just by how he says it, part ultimatum, part plea. But she tries to fend the knowing off. A seagull stalks on the railing near them, looking mean and seed-eyed and wounded. She picks up the cup that she bought at the gallery, where they would never have stopped if she were faithful. It is porous and coarse and she dips her face into it and breathes and tells him, This smells *exactly*, it smells like the road on a summer day before the rain gives . . . She is going to say, *way*, gives way. But her husband has let go of his own cup and put his hands down flat on the table. He is crying before she ever gets to the way at the end of the sentence.

On the drive back she is closer to the sea so the road feels even thinner. Every summer at least two cars slip down onto the rocks beneath. There is always one rescue, an image in the paper of somebody who was saved, a headline about the heroism of a stranger who climbed down and pried out victims. And there is always one whose drift off the edge seems jagged and deliberate.

It is hard to take sides.

*

They are sitting in a car in a neighbourhood where nothing good happens. They are parked up, dead-end. They are talking. But you can hear there's no real hope in their voices that talk will lead them out of here. It is early, the morning is only half-formed, they have borrowed these streets from other people's lives. Something about the way they have parked looks seedy, unplanned, like they've woken up liquored, awry with the curb, memory off-cue. They could be two strangers coming around in a car with no recall, half-cut and wan. The street is calm, low-decile and couldn't give a shit either way. Through the passenger window there is a woman mowing her front lawn. She is old and thin and wearing a polyester nightgown and gumboots. The straps are frilly apricot and match the wrinkles of her throat and breasts. Through the driver window there's a family who have hauled their belongings from the state house onto the grass. All the doors and windows on the state house are open. There are three or four generations squatting in the sun with objects dragged between them: a red towel, a blue-green lampshade, a curtain of plastic flowers, a wire heater. They are not talking. They are blinking and waiting, and letting a brown baby crawl. And topple. And suck. Only the lovers are talking. There should be dialogue here. But I don't know what to tell you. They're not talking with any belief. They are not bothering to shake their heads. He is looking through the echo of his own eyes in the rearview mirror, refusing to run. She is trailing her hand on the dry rim of window, she is blotching the light. >>X2. He is turning the circle on his open ring-hand. He is draining the battery with a useless foot on the brake. >>X2 X2. She is staring at a pair of sneakers, bound and dangling from a powerline, flagging, half-mast. >>X2. He is tapping out a cigarette like it will be therapeutic, he is slamming it back in the glovebox. There is dialogue again: Fill it in. With her index finger she is pushing hard at her breastbone. They are both finding it hard to breathe. The knowledge of everyone they're about to hurt is not an easy element to breathe in. They're the lovers. You can blame them now, if you want to. That's your choice: this is the director's cut.

go home, stay home

You get to the age when you start to leave parties separately: that's when the trouble starts, the drift.

The drift: she stands at the door looking back for her husband, and feels it, with the rhythm of the baby's breath gluey at her neck, the crinkle of mucus she can hear in the tiny lungs . . . But no, the kid's out to it, angelically slumped, cheeks rough with heat, drool curled through the collared wool.

She should stay. Stay. There's nothing wrong with the baby.

There's nothing wrong. There's everything.

She stands at the door, searches for her husband, makes him out at angles through the smog and thump of dance, bodies groggy with the soundtrack, the slither of dress. It's a work do. All the other women here *work*, and even now, at the party, they're still working, working themselves away from their kids, working the free booze into their glasses, working their hips through the calculated gloss of their get-ups, working their way round the room . . . towards her husband.

She stands at the door, looking back at the party she's about to leave. First.

She knows she's not really the one leaving. She's the one left.

*

Once at a party he burnt down a garden shed. Doesn't know how it started but remembers the puncture of his fist, slow-motion and crisp, through the wall, then popping his hand back out from a socket of fibres. He'd been wearing a ring when his fist went in, a silver band his first long-term girlfriend had given him, so he'd started to thumb off chunks of the hole, grope his hand round in the gash of plaster. He remembers feeling the whole shed creaking on his forearm, as if all its slats were going to bust and engulf him, old planks wither and suck him in. So he stepped back, gave it another bash, a crunch with his boot, and before he knew it a line of blokes joined in, bottling and battering the slanted old structure, taking to it with roars. They were all thoroughly lagered and what have you; all sorts of chemical party snacks had done the rounds by then. But it didn't seem so much a pharmaceutical tantrum as a cosmic one. Something animal. They thrashed the shed to the ground in a kind of trance. Some hot old energy splattered through their blood as they hacked, derailing panels in spurts of curse and dust. None of the sheilas had joined in. They'd stood back: he remembers a silhouette of thin girls grouped under a washline, crooked wires cut across a dry-ice moon. They'd all been standing, arms poked at right angles, aimlessly holding the booze their men left behind.

Everything was rented in those days. They were all young and no one owned anything. They couldn't have given a shit when the old hut dropped right down on the grass. It came as a bit of an anti-climax in fact, after their scrum, how madly they'd stuck into it. The final flop, the last timbers whinging and shuffling, the slush of tin, were sort of feeble. The boys kicked around for a bit, puffing, feeling gutted. But then somebody, maybe it was him, had suggested they might stand a chance of getting it past the landlord if it looked like it had somehow caught alight. It was the kind of city where things burnt down, a row of streets just waiting for an accident. And the shed was chocker with weird old cans of poison and paint. So they'd fished out a few and set about torching it. The boys got a second wind waving the tins, coils of kero and toxic whatnot, pissing wild into the sky, bottles tagged with flame and bombed at the carcass with howling run-ups through the garden. They sang in raucous gulps, any crap they could think of, just to hear the words explode, an anthem of destruction. The fire made them operatic. He'd never heard his voice pump out the way it did that night, not before or after. The trash crawled and dissolved in the flame and sang its own chorus.

When the girls came close he managed to get his arm around a good one. She was a ripe one-nighter with a large arse packed under silvery jeans and a healthy portion of boob that was already turning lax and motherly. He couldn't recall her name but he remembered that: the texture of the tit he'd got his hand around, glossy and young when she lay back and let him gum its lustre in the open moonlight, but when she rolled to pull him towards her, tugging unhappily with signs of how the skin was going to give. Couples teamed up like this as the fire dropped and glowed, some matched by desire, some by default. The ones who just paired up with a shrug got stuck into each other faster, got busy humping under the old coats or sleeping bags that'd been dragged out, didn't bother wasting time criss-crossing whispers and limbs, tracing eyelids in awe through the firelight. Not that he was the kind to go boo-hooing because no girl unknotted his long hair or stared at the ridge of his jawbone through that foreground of flame. He'd proven that he wasn't that type, after all, he'd never had a girlfriend do that to him, or one he'd done it to, and not so much later he'd married, to be honest, by far the solidest shag he'd had, a girl with a monumental lower-half and a rigorous, strapping attitude to life both in and out of the sack. And he could not complain: she was the go-ahead type, productive, full of get-go. A model of old-fashioned drive, his dad had clucked and nodded his head. Without much input from him, really, a household, packed with enduring blocks of furniture and placid kids in bunks, had just seemed to assemble itself around her and thrive. It wouldn't be fair of him to make a complaint. Biologically, practically, she was a sound partner, good value. The one thing he could say, though, was that sometimes, through no fault of his own, he'd be standing in the clean kitchen opposite her, that dull, strict look of habit in her gaze, and it was all he could do not to walk right out.

Lately there had even been once or twice that he was not fussed when she'd clambered on top of him, the stronghold of her lower-half grappling him from all sides. Even then she'd been convinced old-fashioned drive could sort things out, rubbing him, tersely, the right way with serviceable kisses.

Not that any of this had bothered him too much, outright. It hadn't been a big issue. Not until tonight. But tonight, there was a new woman here, at the party, and just looking at her had jarred him, caused him alarm. He'd gone out and crouched on a kid's plastic seat by the barbecue, made a hard effort not to look for her again. But she seemed to be drifting the party, trembling with the load of a tiny, over-wrapped kid, not catching anybody's notice or managing to fit herself into any conversation. She hovered alongside groups, giving wan little grins as if she was joining in, shifting the burden of the baby with shivers that gave away how she was feeling, a kind of loneliness transmitted through her thin grip that he'd never seen when his capable wife grabbed their children, tidied and tucked them in. And then, as he watched, a guy from the last group actually sidelined her, stepped across her to crack a joke, and without even knowing it, pushed her out with the brawny wall of his back. And she stood there for a moment, dazed, with a quivering smile still on her face, staring at the man's thick shoulder as he shoved his drink in a punchline across the group, then she stared down into the blankets she carried, down, as if something life or death would happen in there.

She'd looked around for a way out through the bodies as if the house were on fire.

And that move—flinging her head around, with her hair coursing down from the fretwork of hopeless clips, and the neck of her dress yanked aslant with the baby so he could see the echoes of blue veins making their descent—that move had started it. Not long ago, he'd thought, at a party, I knocked something down. I burnt a place right down to zero.

*

When Rigg was a kid, his mother called a party a hooley. The street he'd grown up on was known for hoolies, and his house, smack in the centre of the cul-de-sac, was hooley headquarters: once in a while the gang would troop round to another place and try to stage a bash there, but it always fizzled, and everyone would drift back to their pad, sometimes on the same night, adults with their plastic goblets and their hair in splurges and their sexy gibberish and their tendency to snuggle together vomiting or pashing or squabbling on the kerbside, skipping back down or up to his house, thudding into each other with gropes and sways as they tripped around looking for the key. Usually it would take a kid—from the line of kids that had tramped back up the road behind them, rambling along, still dozy in PJs or jousting in their sleeping bags, racing them in wriggles up the grass verge, sometimes whooping, sometimes listening just to the silver soundpattern of their haul, their hiss—to fish the key out from its hiding spot or slither up to some high window and let the tribe in. Then the hooley would restart, a junction of drunk bodies, trashed and succulent through all the rooms, leftovers plucked from the fridge, smoke oozing and poised between mouths, guitars slashed and brushed, kids clumping in corners, on beanbags, and blinking in time to the song and puke and politics and lunacy as they burst and faded, rose and broke back out. He loved drifting in and out of half-sleep to that, as a kid, sprawling in the hazy liquidity of hooley nights, the rumbling of joy through the walls of the overrun house. He'd give anything to sleep to that soundtrack again: here, at this party, he stares at the couch, in fact, and finds himself longing to curl up and nap with the buzz of the adult world cupping his head, humming him to sleep with a rugged, sleazy, irresponsible symphony he has no part in.

None.

Nothing the adult world has to offer can take him back to that state, let him freefall, to bliss, against a background of wildness like that. Here he is, in hard fact, the Boss Man at a party, the Big Rigg, and everything he does, what he wears, what he says, what he drinks, is a part of that. He took the precaution of getting himself high before he came but that does nothing to excuse him from his role. And just now, seconds ago, he took the liberty of letting himself into the loo while the hostess was still wiping, he took the chance of pinning her back on the seat and rummaging under her skirt, while she squirmed and nestled and pulsed out a little more urine onto his cuff. But even before he withdrew his fingers he knew it wasn't enough. Because he still has to walk out to the party, to his part, stand around, making chat, trading industry pointers, talking profiles, portfolios, means, percentiles, projected returns, expedients, fuel injections and miles to the fucking tank.

His mother, if she walked into this room, this party, if she stood here barefoot and bombed in her rustling dress, with her unhooked pouches of hippy breast and her clinking beaded hair, would not know who he fucking was.

And here he is, having judged her, somehow, having left her in every step he took, to study, to exceed, to invest, to achieve, to outclass, to possess, here he is, and he'd give anything to walk back out now on his rank, his code, his successful model and find a world of dropouts, a loungeful of stoned, fondling, amoral lovers and lie down on some handmade rug, let their laziness bury him.

*

Derek goes out to the garage for the ice. Just a plastic bag of ice is all he wants. He's not thinking of much else, except maybe dumb things like how the metal on the drive reminds him of how he used to have to put the milk bottles out as a kid, six bottles in a crate that had a rust-milk-rubber smell, a bloody long hike up the back drive, maybe a whole K freezing in the sheep-shitty dusk, and he used to have to take a big hunk of batten along with him to fend off the fucking mad ram his father had trained to bowl everyone. How he loved to whack its wild head for a six, back up and wait for it to bolt, then swoop the batten down and listen for the crack, which never finished it off but made its lizard-eyes flicker, its hooves waggle, cartoonish in the half-dark. What a mean little shit he must have been, but then his father hadn't been much better, egging the beast on to tackle everyone, as if there weren't enough backhands going round ... How does he start thinking that, just walking down a stone drive, slipping out from a party to fetch ice?

Did he volunteer to go out (*Hey, not a problem*), or did he get sent (*You couldn't be a sweetie, could you*)? Derek doesn't know, but he knows his way round, knows his way out back to the big chest freezer in the workshop; he's the kind of guy that does this helpful stuff: picks up, pitches in, drops off, lights up, barbecues, gets thanked with sexless cheeky pinches (women) or with clobbers on his broad back (men). Even in the mirror he finds himself offering his copy a chubby, charitable smile, clucking at his image in a *No worries mate* way, amenable and keen, full of blokeish utility. He's the designated stand-up guy, the shirt-off-your-back type. Even now, crunching along the drive, he gets a boost just thinking through the grins and *Onya mate* pats which will greet him when he lugs the ice in. He plans how he can carry it to best effect, heaving it over his shoulder like something he gunned down in the night, a hero.

But the garage door is ajar when he gets there. He freezes, peers in. There's a fusion inside of knees and tongues and T-shirts, a belt half-unhinged from shucked denims and flapping at the freezer with a sequence of small, metal pings. They're young, a couple of teens no one's noticed for hours now, rubbing at each other, hands crowding under sweaty seams, getting each other to the urgent stage. Or maybe, just he is: she seems fevered but also a little shy, perched on the freezer lid, her rump flinching and scant in the boy's hand, him beginning to pester a bit, cramming forward with a stubborn rhythm, his talk as he kneads her, teasing but hazardous.

At the door, Derek thinks for a minute he should clear his throat, break it up, step in. But the thought doesn't reach the gap in his gut that has already made him creep closer, stare harder.

Then she does say no, with a kick at the freezer. The boy kicks out after her.

'Anyway, you've got a girlfriend,' she says, plucking her T-shirt down.

'I'll dump her.'

'You won't.'

'I will.'

'What*ever.*'

'No shit. I'm telling you.'

'I can't.'

'You're halfway fucking there.'

'Yeah, but like, I don't want a baby.'

The word baby warps in the cool of the garage, and you can tell the boy doesn't take to the echo of it. Even Derek feels dislike: the scrawny woman he's seen walking round with a baby, earlier, looks like she's set to pass out under its weight. He's got no time for women that fold up so pitifully, that trail around with kids like they're dazed, fatigued. His mother had been one like that, always wandering, dreary, staring at her house-load of undone tasks as if she were disabled.

'Just a blow, then,' the boy says. He smirks at the compromise. 'Eh?'

'You give me a blow, and I'll dump her. Straight up.'

Maybe he would've, or not. But the girl isn't gambling. She pokes a hand round in a cast-off jacket, produces a phone.

'What's her number then?'

He tells it, scraping his sneaker at the grille which is rusting at the base of the freezer. She taps, rapid, tilts it to her head, connects, stays silent, passes him the cell, and he speaks into it, sure of himself, brutal. He moves with the phone, scuffing, a language of cool, his eyebrows flicking as he grunts. He's so offhand he even cracks a funny.

From the door Derek doesn't watch the girl's face for long. But it's not blank for the second that he does and he thinks he can feel the hot hole in her belly that has drained all the blood from her face, that makes her close her eyes, stoop. Still, she gets on with it, bucks herself up, fakes the sluttish. She's crouched before the call is even finished. The boy's last splutter of breaking up into the phone is hoarse, hysterical, on the verge of come.

Derek would imagine that it's not the best blow in the world. But he's not sure he ever really got one so good himself. And there's so much triumph in the boy's face, so much cocky ecstasy, he looks so smug as he spasms, that Derek can't cope.

There's a stack of timber by the garage door. There always is at these lifestyle blocks, old tongue-in-groove, joists, fluted verandah rails. Take him round any of these work dos and Derek'll know where they are: he's the guy they always rope in, the hub of any DIY off-day, handy, eager to muck in, whip up smoko, lend tools, forget to grumble when they get buggered or mislaid. *Whatya reckon, Derek, mate, kauri, matai?* He stares down at the demo planks, the kids still hurting through the corner of his eye, through the chink of the door.

He would like to pick out a tidy little length of four by two, he would like to stride, yes, *stride* in, hearing the metal door screech as he swings, he would like to organise the wood in tosses through a loose fist, chuckling, until he's scared the two of em white and shitless, until he's got the grip of a lifetime, he'd like to hoist the thing up two-handed and feel the drag, the resistance, the air blast up at all his arm-muscle as the batten drops.

But he's Derek.

In real terms, Derek's the sort of bloke who worries about the looks he's going to earn if he goes back into the party without the bloody ice.

*

Jackie didn't get off the bus. This is what amazes her, what she carries around the party, this thought, uncertainly shiny, like her drink.

She could've got off. She could've yelled, could've struggled from her seat, could've clawed at the bell, torn down the whole string if she'd wanted, could've sprinted the aisle with the bell-cord whipping from her hand and made a scene, could've strangled the driver if he didn't pull over, flip the door and say *Get out then, you mad bitch.* Isn't that what she could've done? Would've done once?

Yes. Once.

Once, she would have said that to see him like that, walking down a street in the middle of a city past exactly *her stop*, was Fate. The odds, the chances, the random criss-cross of events that had to splice to bring them both to that same time and turning, you couldn't possibly calculate. Only Destiny, once, she would have been *sure*, could drive such an equation; when Jackie was a teenager, x always equalled the meant-to-be of true star-tangled love.

She didn't recognise him at first—perhaps that was the problem. He didn't look like he used to: it looked like the basic outline of him, but he was missing something, an attitude, an angle of cunning, a kind of syncopation, horny and fun like the rhythm of back-seat sex, which always used to be there in his walk, shoulders poked back, grin sleazy, eyebrows in on some big cosmic joke. The personalised shrug of his teenage walk, with its blend of sloppy I-don't-give-a-toss outlook and promise of a muscly fuck-beat in it: that had gone. It was his prototype, sure, his model, she could see walking up the street as her bus passed *her stop*, but it was in a suit, and its steps were regular. The rebel come-on, the dirty-cute shove of the ribcage taking on the world, the shock of gritty hair: all that was gone. He didn't even swing his briefcase—he just seemed to guide it smoothly down the street, keeping it level beside his groomed suit. His face looked concave with monotony. His balding head, shining back the chrome of the shop-fronts, made her somehow think the word *high-rise*.

No doubt he was successful. So maybe that was why she didn't get off. She was hardly a success now, was she? Unkempt kindy-mother, dangling a nappy bag from part-time work to part-time uni, a plastic pod of vege slush already burst on her philosophy book, Nietzsche glugged with pumpkin, last night's half-hearted make-up a decomposing yellow round her chin and glittering blue in her eye-wrinkles; she looked, in fact, like van Gogh's self-portrait only without the goatee and with her kid's ladybird scrunchy tied in desperation up into her smelly trail of hair. She was hardly going to knock him dead, was she, if she jumped out down the bus-steps at him now, such a slouch, no one's yummy-mummy, no one's MILF, but a kind of waste product of domestic chaos, a pile of whatever was left over from the morning's scramble to get-kids-packed-and-out-the-door. But she didn't have the kids now: she couldn't use them as an excuse. They weren't the reason she didn't stop, didn't wave out. She'd already dropped them off, at school, at playcentre. She was alone, she could've gotten off. Although, maybe, they were with her in habit, in a general weary principle of shortcuts and whatevers. *Slack Jack*, her husband called her. She didn't carry a briefcase, just the woman's version of it: the middle-aged, motherly, too-hard basket.

That was all true. But it was also more than that. And somehow, the more-than-that had made her get dressed up tonight, slide her body, still lithe, into the slinkiest sheath she could find wedged in plastic at the back of the cupboard, weave herself through the party with a bare arm waving a few too many topped-up gins, sexily colliding with the guests, tilting her frosted face in the chatting groups with a flushed, potent look, as if she might suddenly shout, spin, strip, let her body show off the lovely freed-up thumping of its blood, the giddy knowledge of no longer being in love . . .

No longer in love with the boy she thought of as her one-and-only, her true-and-for-all-time, madly-deeply-despite-her-marriage-and-three-kids, miserable, slavish love.

He was now so dull she could see him walking down a street and feel him *bore* her from a distance. Bore her so badly she sat, blank and yawning, in her seat and did not even bother to think about getting off the bus.

*

It is possible to say it.

The doctor had said it, several times, and nothing happened to the muscles of his face as she heard it, that word, clipped onto the others, simply lined up with other words, stapled into logical, colourless monotone, pronounced, repeated by the doctor's accomplished mouth. He has no lips, Monica's doctor (she'd once joked to her husband—*ex*-husband—that this seemed respectable for a gynaecologist), just a pair of dry stripes where the words exit, each one assembled like the next. Yes, once she'd quipped to her husband (*ex*), fresh from a probing check-up, that her doctor's lack of any pert, flushed pout brought a balance to their intercourse. But sitting in his office this afternoon . . . oh, the joke was on her today, *in* her, wasn't it, and even more so because now she had no husband to tell. She studied the doctor's watertight, linear mouth, working blandly through the contents of his notepad. Without underlining or pausing. Not even for effect.

So, it is possible to say it. That word.

She tries, in the kitchen, at the party, to say it to someone, to say it to one of the women as they twist the trays of ice and clunk them in the buckets. She tries, as more women arrive and sing out offers of *a hand*, as together they ring little gourmet dobs of finger food around the trays, squelch out dips and spray bowls with clattering chips to get rid of the kids. She comes close, the gulps of gin bringing her closer, but the word only skims off her eyelids, past her tight mouth. She shakes her bracelets down, pats hard at the cup of her bra and waves away questions. The women laugh back, relieved to see her giggling off whatever-it-is, flicking at mascara that's dripped along her eyes, left a hologram of lashes: none of the women are here for dramas, or at least, only dramas of their own making, slinky scrums forming as they weave through the talkers on the dancefloor, tongues flirting around a glass, just enough to leave a horny buzz but avoid a husband cutting in. She knows this. So she yells out the window to the men round the barbecue, tosses them loaves of buttered bread, makes a frisbee of the plastic plates, dumbbells from the Watties cans. When someone totes in a gift basket, full of luxury pre-wrapped thank yous for hosting the do, she undoes the silver raffia bow, stakes it in her hair. She bellows that the music needs cranking up, she finishes dressing the plates with a groove around the kitchen.

It is not possible to shake your thing, to circulate, gossip, knock back gins, while saying that word.

But she says it later, says it and says it, squatting on the loo, wiping herself, still sleek with the doctor's gel. She drops her head down and sees it, the doctor's clear emulsion drizzling from her in a string. She puts her palm against the warmth of herself. Skin laps at her wedding ring. The word, the word is. Muscle moulds to her hand as she sobs.

Then he comes in, blunders, with his zip already open, overbalances to see her on the seat, drops to his knees, without really looking, and his hands replace hers. He's the boss man, the top man, doesn't notice, or care, whose hands he's knocking aside, just knows where his own are driving. Soon he'll be signing off on her application for sick leave, he'll be giving her company clearance to crawl off officially and die, he'll be authorising, *okaying* that, he will *manage* it, as if transferring her to suffering is just another relocation, death just a different department. But for now she stares up at his stoned grin, kneads down on his knuckles, braces her stilettos on the lino, grafts onto his hand. He extracts it, shakes, strokes one of her earrings for a moment, then leaves.

She leans her head on the wall and says it. She feels it move in her mouth the way it's moved in her body, swallowing, spreading. Eating every other word inside her head.

*

He had the kind of wife no one remembered.

Not her face, not her name.

You could see it in the bored haze of everyone's hellos. The tensionless smiles and handshakes. They seemed to get duller as Stirling led her round the room. And you recall my wife? Oh *yes* of course: blank nods, blah-blah monotones. Flimsy grips, glances past her hairdo at the wallpaper. Weary displays of teeth, interest-free.

He remembered girls he'd had at school, how he'd lent his first XV jersey to them, the chosen ones, how they'd strutted up hallways, anointed by him, or arranged themselves at lunchtime along the wooden seats, uniform skirts slashed way past regulations, bald thighs shining in big, fresh chunks and the crest of his jersey a tangled gold star on one tit, like a stamp to show he'd wrapped his sports-hero hand round it: Stirling (head boy, first XV, just missed dux, with Toyota hatchback) Was Here. But apart from the show of it, Stirling hadn't ever really liked that kind of girl. Permed, flashy, unshrinking in their slutted-up uniforms, webby black bras like splashes of Coke under their shirts. His wife, overall, had seemed a much better option. She wore rolled socks in nice lace-ups all year, not twinked-over romans, and she smelled of talcum, sammies of luncheon meat, fabric softener, chapel.

But no one remembers her.

Half the time, more, if he's honest, that includes him.

And tonight, on the way here, they'd stopped at a one-way bridge and there'd been a roadside sign. Home-painted, half-arsed on warped Gib, hanging by a nail: Greenhill High School Centenary, it read. Beside him, his wife had given a small woof of laughter, one or two follow-up talcumy puffs.

For a minute, she said, I thought it read High School *Cemetery*.

No one, he realised, would remember her next time either.

*

Stoned, Blake lies back in the paddock, gapes at the veering of stars. What the fuck is it with him tonight? It's the farmhouse feel of the place—might be a lifestyle block, but it still gave off that cabbage-tree, offal-pit, flannelette feel, still had the sound of windblown fence wire you could taste, that chilled tin tone that hummed along your childhood teeth. And the dark was the real dark, the dark of the farm he grew up on, homekill freezer-lid dark, that strung-up meaty blackness he'd always held his kid-breath to get through, praying that he never felt the veiny punch-bag knock, the fatty kiss as he shivered past the creaking sides of meat. Now it didn't get to him so much, of course, as a grown-up. Just that tonight he'd rolled one too many, had too many workmates turn down a joint, look shocked at the offer, look like they might want to make a fucking memo of it, inform the boss (apart from the fact that he looks totalled as well). Blake'd grinned, shrugged, woven off: uptight blokes turned to speak to the women beside them like they wanted to dictate a formal fucking warning. He'd polished the stash off himself. First he'd lost feel of his limbs in the boozy, rocked room, so his torso had bobbed around like something in a trough. Then his spine had zinged into his head, rolled up into his skull with a final stinging flick like his dad's old *don't-fucking-touch-it* metal tape measure. He was blessed he'd even made it out the swinging room. Coming round, helicopter style, in a paddock, even conked out like this, on black sheep jellybeans of shit, could be counted as lucky, could be counted like the big bolts of star that stopped the frozen sky-lid from locking on his head with a whack.

Yep, it was the farmhouse feel that did it. The drench-gravel-dahlia-twostroke-creek smell: they couldn't lifestyle block that out, couldn't subdivide and run the ride-on mower over it. It made him think of her. It made him take too many hits, and think her back in, think her back through the green bedroom door at the edge of his skull where she smiled a half-girl, half-ghoul smile and slid the yellow light out with a cracked liquid click.

The babysitter. Tucking him in. Tucking him too long in.

He could only half remember. And that half was mixed. So she sat on the bed, just the nice girl minding him at milking time, as if she would tell him a story—and she sat on the bed, as if she were the monster from that story herself. He remembered the thickness of her big, blunt half-adult teeth pulled into a smile of pure loneliness. The loneliness of all those farms, packed into clammy bulk around her singlet, bicep, chin. There was no one else but the two of them and miles of outside hissing fenceline. He could feel the warm, heavy nowhereness of her, dwelling, dwelling on the end of his bed. He could feel the warm wet burden of her eyes, like a cow down and doomed in the drizzle of barn light.

He could half remember a friendliness for the hand she put

under the sheets, a recognition, her mouth on his a sob of sour comfort. And he could half-remember the heat of his stomach rolling a cry hard up into itself. Nights curled round the bad dream of her, like the pumping acid pod of an appendix.

He's way, *way* stoned.

Nah, it was too long. He was too small for that kiss.

He's lonely, lonely, stoned. He wonders if he's making her up, that girl, lumbering over from the next-door property, her old cords garnished with the loose slime of grass and her hair in stumpy plaits. But if it isn't real, his insides shouldn't feel . . . feel *gristly* as the carcass his father would slip the good butcher knife down, in one gliding hack. If she's real, he misses her, hates her, misses her, however that works. He never, and always, understood. Suppose at least he had her, if she was real: other little kids at milking got tied in their beds, his mum and dad had said. For safety. That's how they did it round their parts.

It's the farmhouse feel. The nothing-else-ever vacancy of the place. Some party, some fucking do, yahoo. Back-paddock freezer-door dark. Stars and animals swinging. And the whole fuselage of the sky about to drop down on you.

*

She's a hard woman. Ian can't take his eyes from the rod of her collarbone, steely under silk-strings, and even her cigarette shines hard as bone in the outdoor light. She breathes long lashes of smoke, sneers, angles. Brackets of bone rub the dress's surface: he hears static. Everything she does implies, leads: her sharp tongue-tip, the vapour of ribs along the sheath, the teeth letting out their smooth nicotine shiver.

It seems to have been decided that they'll disappear and fuck some time. It's a done deal. It's some contract they made in the spill of drink-dance, in bumping with a laugh through the ranchslider, the blur of lighting up. His wife has gone; her husband's had a skinful and is trampling solo to old disco tracks, couch waiting to catch him, comatose for keeps. So Ian's just a few cigarettes away. From shoving that fabric upward, thumbing at that sleek bone, hoping she's tight enough to sprain him.

But he thinks he should say something. Should talk to her, before.

A teen silhouette shrugs over the lawn in front of them, moves with a thrum out through the fence.

'I reckon ... I thought the 30s would be different,' he finds himself muttering. 'I thought I'd be, I don't know, looking back and feeling ... somehow wise. Like here tonight, seeing these teenagers. I thought I'd be all like, *If only I'd known then what I know now.*'

She's a hard woman, exhales a hover of smoke. Her mouth looks leathery. There's something bitter, sweating through the skintight of her metallic dress. Her eyes are an empty glass.

'If only I *felt* now what I *felt* then,' she says. 'That's more fucking like it.'

*

Somehow Sonia finds herself rubber-gloved, scraping the plates into a rubbish bag. Gown bunched just-a-bit into her undies so the hem doesn't dangle into the mulch. A plastic peg in her hair to stop it sweating into weeds around her face.

Her face in its Maybelline leftovers. Crikey, what a hoot. She catches sight of it, doughy and dun in the oven door. Lippy slithered into wrinkles and blue syrup stuck in ducts. What a real hoot she is.

Ah well, no sense moping. She belongs in the kitchen, in the guts of a party, on the run-up or the clean-up. That's who she is. She's a vending machine of a woman, or one of them big squeaky trolleys, kitted out with clean towels and bleaches.

In herself, though, she doesn't scrub up well.

Turns out she's not the only one, either. Another woman wanders in, semi-grins, sets about gladwrapping, jamming the washer tray full. Her frock's an eyesore, too, a lolly-coloured flop like something the shop spat out half-chewed. Big wombly bosom, asymmetrical, a tea-towel smell wafting out from its sides. Still, it's something, not to be the only one. Something to have a sort of mate. Once they've had a wipe round they share a dish of tidbits that won't fit in the fridge, smirk at each other with grease, the companionable sludge of pastry along their teeth.

A thick dusk, ripe and silent as tree roots, trickles towards them over the paddocks. They stop on the lino, in the last block of honey the light leaves, and sway with it, nearing touch. Side by side, the bowls of their breasts almost slope to each other, knock, damp with love.

*

He's going to take her home, because how could he not, when she comes out to sit on the deck and smiles at him, such a feeble smile, her upper lip rising so palely, it cuts him to bits. He's a dismal flirt so doesn't try it. Just hunches where he is, on a plastic kid's chair, and watches her, nudging about the baby. Watches, looks off, swallows, stares again. It's red-hot and hellish—all the blood in his torso, slowly detonating.

'I think there's something wrong,' she finally says, not so much to him as the dark along the decking. Her voice isn't sweet, but even so he gets a rush from it. There's the sound of a brink in it, a shiver, breaking-point.

'Bubs?' he says. 'Nah. Look's KO'd to me. You want to leave them while they're kipping. Take a break from worrying.'

'No. I feel it. You see?'

'How's that?'

'I know he's asleep. But ... I think there's something wrong with him. I should get him home.'

'Give it a bit, eh? You don't want to bail too soon. The hard bit's getting them off to sleep. And that's done.'

He's never had to give comfort like this, to reassure anyone: his durable wife never needs it. There's so much contentment in it, he feels like extra stars have cropped up above them, stars as cheap and breakable and surplus as the clips achieving nothing in the shambles of her hair. The plastic cup starts to crack in the compassion of his grip. He reaches out and pats a little friendly drum riff on the barbecue. Through the grate the smell of char tingles. Love relaxes in the thump of his hand and he longs to stretch it out.

But she doesn't pick up on the solace of it. Fumbling, sober, she knocks the kid awake. Fist-sized, the face wails out from its woollen stranglehold. She starts to scrabble at the neck of her dress, as if she might haul a breast up from it, then blinks across at him, eyes wet.

'I put this dress on,' she shakes her head, 'without thinking of how . . . It was my first time out since . . . Oh god, I'm an idiot. It does up at the back.'

So this is how he gets up and goes over to her, how he scrapes aside hair from the apex of her back, how he feels the tender hunk of bone there, buried in the thinness, the size of a grenade, how he thumbs around the gauzy neck for the zip, almost pierces the dress as he tries to steer it downward. And this is how one side of her body almost slips right into his hands, outside the oblivious house with its packed thudding of half-cut dance, its lonely buzz of prattle and boozy clink. This is how he finds himself bending towards the shoulderblade that rises, that flinches, wing-like in the chill, a structure his hand could crush, that almost meets his lips. Almost: he feels heat run along his teeth, the sting of almost. In half-light he makes out a birthmark on her shoulder: as he pulls away the shape of it blots his lids.

A rough guide to the rest of the night might go like this, although he hardly remembers: she asks for the dress to be done up again, thanks him, backs into the party to mutter to her husband that she needs to leave, can't feed the baby, has to go home. But the baby has dropped to sleep again; her husband tries to woo, distract, bully, then snaps, slaps the keys at her. She walks to the door, turns, watches her husband for a minute. He shakes his head, sulks, flanked by a trio of women who soothe as he grizzles, gulping his next drink.

Stepping in from the deck he clears it with the husband: *No worries mate, I'll take her, nah, some women lose it after kids, eh, not a prob, no biggy.* It's easy to stride to her, retrieve the keys from her tiny fist, pull off the one she taps as house, flip the rest back across the lounge to one of the women. The husband shrugs, the women gleam.

Either no one gets the drift, or everyone does.

But the rough guide to how he gets her outside is irrelevant. What he remembers is what it looks like out there: all the kids that everyone's been ignoring have torches or cellphones out in the fields, and the lights swing and blister unsteady stains in his eyes as he walks her down the drive.

'Go Home, Stay Home,' she says, when he stops her by the car.

He stares back. The children scuttle through the iridescence, shrieking. The fence wire they slither in and out of drones in low-pitch ripples through the night. Then one girl veers up the driveway past them, pulls to a halt, turns in the stones and, staring at them, thrusts a torch under, then into her mouth, her teeth clunking plastic. Her face blazes, the meat of it translucent, its shape inside-out, tongue twining with wet light. The concave phosphorescence of her face drives her eyes back under bone hoods. Then she gags softly, the evil of the joke gone in a flash. She dangles the torch away from her, drops it, listens to the blank bump and runs off up the drive.

'What the fuck,' he says as he bends down for the torch.

'Do you remember the rules?' the woman asks him.

'Eh?'

'For Go Home, Stay Home. Do you remember the rules? How you're meant to play it?'

He hits her with the beam so her eyelids flick, wrinkle away from him.

'I think,' she says, 'I remember my first game. I was little, you know, always the littlest kid. I thought it was magic to start with, how you could have a home in it, how you just *say* where, choose a place where you're just . . . safe. But then I learnt how you had to go out from it. They made you go away, that was the whole game. And there was always someone to stop you coming back there. And the longer you left it, the more you got scared and hid and crept, the more people there were to stop you. Getting home. The longer you left it the more the tagging spread.'

'I don't remember.'

'I think . . . my husband got tagged tonight. Do you?'

The question shivers, slips. But she seems to have the kid in a sturdier hold now, and with her free fingers she's running the trim of the car door. He listens to the squeal of her fingertips, not saying anything else except 'I'll let you in'.

In the car she looks straight through the screen and talks.

'When I was little, our street was on a party line. You remember them? Whenever you were on the phone you could feel the others listening in. I could feel their voices, feel what they'd think of me, how they'd be saying it. My mother was like that too. She'd hardly use the thing, because of everyone *in there*. You could feel their voices there, I mean that, humming through the line right into your head, even though they weren't saying anything. It's like that all the time now. What I do with the baby, how I don't do things right, with the house. Like everything I do is . . . on the party line somehow. You ever feel like that?'

He says, 'I'm not the type that . . . stuff gets through to. Most days. I'd be stoked to feel . . . much at all.'

'You don't seem like that.'

'Tonight . . . I'm not, tonight. I'll . . . let you in.'

He says it again, pulling up at the house she's directed him to, walks ahead of her to the front doorway and jams in the key she's selected for him. It's a brand new, clean, metallic and up-and-coming house, executive and symmetrical, but he feels something collapsing as he steps into it.

That's what he wants: a demolition.

He stands in the dark lounge as she skims past him, puts the baby in its crib.

Muscle overheats in his torso, smacks in his chest, waiting. When he feels her come back to the edge of the room he can't believe the battery of hot blood that speeds through him, hair-trigger, toxic. Can't believe it doesn't ignite, splash the place with fire. But she doesn't come closer. And he doesn't know the layout. So he strokes around for a switch and reaches out to punch on the light his hands have found. She's bright for a heartbeat, but at the last minute, his hand knocks the dimmer. And he has to watch the room sink, down through levels of dull, opulent, orderly loneliness. Back to dilute black.

He hasn't thought to bring the torch. He has to rely on her, in the vague room, to have the motive to drift towards him.

the next stop

It was the kid who saw him first. There was a line-up of orange vinyl chairs on the side by the Coke fridge and you could guess that's what the kid would head for, flat out. He was rarked up, jumpy, my kid. Like half the South Island, I suppose. Only he was extra jumpy, being thirteen, or just about. So he got into the shop ahead of me and took a jack straight for the Coke. Dropped the chain fly-screen back at me and Bubs with a slap.

There were maybe five vinyl chairs, or seven, to wait on between the counter and the corner. Orange, with black metal legs, and if you sat down on them you'd feel fish and chip grease suck up to your thighs. Half the seats were gone black and slashed, so there'd be this bubble of fatty air squeak open under you. You wouldn't want to even pick up those thin, oily mags, but you'd probably get desperate not to stare into space at some point. The air tasted soggy and chocker with salt from the vats. Plus, there was this 70s rope thing rigged in the dirty wedge of window by the very last chair. You wouldn't want a bar of that. It was this sticky net sack with a gross glass tub stuffed in it. Tucked into that there was one of those plastic spider-ferns that the sun had made an even worse joke of.

But I didn't pick up on him, sitting right there. It was the kid that did first.

I'd got through the fly-chains at the door and grizzled at the kid for just swinging that flap at me and Bubs. She was being a major handful, Bubs, and was due to pack a real shit if I didn't let her down out my grip, and I don't know, odds are it was already too late. But we might of stood a chance if the kid hadn't made it so obvious. There was some station half-tuned on a beat-up radio propped out back over the vats and they had the Eagles jangling a four-part whine about sunrise. Plus there was the buzzing of the fryers and stuff, and hooked above it all there was a fan pumping around, a big flywheel of grease that was off by a fair few degrees and squealing, making everything feel tilted. Plus, you know how they sink those metal tubs down in the troughs. They shunt them in the vat and everything froths. They tip them on the paper and whack them back to drip off the racks. So my point is, there was no shortage of noise. If the kid had kept it quiet, we could of maybe pulled a uey. Just backed out through the chain strips where we'd come in. (They use them to sift out the flies, but it's not like it made a diff. There was still a tag team of black flies twitching round the shop.) But he's no good at covering, the kid. Straight up, he made this dumb gulp: there was some word in it, but I couldn't tell you what it was. Then it was too late. Plus Bubs was wriggling big time in my arms. She was full on by then and I just felt like dumping her. I'd done my best to keep her topped up on the road, but she'd had a total gutsful. Fair enough, I suppose: me fucking too. The whole day had just lasted too long on that bus. I don't know. It was like we'd gone past the point of any way out by hours and hours. Drove off the edge of any plan to get things straight. I'd done my best to get us sorted—last stop, I'd gotten hold of the timetable and taken a crack at making our trip stop somewhere decent in the island. But it didn't matter what we tried to catch. There was no good road that was coming to meet us.

Then I knew he'd seen me before I saw him. I knew because when I looked at him, his whole head already had a fix, that stage before a low smile he gets where his eyes are jammed on target and the only thing moving is this tiny shiver in the thread-veins just above his beard. He had a cap on that smelt like something mowed and read CREW, and when he came close the red of it picked up those veins. They'd been in his face as long as I knew him, weird strings hanging like an inch above where he'd shave. Looked like red pen someone had been testing out in scribbles on an old beer box. Before she learnt better Mum used to take the piss. But I didn't. Plus he was wearing a shirt the green of the pine needles you could see clumped in the clay of his boot tread. There was this blowfly that landed on him later, when I was having to talk to him. It dozed around his collar, interested in some stink built up there. I watched it. The edge of the shirt was dieseled, gone the colour of that fly's back-end.

But by rights it was the high-vis vest you saw first. Zipped up the front, with chunks of pocket plugged full of work tools. He gave little Bubs one to play with later, pliers or some shit. I wasn't too fussed on it—I'm no prize mum but even I could see that was a hazard. But he just laughed and said, You gotta shut them up somehow, eh.

That was later, but. First up he just walked close, easing CREW back on the sweat of his head. Took his time looking me over and said, Hard case.

Suppose I just froze for a few secs. While he went on clocking me. Hard case, he said, hard case seeing you here.

Which is where it went to bits. So let me back up. Righto: the kid had gone hunting for his Coke and, instead, got the chiller halfway open and made this yell. It rebounded off the rows of cans. And too late, he looked our way and scoped me and Bubs, straight off. But it took him a couple of seconds to click with the kid. The kid has grown: thirteen is that point where your body gets away on you. He's all shins and collarbone and doesn't matter what you put on him, his corners poke out all his gear. Maybe the hair reminded him. Now the kid's stopped being such a runt he's got hair like I used to, that same colour, flicking out wide round his head. The funny thing is, it even smells the same to me. When he lets me lean in to get a good whiff, which isn't much, there's something I can breathe in off his neck bones and it's stale and wet and feathery like something left over from my own self. Like the smell I used to wake up with coming off my pillow where my own head was sunk years back.

By rights I should of stopped him. Getting a Coke I mean. He was wired enough. Been cooped up in the bus and he'd never exactly been into sitting still. But it was better than that other drink. He tried me on for that one first. That Red Bull they reckon gives you wings or the one in that booze-look black bottle they call Mother. Mouthful of that shit just about makes my heart cave in.

So the kid wasn't waiting. He had hold of his Coke while the talk got underway. Started full on glugging. I can't be sure word for word what happened then. The guy behind the counter just picked up the kid necking his drink and came out with this high-pitched yapping about how he was into it before I'd fixed him up for cash. So I was kind of half into the catch-up at my shoulder and half-staring up above the counter to get our order square, get the yellow guy paid and get him off my back. And the issue there was being skint for starters. Or as good as. Which the little shop bastard figured out no worries. No prizes for that, with me fucking fidgeting round in my bag to check for any loose pingers, and trying to add Bub's hotdog onto the four-fifty chips and fit the kid's fucking burger on top of the Coke he'd already sculled, and then the guy slamming his till tray, still ranting, and having to ring the order on again with two dollars chips taken off and me telling him to keep the fucking egg if the fucking egg cost me a buck. Trying the whole time to keep an ear out back for him. But like I've told you, the Eagles were twanging on about motels and desperados, with the fan cranking through them and the foam in the vats going spare so the whole shop was a boil-up of hollow metal noise. Everything clattered as they shovelled in chips. I don't know. I wasn't even blinking by then. I was parched as a bitch and the air in the place was so groggy with fat I couldn't get a breath. I was trying to count and the answer wasn't coming, and between the cruisy flies and the Eagles and the chop of the fan I was totalled. I just lost track of what was what.

But he kept up talking. He wasn't letting me off.

At some point he said, Fuck, you look old enough.

I said, Yeah, well. You get that.

He said, So. How's your mum.

The guy behind the counter was ripping off a ticket from the book to give me. It had a three and a spade on it but the spade was red, like a heart wrong way up.

I said, Same old. Yeah. She's right I suppose.

He said, See much of her these days.

I said, Not a lot.

He said, Shame.

I said, It is what it is.

He said, True.

I said, She turns up when she wants to. Whatever. Suits me.

He said, She get through the shake okay.

I said, Unit's a write off. Not a scratch on her though.

He said, That'd be right.

I said, I reckon.

He said, How about yous.

I said, We're clearing out.

He said, Aftershocks.

I said, Among fucking other things.

He said, You got help.

I said, Yeah right. Who the fuck does.

He said, So where yous off to.

I said, That's what I'm on my way to jack up.

He said, Nothing sorted then yet. At a loose end.

I said, Too soon to tell. Suppose something'll turn up.

He said, Early days. No worries. Early days, eh.

I just stood there and listened. It was when he said early days again. I don't know. Some cold idea just spazzed through my head like goosebumps.

Which is why when Bubs revved back up I whipped off one of her jandals and gave her a good one. They were the jelly kind, thick with glitter on the inside, and I can dish it out when I've had enough. The tread stood out on her leg like a fish, even before she got the chance to start up a howl. For a couple of secs I just stood with the stretchy strap flapping in my hand, staring at the little red fish bones squiggling up out her skin.

Then it was all on.

Behind the counter the guy started kicking up at me again. Loud as, to get it over top of Bub's screech. He was waving his yellow hand at a jar on the counter, which had a stash of coins poked through the lid, and a pic glued round the side of some black kid's head saying you could donate and be an Angel. I said, Yeah, well, you can fuck right off. Let the angels pay for my feed. Or you're so fucking holy, why don't you make it free, eh.

I suppose I was hardly toning anything down by getting in his face like that. I suppose I have to be thankful that Bubs got taken off my hands and propped over on that corner seat. And thankful that he reached her a tool out his high-vis jacket and started doping her with it. I suppose I shouldn't of had this jet of panic shoot out around my back teeth. I shouldn't of made this choke, like bad luck was dizzy and sticking to the roof of my mouth.

Suppose I should of sat my arse down, like he said.

But as it was, I just paced. I looked down at the manky vinyl squares and raced round them, scuff by pissed-off scuff. Even worse than the kid by the finish.

And where the kid had fucked off to was through another grotty blind, but this one was green beads in jingly plastic blobs, and you went through to a restaurant. Not that anyone would want to. The kid was just standing there, in the empty diner where the lanterns hadn't even got bulbs and red tassels dangled off everything in the dark. The only thing lit was the fish tank, filled with a thick green the creatures were straining to swim through. And just looking in at the scummed-up glass you felt like the lonely fucking hard work of their fins was leaving some kind of filth in your throat like your words couldn't hope to ever float to the surface. I wanted to explain to the kid. I've wanted to for years since then. He was looking at me, and the chunks of sick green bead went tingling over his face like the bubbles in the fish tank you could tell held zero oxygen. And back there is where he should of stayed. Maybe he would of, if I'd found a way to explain.

But everything was fucking with me. When I turned back, there was Bubba sitting on the chair snot-faced and grinning at the tool, and above her head the gross sack was swinging and the bubbles of glass that poked through the rope looked like fish scales. So I knew I was out of it. The fact that those weird bits could match, but I couldn't get our trip straight to save myself, that was proof to me. I wasn't going anywhere fast, even if I tried. Not without him.

Which he'd figured, by then. You could tell by the veins, the smile that kept lifting their red-brown ends. The fly lazing round on the fuel of his collar.

He said, Where'd you say your next stop was.

I said, Fuck knows. I don't.

He said, All right. No need to spin out. You should calm it down.

I said, Well there's not many fucking connections from nowhere to nowhere.

He said, How many of the crew you got with you. Just these two.

I said, The others got fixed up.

He said, How's that.

I said, You know. Out of town. Into care. After the shake. Until I could get somewhere sussed.

He said, How many you got now.

I said, Just the four. Three boys. And her.

He said, Oh, yeah.

He looked at Bubs and said, Sweet as. Heard you finally got a girl.

Then he said, You see my story in the paper. After the big one.

I said, Nah. What's the go.

He said, I was right in it, mate. Took on the quake. You should of seen me.

I said, Missed it. Must of.

He said, Yeah, well. I was all over the paper for a couple of days. Plus TV. They made out I was a lifesaver, mate. Digging people out.

I said, True.

He said, No joke. I was a bit of a hero.

That's when the kid came back through the curtain. The flight path of green beads went mental as. He's never learnt to slow down, my kid. That's what I always see: my boy launching his face through the beads at us. The bubbles of the blind going ping and clack. And his voice sounding squeezed up out his skinny body.

I saw that bit, the kid said. I saw that bit about you on TV. They interviewed that woman after. You made out you were some superhero. Then that woman came on and said you were full of shit. She said you weren't anywhere near.

The beads were coming to a stop like air running out. I had the ticket for our feed screwed in my hand. The jar on the counter wanted money for angels and in the poster taped round there was a sad black kid. And in the chiller staring back at him there was a high-rise of Mother cans. On one side of the shop there was the line of orange chairs, with Bubs sulking and squelching on the last one and the spider plant drifting in its glass bin over her head. She was waggling a socket in her hand and he was tickling his thumb in where her T-shirt stopped. When the kid said that. Like I've said, the kid's memory was none too sharp. He moved way too quick, my kid, but he wasn't the brightest.

I didn't move when he pulled up from Bubs and just eyeballed the kid. Got a mouth on you, haven't you, he said.

He just stood and toed it, my kid. And shook. The shake moved the light in his hair. I would always have left it uncut, my kid's hair. So the smell of our days could keep lifting off of it.

Pay you to watch that, he said, stepping up, closer to the kid.

The kid said again, You're full of shit.

The guy behind the counter had come through and was shoving the wrapped-up feed at us. His mistake was trying to stop it. You could feel where it was heading. And I thought I had given him the ticket with the heart on it. I remember looking at the three and the red spade. But later, when the cop had sat me down by the fish tank, I still had it in my hand. And the jandal, too, with the glitter in the jelly like a held breath. I kept checking back for that dance of little specks. The cop said it was choice, the description I gave him. Gave him a lot to work with. But through the coated glass the traffic was going nowhere and the sirens lit everything with high-pitched fins. He was crouched by the tank and echoes that weren't fish kept trying to spread through the slush. And my brain was full of goosebumps again.

scenes of a long-term nature

They will meet at the east wall of the kitchen, where the last of the sunset runs sour in the tea-towel checks. They will fill the kettle, a joint action, him levering off its stiff oval lid, her taking up the handle and posing it under the drizzle of the cold tap. It will take her both hands. It will cause a quaver in her shoulderblade. But they will sing, a shorthand hum of tune they can't place, the residue of years in its half-vanished verse. They will wait. Through the net-trimmed window, they'll watch the washing line mill the glow of evening. There will be something still strung from a peg, and they will blink, but neither will be able to recall what it is. *Tomorrow, we'll get it tomorrow*, he'll say to her. The base of the jug will rumble and flick itself mute. *Grub's up*, he'll nod. They will watch the knots in each other's hands as they work, the his and hers cups, the spoons with their lacy crowns on, enamel names of holiday towns, the brackets of blue-tinged tendon in their wrists. She will pop open the trays with the weekday pill slots and top up the pellets from their silver sleeves. He will shave an apple for them, ruling off the red with a penknife in a loud frill of peel. They will listen for the theme to their programme, an off-pitch saga beaming through the lounge, a summons for their slippers to aim for their side-by-side armchairs.

*

They will have children. The skin of her belly will swell and split into a mesh of silver ripples, a heel from inside loosening the net. He will remember the evening she sits, no longer agreeing to the seams of her clothing, and the kick of his son will lift the globe, setting the fine streaks moving like he's gazing down through shallows at a flexing school of fish. They will have more. They will sleep in relays, pass in the hallway, stumble for each other to graze at palms and face, then blunder on to the sound of children bawling from sleep like their hearts are stopping. Her nipples will crack, crevices opening and crusting in the pink. She will not let him touch them. He will stare at the milky latch of his son's mouth puffing at the counterweight of breast and feel orphaned. She will steer her body backwards onto surfaces that are all too hard. She will wear puke on her sleeves and nappy pins clinking at the hem of her skirt, for convenience. She will always look flushed. They will hold small nests of breathing wool at chest height in a cradle of elbows and everything will ache. They will sing about pirates, they will sing about ribbons. Everything will ache. The rooms will fill with objects of broken colour, levers that whir, buttons that spin. They will watch them with the ghost of sleep still in their heads, the days out of focus through a cloud of other eyes they can't shut. They will step around unwashed clothes. The grass will grow, to silence the war of the lawnmower. The television will whisper. They will nuzzle the scalps of their children where the traces of palest hair turn down the soft track of spine and they will inhale. And inhale. It will be years that everything goes on aching.

*

They will nearly end. There will be nights when she sits awake on the edge of the bed, the moon a hard rim that doesn't answer her squint. She will know he is lying. She will hear it in his reassurance. In the low gear his car rolls into the driveway, idles before he comes in. She will know it, side-on, in his torso, when she stares at him smoking out the back of the house, the weight of out-breaths leaving his body in low strokes, steady, embittered through the axle of ribs. She will know his smile is rigged. The way he takes off his clothes in the considerate half-light of the bathroom will be too tidy. She will listen to the reasons he tells her she's wrong, all wrong, but she will know even under his defence, the phonics of hunger she'll hear somewhere in his chest. Yes, his diaphragm, moving against his meaning. When she meets the woman, her replacement will only be a version of her, wearing a dress in a shade she might have chosen, travelling the room with a slur she might have once had in her own hips. She will like her. She will want her to die. She will trade grins, click glasses with her, and wish her a future that is too big for him. She will write on the back of a bright serviette while she watches them on the company dancefloor, a Bic-pen parallelogram of bile that scratches down all her petty fears. It will be a cliché. She will stuff it in the dregs of her cocktail. It will soak with cosmopolitan. She will watch the green dial on the dashboard all the way home, snapping at him each time he edges over the speed limit. She will know because he never snaps back.

*

They will fit. They will learn to. She will hoist her skirt and thumb her pants aside with one hand, holding him in the other so she can smirk down and guide herself on. He will run his fingers through his mouth, a long suck, before he kneads them home. They will pump and shudder on each other, laughing at their rude grace. There will be an order to sweeping the drapes closed, a ritual of fingertips slipping down the stiff joins in their shirts, drawing their heads and ankles out the narrowing cloth. When they kiss it will feel like an elegy. When they kiss it will be a dirty joke. She will let him prop her on the frame of the bed and beat upwards until they grunt with rowdy fun-loving come. Or in the winter they will take to the hump of cold quilts and stage a lazy all-in-one fuck, barely peeling the covers off the places they push into one. They will know the poses each other strikes as they wipe themselves clean in the bathroom later, dopey balletic hunches to yank on the toilet roll and ease off the glisten of love.

*

There will be an illness. One will take the other to appointments down the long halls where clocks click backwards. Everything will be too clean for the pain. One will fill out the forms on the clipboard. Everything will be blue or green. There will be the thud of machines to lock one into sleep. One will write details over and over while the other leans back from the waist and splits open. Everything will be too well-lit for the fear. The radio set to mystic static. The heels of the nurses set to disinterest. The fingernails underscored on the vinyl handrests of the endless chairs. One will bring coffee in paper cups with a blossom of milk left on the surface. The other will watch it turn, leaking tendrils into the dark. It will be like the emblems on the doctor's coat. It will be like the danger clotted in their body. It will be like the numbers that drop and hover on the screen. One will breathe in for the other. It will be their turn, another time, to breathe out.

*

They will piss each other off. Just plain irritation. She will hate the way he blows his nose in the shower and it never quite rinses. He will hate the way a rain of beige powder is forever spattered round the basin. He will know it's not fair but he'll still hate the way she bleats bad muzak behind supermarket trolleys. And the way a gully of careless grey will weave up the part in her hair. She will hate the way in middle age he suddenly stops indicating, veering them into roundabouts through a peal of urban fuck yous. No one will come from Mars. Or Venus. They will just get on each other's nerves. Then shrug it off.

They will feel black and blue with talk. A marriage-load of the same old arguments. Money on the A side, sex and children on the B side. Either way the needle will be stuck.

They will fight. They'll stage three-day slanging matches which have the children bolting for their rooms, though once the kids are teens they will stand by their doors, roll their eyes and laugh. She will discover a talent for scrapping which is nothing short of magnificent. She will battle till she feels the pupils of her eyes dilate. She will thrill to the judder of doors, unhinging everything as she walks out on it. She will pick up the vacuum cleaner once and send it in an unplugged wobble of dust across the room. The children will giggle for years about Mum and her spazzes, dizzy Mum and her tiffs. He will know what's at the heart of them. He will load the kids in the Triumph, when they're little, and take them for an iceblock. They will bring her one home, blue with frozen promise and wrapped in a cocoon of fineprint.

*

He will take her on one of their last outings to buy her an eternity ring. They will have to plan for days. He will clean out their handy carrybag. He will pack its zip pockets with tissues, with inhalers, with a brolly, with mints, with personals and spare plastic sealable bags just in case. He will polish their good shoes, re-trim their comfort soles and leave them on newsprint to dry beside the cat's dish. He will flip through the bus timetable to decide the best route. He will have her arm through his all the way, a shivery company. He'll love it, down to its irregular pulse. When they've clambered on the bus, he'll have gotten the money wrong, the driver tutting and the queue groaning behind them. He'll tap her wrist where the bone is a fierce knob of blue with a message of *Not to worry, not long.* When they reach the shop where he's scrimped to let her pick whatever her heart is set on, there will be another couple ahead at the counter. They will watch them, with arms in a doddery link, the gleam of the merchandise like stars on the scrubbed film of their shoes. The couple will linger over their purchase, then head out through the bleep of the storefront, not noticing the selves they have rushed through.

*

She will make him jealous one summer. One of his friends will watch her too closely, tour her movements in the overheated bach, notice the sunburn flex on her collarbone, the peel of her soles from the sandy rented linoleum. She will bend too low to wedge in the tent-pegs, skip too brightly through the taut cord trails. She will bend too low to offer him the can-opener. She will bend too low to pass him his plastic plate, to tong it with a blackened steak, a flop of potato salad. She will bend too low to swing up the children into the greasy cradle of her breasts. Her hair will be pinned off-centre, the ends of it bleaching in the day-long salt. She will not just wade, but hand him the kids and dive out, sluicing with her thighs for deep water. The haul of her torso out the tideline when she returns will be heavy and sated and relaxed, the stretchmarks swimming down into her bikini like secrets, porous and quicksilver. She will make him jealous. She will want to. Tunes will tick around the turntable they prop by the washline, black grooves curling in the sun, and she will dance, on the balls of her feet on the buffalo grass. His best mate will pass her a drink. The ice will clink in the yellow glass tumbler as her hips shift. Her toenails will be painted. There will be jokes about parties where keys are traded, and he will want to kill someone. He will kick the chillybin instead, waking the tentful of grizzly children. And only she will know why. And smile.

*

He will win the prize for *Best Hat!* on *Hat Day!* (the staff will use exclamation marks for everything). They will take his photo, propped in his chair with a red plastic plate that they've filled with a ring of fiddly iced things baked into frills he can't handle. He will grimace and dribble at the flash. They will pin it to the noticeboard, *Winner: Best Hat!*, above the poster of the kitten clinging to the rope which reads *You gotta hang in there!*, below the flyer requesting that residents only use their buzzer when in *genuine distress*. They will wheel him to room 17. He will balance where they leave him on the left side of the bed, trying to unhook his toes from his slip-ons. It will take concentration. It will take swear words. The sight of his toenails, yellow and cracked, will not seem like much of a blasted reward. He will sponge at the drool on his spencer. He will tilt the bed back, careful to thumb the right button and not nudge the alarm again by mistake (*Oh, you naughty man!*). He will look at her photo on the locker, where she's pressed under glass in her white dress, her hair crop-dusted to a bell-curve, stiff and dark below the gap he's found under her veil, the space he's shivered to, lifted. He will still feel it, the scratchy gauze of her crown and its delicate, snagging trims, the warm tremor of her breath as he burrows through its trail, *I now pronounce you*. He will look at her photo. But he will not talk to her. He will not tell her about the fussy cakes he can't pick free from their corrugated paper, the froggy flop of the humiliating hat. All that mess they'd perched on his skull, all that eyesore of beads and daft bloody ribbons: he will thank his stars she wasn't here to see that. He will get himself settled. He will use the button (for god's sake, hit the right one) to steer his bed back and blot out the neighbours, the jerked tide of walking frames, painstaking and squeaky in the hall. He will think of making his way into her, all fingers and thumbs through the silvery see-through stuff that spills at her head, of reaching for the outline of smile he has to blink through, her still face washed in a haze of silky light, waiting in the layers of veil like a ghost he's always known would come.

*

They'll get on the bus. She'll be first, because she's older. A couple of years, but big deal enough to mean she gets to move to the back. But he'll sit sideways, as long as no other bugger nicks the seat next to him, so he can see her. He'll watch the way her jaw moves as she stares out the window, the crimps along the chinbone that look like sad thoughts. He'll watch the way her fingernails drift to the zits on her forehead, poke around in the hairline spray of pores. The way the slots between buttons on her white shirt bulge wide, let him peek bra-lace, grubby, overloaded. He'll watch what she reads, the way she pinches books off the other kids if she finishes her own, speeds through pages with no trace of needing to spew from the bus jump-starting the words. He'll watch the lazy hunch she's mastered, the coolest pose he's ever seen, the slouch of her trunk dead low in the seat with her knees slid up the metal in front of her, spine like a hammock, book on her belly, tongue-tip tapping her top teeth as she reads. He'll think she's the one. The flicker of boob-lace, the spread of text on her pelvis, the untied shoelace she always seems to sport—these things are evidence. But once he goes up to her, full of certainty, to tell her so, she'll stare hard back at him. *As if*, she'll blurt. Then smile. *As if.*

how to leave your family

1.

Drive to the shops with three children, boy and two girls. Load kids, car hot, voices and hands sticky, car seats bulging and scalding, seatbelts whining to cut damp skin too tight. Lean in bodily, lumber, one foot left on gravel, head stuck in their wriggly haze. Smell urine-jelly bloating a nappy, grazed and glitter-sprayed legs, the heated crush of cheese and banana bumping inside a lunchbox. Almost smile, until you get kicked in the face, a toenail (dirty) nicking your cheek as kids chant, *Did not, yes you did, did not, yes you* (foot jolt, violent and final) *DID!* Hear your voice explaining, tired: *We don't hit, and we don't kick* (snickering, more kicks). Give up. Plug in last belt, a *who-cares* click. Reverse. Clamber. Scrape clip through scalp and out of hair in climb from back seat: stand and run hand along skull.

Look down into the hairclip: gaping and cheap, tooth and claw. Useless. Throw it into the gutter (*Mum!*). Drive streets. *Did not, yes she did. Not. Yes she—*(kick).

Park: put face on wheel for a moment. Feel hot vinyl through hair, ridge of string and small pulse coming from cut kicked open on cheekbone. Turn to look at children. One still wet from kindy water-play, one with lipstick and snot smeared up face. Last one barefoot. Almost say, *For the thousandth time, will you please put something on your feet, you know we don't go into shops without our shoes on.* But close mouth, stare down at littered car, at the dirty glinting twitch of feet. Turn and twist down the rear-vision mirror to check face. Stroke the damage, a small raised welt in freckles gathering scab. Black smudges on eyelids from heat, lick thumb then try to rub clean. Shrug, pull out keys. Turn back to kids, murmur, *Hop out then*, but use look that scares them. Look that goes through them, eyes with no mother in head.

Unbuckle kids. Wait for kids to get out. Wait longer, sun on cars like blade after blade. Get kids through carpark, drag, herd. Crouch when son stubs toe, flick tar from blood, kiss, but say, *Well, what can you expect?* Grab girl dancing in path of reverse lights. Give backing driver small hand-sign, *Sorry*, puckered half-smile: feel untidy, spineless, wifely. Get the bird in return, which kids mimic, fingers stabbing with hoots at the sky. Drag kids harder. See red eyes of blue-haired women passing you, heads tilting, sniffing in conference. Mutter: *The world is full of nanas and bitches.* Feel clever, acid, charged for a minute. Then wonder which one you are.

Try to get youngest into trolley. Dancing stops, howling begins. Try again. Give handbag to oldest to hold, shout when he mimes All Black pass with it. Get grip on small girl's arm, close fingers, feel bite of wedding ring. Lean in, hissing. Get more screams. Pull on small body, launch it into trolley, drive chubby legs down through gaps in steel. Push ahead as if small girl invisible, not thrashing. Point out TV screen looking down over screams, see her red face uncurl suddenly.

Stand lost in aisles for several seconds trying to remember list. What did you want? What are you here for? Fail.

Feel it building now, slow motion: loneliness.

Loneliness.

Load trolley anyway, can after bright can, random, clanging. Thud in some flour, some oily packs of *eat-within-one-day* meat and *on-special* bread. Pull sticks of stiff bread from fists of children using them as swords, replace on shelf. Mentally poke tongue at nanas/bitches. Stop. Realise you haven't been adding. Stare in, trying to calculate price. Stare in harder. Remove things children have slipped into trolley when your back was turned. Ignore whines. Walk on.

Walk back. Pull coins out of pocket, wet-eyed dancer out of trolley. Send all three kids with coins to play on ride-on trucks at corner of supermarket. *Quietly, and don't lose each other.* Watch them run away, instantly spread through space. Clacking pink beads, a slight trail of toe-blood, and loud, long, tongue-thick, falling-behind shrieks. An empty aisle, grid on grid of silence. Think: *That could be the last time I see them.* A stupid, chilled, guilty thing to think.

Turn. At the end of the next aisle, see the boy-man stocking the shelves. Man, boy. Wheel towards him. Roll towards him and see his green smock pull at the thick bulb of shoulder, lift up from his low-cut baggy jeans. Shut your eyes but then open them to the same scene, his skin, a strong, hard margin. He holds the stretch, his big hands spread on the box, his booted heels tilting, a black belt edging down hips. See that rise of triangular muscle, sculpted down from his bony hips to the apex of penis hidden below his buckle. Think of it, think of it suddenly: that hot, covert softness. Think of licking it awake.

Stand in the supermarket, soaked in longing. Feel like desire has hit your body from a distance, cosmic and cold, like a swan's tough wing. Like locusts, clicking and jointed and screeching, a plague, exploding on your skin. Like stars.

You're so dramatic. Crisp, evil stars.

Think the worst word you can think under these circumstances. Think: *Fate.*

Stare at him as he stares back at you. Stare at him, still, as the box he's holding overbalances, slides in an arc past his spine. Watch, watch the bombing of cans, their glossy shrapnel, their rolling, chaotic light. Then turn, as he crouches, still watching you, callous, erotic, uncertain. Get straight to the checkout.

2.

Get home. Ring husband at office. Say you went to the shops but the kids were shit so you missed some stuff. Could he go get it after work? Start to give him a list, then hear his sigh, the one he gives like he's run a long way and had to carry you. Hold onto the phone in the silence. Feel its plastic shell warm up with your sweat. Feel it bed down the dirty, raw print on your cheek. Almost smile when your husband says nothing, when he hands you a licence to turn around. Say in your best snarl, your teeth-bared voice: *Fine, fine don't bother, then.* Almost smile, when the last thing you hear him say before you slam down the phone is, *Hopeless. Well, I don't know how long you can go on being like this. Being so hopeless.*

Feel hopeless all the way back through the streets. Hopeless, hopeless like you could keep on driving. See yourself doing it: merging and sliding pointlessly, endlessly, through the streets, no signals or lights to mark you, just loose coils of directionless rolling, the kids falling into their own hopeless curls of hunger and nightmare in the back seat. *How long can you go on like this?* Feel yourself answering, deep in your body, a gargle of blood, answering him.

3.

Pull up outside the playground instead. Unstrap the kids and watch them splash through the bark, hitting the frames with star jumps. Watch their thin limbs grapple and hunch, stand here and let them scare you. Think: Where do they get it, the force of their joy, the electric, animal grasp of it? Follow them as they call, all three, *Mum, watch me, watch this, Mum, look at me.* Have your hands ready, outstretched and trembling beneath them, as if you could break any fall. Feel it, feel the aura of their bodies as they buck and swing, feel their knuckles' squealing grip, the sound of their waists and kneebones orbiting bar after bar, their hair spilled, their small teeth radiant.

Rock everything about them inside you. Think you could live in this echo of their delight, tasting it all in negative. Think you could just sit down here, tired, so tired, and breathe in their distant particles. Breathe in the dust of their vivid life as it rises from their limbs' sheer blast.

Shiver, and think you might just survive on their residue.

Then turn and see him, the young man, the boy from the supermarket, under the old wooden jungle gym. Watch him un-crouch, a slow, deliberate ooze of movement, then see him step, out of the damp fort's shadow, exhaling smoke. Old, knowing smoke. Watch him flick down the relic of cigarette. Watch his hip flex as he crushes it.

4.

Tell yourself all the things that are wrong with this: that he's moving across to blur the image of you and your beautiful children, moving across the picture you'd almost taken of you as a happy mother, moving across like a luminous burn dissolving your face on a photo's surface, moving in to seal the light from the lens like the warm, glowing block of someone's thumb.

5.

Him: I wouldn't have thought you'd had kids.
    You: Three.
    Him: I can count.
    You: Can you count the years on my face?

Him: Can you count the studs on my jeans? I'll let you count them with your teeth if you like.

You: Fuck off, little boy. I can't *believe* you.

(Pause.)

You, again: But give me a smoke. Before you go.

Him: You don't smoke.

You: People change their minds.

Him: I'm counting on it.

(Pause.)

Him, again: I'll give you three. One for each kid.

(Inhale—him, you, him. Exhale—you. You. You.)

6.

Retreat. Withdraw. Fall back. Exit.

Descend from the surface of your face as your husband reaches to touch it. Tell each nerve to contract against his investigating hand.

Fail. Receive the brush of his gentle coarse thumb over the cut on your cheekbone. Hear the vibration in his query through your hair, *Where did you go getting this?*

Swallow as he mutters, *I'm sorry.* Revoke. Turn and shuffle around your kitchen, unpacking the supermarket bags, the items of truce he's carried home, against his better judgement. Make a gesture, an *It doesn't matter* sign, a motion of split love and futility, a shrug only your husband can read, part of the body language of marriage, private and useless. Repent. Nest in your husband, suddenly nest in him, hard, with ribs and head. Remember the feel of the boy's finger hovering over the same location. The rush of gravity into the tiny wound, the voltage of his suspended fingerprint.

Catch sight of your eldest daughter, watching you in her father's arms, just as she was the one to watch you at the playground. Distant, suspicious, thin. The spitting image of you.

7.

Climb into the unmade bed. Know you should take comfort from these sheets, this sour, familiar hollow. Take nothing but notice of knots in your torso. Stay rigid, almost unbreathing, beside the man who married you, and feel it, like snake upon snake, the loop and ripple of snakes exploring your heart chambers.

Get up to a child's cry.
Get up to a child's cry.
Get up to a child's cry.

Call *I'm coming, Mummy's coming, I'm here, coming.* Take a few stumbled, off-centre steps. Look down: find that the dark hall floor is laced with toilet paper, long white strings. A child has pulled it from a dozy midnight piss back into their clothes, their bed. Feel it around your ankles, a drift of scratches, dry, ludicrous, domestic. Gather it, absurdly like wrapping paper, like a prank but dazzling gift in your hands. Laugh. Laugh out loud in the dark hall at yourself.

8.

Sit in the tyre-swing hooked to the old fort. Rock on heels, scuff there, childless, thinking. The tyre is a gutter for rain and garbage. Listen, smell it, black mulch leaving a hollow clunk and slop as you turn.

Kick, circle, drift. *Leaving* and *staying*: let the words evolve, let them detonate, slowly, in your mind. Think them through until even the sound of the words feels like enough to tip you. One way or another. This way, home, over, back, out.

And find yourself thinking other words: *contentment, atavism.* Feel this last, a strange hiss of word, its rhythm, its lure winding through others. This word rising in your mind when you think of the sloping muscle, the smoke escaping through the teeth of the boy. Lean your body back, rigid, use it as a wing, the black mulch echoing you. Think this word until its complexity, its pollution, is all you can feel.

For the thousandth time, you're so dramatic.

The boy has carved an image into the fort. It is you, obscene, cut open. It is him, too, a cartoon, a tattoo, limbs splintered through you, his phone number gouged in a cleft. Let your fingers run through it. Think: Your children will play here, run through the tunnels where you are only graffiti. Cry for a while. Hang for a while.

Dig your feet round till the ropes lock and plait you a cage. Stiffen in it, creaking. Then let the ground skid away from your feet. Fall through the playground in dirty circles.

When the wheel stops, make yourself chant it: *Staying. Staying or leaving.*

Did not, yes she did, she did not, did.

Decide.

Get it wrong.

the wait

We pulled a blanket over her and sat on the porch. The dark was the whole kind, with only the thin end of moon to cut into it and show up the edges of things: the table where she kept that rough shell she knocked full of ash, those feathers on their nail by the door, the bung board step to the gravel track and, low down by the centre post, the slump of a dug-out candle. The shape of what she'd last been drinking from. If there was any light to come we'd see it in that first, so we just sat and watched for it—glass half-something, the two of us staring down at her dregs for a good long while. Some time morning would have to start shifting in the slick of what she'd never gotten done.

But it took its time.

And it was too hard to start, for that first block of waiting, so we didn't speak, we just sat quiet. Any other night if I was up here this hour, which wasn't unheard of, it would have been me and her, rugged up and chanting talk into cold air, her with her stocky limbs packed in a bundle and drink propped on her knees and chin. A heavy vessel. But she could drain them: for long straits of talk she'd just crouch in her cane chair, tip it steadily back. And I thought it had peace in it, some dull comfort, the huddle of her, close on the crook boards of the porch, the sound of her lapping her drink between the words, considering. I'd been known to go months at a stretch without getting bugger all sleep; I'd drop half in, but it was never decent. I knew if I had enough of trying, I could walk up here from my shed and she'd be camped out, too, dry-eyed, tucked into a pile. Bottle of some cure lodged in the cradle of her collarbone.

We both jumped when a bird hooned out from the trees. The leftover sound skidded down the leaves long after, or it could have just felt like that. Maybe that was a low point. In the end we had to start talking, him and me—though we'd never talked about her since she'd shown up out the blue months back, had us both gaping as she shrugged off her swag, two old blokes panting at her sweat-streaked youth, the wet stubs of bush clung to her sawn-off boots. When she shacked up with him, I bowed out, nothing said. But now we had to try something to bridge the place she'd left us—which was an afterthought of porch tacked on to raw boards loosely based on a house. Half of what his crib was made of we'd milled out the bush ourselves, a lifetime back. Felled and chained and split and railed by hand, that place had felt like a mark made, something solid. Now we could feel it behind our shoulders, paint barked, off plumb, only hanging on at the homemade joints.

And what do you say when it comes down to that.

I started nowhere. I said, There's things. You know. Will need doing.

True, he said. I could hear the blunt of his heel hacking at a board. It was the first time he'd moved in a while. An hour or so back, I'd seen him lean out of his chair into a kneel. It was rough, broadside, not like prayer. He was close enough the dark gave way to let me watch his elbows crane. The rugged sound of his hands worked up through his beard, went stilted on his skull and stayed there. You could hear cracks of his thumbprint in it, scalp crossed with fingers, squared off, smoked stale.

Yeah, I said. When we get our heads straight, eh. There's

things'll need doing.

Still, I couldn't have told him what.

I said, Someone. You reckon? Someone I should call?

Then I could feel him look up at the track: I knew in his head he walked into every out-shed, doors off-kilter on their vacancy, splinted roofs, warped cots spread with dust. There was no help to call up from the outcrop of huts. You could howl up the route and get nothing. The community had all cleared out, years back. From time to time you'd spot things mangled into the bank, someone's fork or sleeve, a panel of uke or flag, but you'd just look at overgrowth sprouting through the mud of the weave or the frets and know the place was done. The era was done. The dream of it. Bodies muffled on bedrolls in the evening, lounging heavy with the good we thought we were making real, limbs mussed in a nest under this patch of stars. Like we'd never been up there. Now we'd come to this, there was no one to yell for, and only the voice of the blacked-out valley coming back.

What about, I don't know, cops. Need calling, you reckon? I'd gotten us both a beer when we first came out but it tasted like rope.

He said, Fucked if I know.

Reckon they'd even find us? Up here.

They always used to know where to come. When it suited them.

Track's a mongrel coming off the main road now, but. I could go out and wait for them.

But he made a sound like he'd had to let out a backlog of breath. And that was all for a bit. A cry like that is a closed circle.

If I looked down to the left I could make out the tank he'd halved for her last year to plant out. I hardly ever saw her any other way than hunched up, messing around with her hands in the soil, grubbing scraps of dry plant in and out, flicking down seeds into thumbed-out gulleys. Mostly we'd mutter through hours that way, her back to me, all-fours, inching round her plots, the hair she dumped upwards and forked through full of unbrushed sun. I'd pace near, or drop to a squat, and we'd just keep that trade up, low-key sentences, easy as a shrug, but somehow it felt like we were sorting through everything just by talking. Nothing major, just clearing up our bit of the world. When she stood up and knocked dirt off her knuckles, a smoke would be in them before she took two steps. She'd make chops at her knees to clean up but there were always dents, muck lodged around the joint. She only had stringy, bleached layers of singlet and rugby shorts, caked with dust around the arse. You'd watch as the smoke drifted down through the armholes, yanked wide enough to see ribs unsettled. Her hair was close to dreads, a mix of suede and straw, and she'd rub at the crown, leave a halo of scruff round her head. She'd reek of earth, stick her face into her armpit and poke out her tongue. *High fucking heaven*, she'd say.

She got people? I tried again.

It didn't seem right that there could be a sun coming that wasn't going to land on those creases of her body, her face raked with clay at the grin lines, the bulk of her forearms, the drum skin of gut gone dark below her tank. It didn't seem sun could get a grip on the valley without her skin to fix its glare in place.

He said, She tell you she had people?

I shook my head. I was trying to pinpoint anything we'd talked of, but all I could get to was her voice, the murky honey timbre, faced away from me, murmured down in the rubble of her garden. The way it smudged with tar when she laughed, like a lullaby winding up in the rough. When she crouched for the dig, there was a bared stretch of tendon and above it in her groin, a pale cove.

Know what she told me? She told me she'd been up here when she was a kid.

Eh?

Back in the day. When the place was packed. She said she came up here with her mother.

No. Who?

That friend of Parsons. Did pottery.

Eve?

That's her.

Don't remember her having a kid. Do I?

She did.

Suppose. Could be I didn't notice.

There was the splatter of another bird through flax. Nothing left to do but pore over the dark that would hardly let you see a world through it.

No, he said. We didn't notice.

That's not what I meant.

But that's the point, eh. That's been the whole point.

Something made me want it to rain. Just seemed the smell of wet earth might give us something to breathe in. But out from where we were sitting, nothing moved, nothing crowed or dripped. You could just hear the pull-back of trees right at the sky-end. It seemed like the porch had become unmoored from everything.

The place was full then, I said.

Still.

Look. It wasn't us.

The *place* was us. That's what it was about. We *were* the whole place.

Not her.

You never noticed. You just said.

She wasn't one of them.

Righto.

She tell you she was?

No.

Well then.

She never went that far. All she ever said was, she was there. Back when.

Then why was she here now.

Maybe, he said. Maybe this. Maybe she came back exactly for this.

He was steady now, I could hear it. His voice was like a brace knocked hard into the lean of the dark. He wasn't going to need to go aground on the boards of the porch again, like he was steering his body down through its last collapse. He wasn't going to coast his hand around his head like the ruts left in bone might hold some answer.

We thought she was something new, he said.

Did we?

Don't bullshit me. I know you did.

Like what?

A sign of something coming. She brought it back, that feel, like we could build it all up.

And that made me hunch. The blanket we'd lowered over her was earth-toned, saddle-weight. You could smell the clay dried in between the weave, turned to seed. The smell of her skin couldn't muster through it, which I suppose was a good thing. It wasn't going to keep, her odour of sesame, leather, overripe apples in the heat. I'd loped behind her so long when she was at work, to breathe that in, but I knew it would be lost. When a loose rain did start to sift down I could hear it, rinsing the cloth-end her barefeet were stowed under. I would have stooped to hitch her closer, but I knew at least it wasn't the hollows of her face that would be taking more weight. It was too much to have to think of her mouth, her gaze, thatched with canvas.

He said, She came back for this.

No, I said. Because you had to shoulder it again when he spoke it, the buckle of her nape. The loosened trunk, its weight cut free of her face, the stumble of us sawing her down from her harness. And who knew the vocals that a body could make, when you try to bully the life back in. I could taste tears I hadn't got the stomach for, spread on the roof of my mouth like they'd stay there, for good, in the grip.

He said, I know she bloody did. She did. She'd been waiting. She came back for this.

Then early traces of light just started to wheel in the base of her bloodshot glass. You know when you have ambled to the end, when you've reached the numb final thing that was always coming. And I wanted to shake my head, to keep my *no* going on repeat, but the twitch of the dawn had got up into the trees. The wind was just a graze but it took to her bindings, flicked the ends gentle as an omen. And then you had to think of her fists and the way, when they weren't sporting tools or fishing in the dirt to tie down tendrils of plant, they were stringing on the porch, hooking oxidised arches of bone-coloured wood and bead into chimes. It was me she'd got to lash those catchers up round the place, climb up and puzzle out all the fault-lines of knot and rod until they dangled free. I'd look down and in my chest her grin would leave an aftertaste. Nothing much moved now, but it wouldn't take an hour for the weather to turn, and it would be over. We'd have to sit here listening to all those things, tingling on their pulleys.

7 images you can't use

1.

It would be good to open on an image here.

Use an image, they say in class: dirt in the bed of a silver ute, tools and thick grit sluiced on the hairpins, a rotted-out bird nest, beer cans ricocheting light, the white crimps in his iris, the murky park where he pulls off-road, breathes into the rearview. Look how much you've got to use (it rhymes with lose for a reason). Draw the reader into the details. Be concrete: oh, the concrete stubbing your tailbone, the ramp you can hear kids flogging their bikes down, the plywood hauled circular and hollowed with mould, your landing mangling the clay as he grubs under your jeans, and you grub back, to cup him unequivocally with muscle, close your lonely cunt on fingertips. Get the picture? Use it any way you like.

2.

Stay with the image. In the image, he withdraws. There's no background, there's no foreground. You lie face up, let your

breath resettle your trunk, his come cool down on your hip. The
concrete on the back of your wrists: Ah, you sad bitch, there's
the rub. Everything grazing you, except for his kiss. You are the
place in the world he won't look at. He's interested in getting his
gear straight, his smokes out, his boots on their track through
the pines, ute-wards. He's got shit to do, right? Don't pretend
you didn't know it. When you get up, in this shiver, this clamber,
no one's feeling sorry. This is the way it works. Tipped upright, a
trickle still winds up in the jeans you drag on. Warm and rough
on the seam, dead-centre: you blunder back after him with that,
adrift. He's a diagonal of dark pines ahead. You watch him kick
a nest out left, so it's loose-knit, up-ended and grey at the base
of the trees. Nothing lives in it. That says something. Driver's
side, he'll rev the ute engine maybe once, then bail. So you hurry.
There's a sea that slumps at the bottom of the gully. Nothing
ride-able down there, just low-cut humps of dirty green. The kids
have got fuck all air off the half-pipe. It's spongy with weather
and the nails are squeezing back up. It's good of him to give you
a lift. You suppose.

3.

Grit on silver, travelling in half-light. Tools vibrating in their
metal slide. Stars of egg white glinting on your belly. The view:
nothing but tremors at a distance, silt and liquid the woman tells
you is limbs. The wand runs down your gut. She nudges it into the
give above your pubic bone, reading the bulges of light that come
from its bounce: spine, fingertips. There's a click of numbers on
her screen to measure it in weeks. So here's an image: accidental,
the shape of a kid, like a mess you trace in sand, unthinking,
with a cracked stick, all those hours you wait on the beach
and stare out, watching the glide of him when a swell gets up,
unloving you.

4.

The counsellor passes you an image, too. It's a face in a pale sac, a fleck of baby. Bud hands, bloated head, a dob of black eye under film. A pink squirming rope, afloat. In her office, there's a skylight in four metal squares that stamp the light down. She is not helping you. Not the way you thought. She twitches her chair close, pats you, underhanded. The image has fine veins that fill as she licks her index to turn the next page. Now the image has fingernails. You thought she would give you procedures. Book times, count you down. Instead she gives you prayers. It's too late to back out past the pot plants, the doll-pink plastic guts with their snap-on kids. The layers of organ cupped around the foetus look made in China, wipe-clean and toxic, like things you used to line up on plates as a child in your playhouse kitchenette. You can see fillets in the image, see-through muscles binding to a tiny backbone. The woman has a file of hole-punched options and you feel it in your teeth when she clicks the steel rings closed.

5.

There's a shaped glass so you can see who's coming in the pub door when you're out the back. You're rinsing the dishes: people slide over the dial of it, magnified. The apron, taped at your waist, is where you wipe your hands. Your belly ends the night in a wet sail. You don't think about its passenger. Your hands look chlorinated.

Except when it's him—his image on the mirror, taking a slow dive from left to right. He goes to the bottle store side of the bar, not where the usual losers are dozing. Your palms are heavy with what you've got to hide.

He's stocking up large—must be a big night on. You rack it up on the till, but the cost comes out sky high—a trail of zeros he's not fucking paying for. As if, he leans in and tells you, as if. You ring it on again, damp thumbs in a slow thud. He guillotines his wallet on the counter, a fed-up tap. You try to read a pattern in his stubble, like it could map where he's been, who he's hanging with, whether he's got two fucks to give. But he's not interested in you. Why would that change? You can't take his eyes square on. You think of the girl he's bound to tip this booze down, the nest he'll punch between her open legs, the seconds she'll lie down in, see as love. The thing inside you swivels and makes no difference.

You have to be careful opening the till, so the tray doesn't whang out and munt you in the gut. But you're not. Big deal. Like he was going to flinch. He wants his change. You scour it out, count it back into his hand. And that's it. You've got a sink to get to. Strips of fish to swab in batter, drop into a gush. Order up. People wade across the surface of the mirror. The thing inside you is a sigh, or just as pitiful. All those dishes won't scrape themselves.

6.

If you need a wider angle: stand by the sea. It won't help you. All it does is tip the horizon to ankle-level, swish by swish. Gulls black out bits of the sky. Where the sand spits out there's a park with some mongrel swings, bung chains on slipshod legs. The picnic tables are meant for knives and bird shit. A cast of kids hoot from their hoodies, getting good and pissed. The cloud looks tidal, shapes washed up in it you only half recognise. Behind you the rest of the town backs down. The church, the pub, the dump, in a line. Where else would you be? Even the kid's got no exit.

7.

What does it look like from inside?—your black bush singlet the only thing that fits, the cross-hatched slack of it, and under that a layer of belly, pulled hard in a bloodshot swell. You're like a giant eyelid. Sometimes he drives past you in the main street and doesn't blink. You stand and watch—the afterbirth of green tarpaulin flapping on the ute bed.

8.

The class is on a truck they drag round coastal towns—there's no shortage of them, sun-lit and shit-house. They call it a foundation course. The social worker sends you down. The writing teacher has a lesbo hairdo dyed malignant blond. She believes in all you losers. Use an image, she says, use your voice. Give the reader the details, specifics, so they *see*. All the other women, run to fat in their marl tracksuits, have brought in a long-ago photo in a white gown. Boobs boned up on budget satin, a tinny ignition of cut-price sequins down their frocks. There are men in the shot, but it's their own face they mostly write about, in the only day of make-up that ever stuck right. Their poems sound like smudge-proof adverts. The teacher's earrings are branded dyke artillery and they lurch when she nods at you. Your turn. But you don't have a photo—why would you keep one? Detail: his hair came out tussock-coloured. Detail: he had blue-brown fists. Detail: they dumped him on the wet bed of your trunk while you feathered the blood in his hair, left-handed. There were some seconds where his mouth went, *specific*, easy-does-it around your nipple, browsing for some love you couldn't stock. And that was it. No one took a photo. So you don't have an image to end on.

short for the sea

Slippers.
Out here in slippers.
You wouldn't credit it, she mutters at the door-glass.
Put out here. Tipped out. Like some mangy cat.
Like some dero.
Like some dero they used to wind up at the bus shelter when they were bits of kids, old winos with piddle-stinking coats baled up with snarls of twine, goat-greasy hair in dags. Once, another girl said she'd seen a stringy dangle of a willy but Mer reckoned it was probably the twine undoing. And their eyes. Eyes just blinks of grit-bewildered wet in their paper-bag-coloured faces. Those boys—the boys Mer got round with in them days—they'd poke at the winos, rip up sticks and stab at the humps of old-man till they growled and limbs shot out in a scuffle from wild sheets of the *Star*. But Mer never did. Couldn't bring herself to. She never got into it, poking the scruffy old hulks along the bench. Because of their eyes. Their eyes took too long, so long, to unpucker the crinkled smut of their faces, and even then you could tell they didn't pinpoint anything. They blotched and unblotched, the way that a baby's eye does, never really getting a sense, a grip. Slimy

eyes, helpless. Like two more tiny mouths.

She blinks her own eyes, now she's shoved out here. Old Mer, on a doorstep in who-knows-where, and getting bloody cold on top of it. Freezing out here in just her slippers, thank you very much, and her good light frock with the daisies on it is no guard against the night. She squeezes her own eyes, looks down the hill, tries to spot where she is. But her lids go and drizzle. And the dark has pretty well blocked the town out—when you could have turned her round three times and lost her in the daylight.

Wes would not have stood for it. Son or no son, Wes would've squared up for her sake. Would not have stood by and let his own son turf her out.

She tells him in her head: *Wes, no offence, but that boy of yours has proved to be a proper so-and-so. You've been singing his praises all these years, puffing him up as a decent young chap. A company-car type, up-the-ladder and on-the-level. But don't you believe it. Wes. I'm booted out. He's booted me out. And I don't have a clue where in the blazes I am.*

Simple, Mer: You're in your slippers, aren't ya?

That's what good old Wes would've chuckled and said.

He liked to have her on, to rib her. She misses that: being egged on, teased, when she's grumpy or prim. Wes always knew how to tickle her. Simmer her down.

From the very get-go. When she was sat there, plonked there, right out of sorts, on the seat outside the finance place, that day he met her. When she'd been in, in her mightiest shoes and the owl brooch that Arthur had given her (*May he rest*), and the papers all folded neatly into her stiffest purse which she'd buffed last night specially, and she'd licked her good finger on the right hand where the tendons hadn't snapped and she'd used it to swish up the corners of the pages the way she'd seen officially done in the bank, and she'd eyeballed the upstart in the suit behind his desk, and tapped at the bottom lines, all the numbers she was due, she was owed, that should be coming to her. But him saying no, *in fact*, she was cleaned out. The whole thing collapsed, and that was that, *in fact*. Kaput, her life savings, every shilling she'd put by; her nest egg, snuffed. So she'd stumbled out to the seat, and had blinked at her bloated feet in their high-and-mighty buckles, and grabbed and grabbed at Arthur's owl with its plumes of cut glass coming unstuck and tried to look down and excuse herself into its gaze with ugly, sorry belches. *Honest, Arthur, I couldn't have known, luvvie. I could never have seen it coming.* Then Wes, out of nowhere, had parked himself, not too familiar, a bum-span away, just rummaged around with his few bits of shopping and whistled to himself, a sideways squeak through a gap in his teeth, a ditty from her childhood. And when Arthur's owl had dug in its claws, all screech and reckoning, she'd begged it out loud, *Please, Arthur, I'm not up to it, if you take on it'll be the ruin of me.* Wes had just leaned over, given her a friendly nudge. A ruffian grin. A perk of the higgledy eyebrows, half-long sprouts, half-bald. *Don't want to get your undies too bunched, love,* he said, with a cluck-wink like her dad used to give her, a cheery wet quack of the tongue, *she can't be all bad.* But Mer didn't know which way was up, so she let him deposit her next to him on the bus, let him rub against her as the bus chugged along, let his bony odd little knees with their flakes of psoriasis swerve against her purse. And she let him lead her through his little front gate, and let him mine his scungy sink for one or two tea things—*have them rinsed in a jiffy*, he said—and she let him plop a few sweet chunks in her brew, and my word, that was what woke her up. It was a rugged cup. And she told him. She came to her senses with his fag-end of china in her hand and said, *Oh, my word, that's a rugged cup. You could stand your spoon up in that.*

Put hairs on your chest, love, he chuckled back.

And she'd stayed on. A shocking turn of events, Mer knew, but you see, it was the company. You wouldn't trade that for the world, the company of Wes, with his antics, his monkeying about, his cheeky quips and the lovely tobacco-cackle he fired at you if you got lofty on him. All phlegm and mischief: he near fell in half-laughing at how grand her little ways were sometimes, and she swatted him, giggling back, *Oh, you're the limit, you are.* He was a kid, most days, and in need of his bum paddling. Certainly, it took some time getting used to the sight of him blundering about in his PJs, the wishy-washy flap of which was never quite hitched respectably. But you could fall into step with him easily, move in, bit by bit, watch him trek back and forth to fetch your few belongings, waggling his string bag, his eyes twinkling like lozenges. He'd convinced her, when the corns on her big toes hurt, to keep in her slippers. *You don't want to wreck yourself. No one'll see. You want to get off your high horse.*

And now look, she snaps at him, dear old Wes, in her head. *Now just look at me, out here in slippers.*

In her head Wes, ever saucy, replies: *I tell you what's worse love, you don't have your teeth in.*

And she feels her gob drop open in the black air and half the night suck into her chest with the shock of it.

Oh, where is she? How many jolly steps has she been? She's been trooping about without thinking, and the town is pitch. Certainly there are poles but they hardly gush light. There's great brackets of blackness around those light-blobs, whole nowheres the lamps do sod-all to alter. Her eyes only make them fizzle more. One or two cars throb past, and she almost has the time to shake a hand out, shuffle to the kerb. But she's too late, ignored. Wobbles on. Hears a dog jack-knife on the end of its chain, someone's tin-lid shriek for the slither of scraps, another mutt hack and banter at the gaps in the fence. *Don't get your dander up,* she tells it, puffing. There's a vegetable pong of leaves going off in a swimming pool, someone's tea gone black on a stove, the *phew* of a dollop of catshit nearby in the darkness. She is glowing (*Yes, Wes, ladies* glow) as she trudges, peering for the letterbox. A couple of young blokes clump down the road, their jeans flapping. Black hoods make them eyeless. She pulls up, clutches her collar, tries to ask, but it comes out as wheeze, gobbledy.

Foo-hoo-hoo, she hears.

Please, she manages, gummy. *I'm a bit upset. Could you tell me where I am? Could you please?*

Ol' lady, one of them scuffs back around, pulls a slug of spit up and launches it, *you in hell.*

Please. You see, I'm just a bit upset.

Said you in hell, ol' bitch. You in the right place.

The boys punch each other, gung ho, move off blurting rap. Mer hears a dog flail up against the fence again, clawing. Other mutt-allies clatter and huff.

Bits of kids, she says to Wes. *Would you credit it? But I have to fetch my plate back, no two ways. I can't get by, I'm sunk without that.*

Well, it'd match your slippers.

Slippers, she sobs at him. *That was your bloody doing.*

And the tipple was his fault as well; his favourite sherry she'd gone and bought, and had ready when they'd picked her up this evening, showed them proudly, such a lovely drop. And Wes's son and wife had seemed to nod so kindly, tilt it gratefully under the hotel lightbulb. Margie, the wife, chipped in with some very nice things about the way Mer had flossied-up the bottle with a fancy bit of ribbon, and Mer had said, *Yes, it wasn't easy, mind you*, the way the mucked-up tendons had left most of her fingers swinging like broken clothes pegs from her hand. And the evening had seemed to get off to a fair start. They'd taken her out to their car and Wes's boy was the sort who you felt *escorted* you, just that firm type that you felt ladylike around. Handed you into the seat and attended to you, helped with your belt when the bugger of a clip got stuck and the tendons turned it into a silly performance. *That's not a problem, Merilees*, he had said, Wes's boy, as he leaned in to sort it. And a rather untimely pop of wind had squeaked out of Mer as he levered over the vinyl, and she'd blushed, *My goodness, I don't normally fluff*, but he'd only smiled and pretended not to hear. And she'd had no option but to let another trump go as she'd heaved herself up out the car, and it seemed like a fine forecast for the meeting that no one remarked either way, although Mer could hardly stop a murky bubble of laugh thinking of how Wes would've had her on. Wes would've giggled up a burp and said, *There you go, Mer, it's a smart fart takes the elevator up.*

Mer had carried the other parcel to the dinner table: she was getting around to it, you couldn't rush. And there certainly were a few awkward points to begin, as they'd settled into munching. But the tucker was lovely. *This is such a treat,* Mer kept saying, *such a real treat,* and the fuss over the seeds that jabbed under her denture and meant she had to slip it out had not spoiled the occasion too much. Not even when the ruddy thing caught her by surprise and slopped out and battered on the table before she had a chance to catch it (*Oh dearie, my tendons*). And perhaps it was just how gracious the two of them were, overlooking the gaffe and the gravy-spurt and going on smiling, that sped her up, that made her get to the reason for the visit, the parcel and the cause for her trip in person to see them. She'd come a very long way, and stopping off at a hotel was not something she was used to—but that was what it called for, the parcel, it was delicate. *You see*, she said, scrabbling at the worn paper wrapping, *You see, it needs . . . it needs . . .*

It caught at her heart to unpack it. You couldn't tone that type of sadness down: her heart was all over the show to see that dress. It made her scrounge about for a way to explain things, it put her astray with its pumping all funny, its wobbling about in her chest. But she'd tried to go easy, to warm up to the exact thing, because the truth was when Wes first told her it came as a terrible shock to her as well, it gave her a mighty turn to see him step shy and doddery up the hallway until he stood, as good as starkers, in the kitchen bulb which whined with the back door breeze. She'd backed into a chair, she'd folded up, she'd felt crook. A bloke in a dress made her queasy, and what's more it was *her Wes*, her mate, her fella, balanced there with his jittery ankles clearly not cut out for those sort of perilous patents, and his leg hair squished under pantyhose the colour he brewed his dreadful gumboot tea. The frippery of the whole get-up just bulged at her, the pecking of plastic beads, and his half a dozen hairs wetted back and clipped with bobby-pins. It had not been easy, to take it all in, to get her head round it. She felt like bolting, to be honest, for a spell. But his eyes were like lozenges, like little dobs of honey, and she'd come to be almost giddy with love by that stage. Not that it ever took the form of more than a cuddle, mind you, a steadying hug, a nudging little lie-down for comfort from time to time, just a nestle in the chill, in the scrum of old blankets, against each other's joints, no fiddling about, just chat. Like: *Mer*, he'd said to her one night. *What's that short for?* Short for Merilees. *Oh*, he'd muttered. *I'd thought it was French. Could be wrong, but I thought it was French for the sea.*

She had somehow ended on that, telling Wes's son and his Margie. Stopped because it swamped her, the romance of that. *No one had ever said anything so . . . magic, in my life*, she ended, holding out the dress. *My name's . . . Wes said my name's short for the sea.*

And she looked up into the face of Wes's son.

He had a terrible grip on him. No more escorting. She rebounded, fluttered. What's more, he was raving. At the end of his long driving arm, her head went bumping, her legs sprawled. She was hoofed out. Reeled. Came to her senses in spirals against the glass back door. Heard a noise like the buzz the old tellies used to make. Bright black and white, big bars of tuned-out squeal.

Got a hold of herself. But didn't think to ask for the bits she'd left inside. Her plate. The parcel.

The dress, Wes, she tells him on the roadside, *the dress. What you should've been laid out in. Tomorrow. What I came for. What you should've worn.*

Where's that letterbox? Where should she turn in? The bloody house has evaporated. Where has it got to, Wes? She's come to an edge, a fork, and the lamp lets a ruffle of light down. Her dopey slippers glow in it. A cluster of milk bottles glint like balloons on the verge. A kid's trike has toppled. Someone's squelched a handprint in before the concrete got dry. She sits down, suddenly, down by the hand-hollow. Lets her useless fingers dangle in it.

When the car pulls in nearby, a kid is half out the door before it parks. Muddy, kitted out for rugby. She drags herself up, all trunk, hears her frock snag, treats her knee to a doozie of a graze. Croaks out: *Please, please.* The kid jumps, rams his hand up to his gob. Shouts, *Da-da-da-daaaaddd.* She must look like something the dog sicked, a monster. The man swoops out, the handbrake wrenched, the motor still on.

Please. I'm very upset, she tells them. *There's been a bit of an argument. I'm only in my slippers.*

He's hardly impressed, the man—in fact, he needs it like a hole in the beeping head, Mer hears him tell the woman who half comes out the house, toddler rucked up and grizzly in her arms—but he puts her in the back of the car, says he'll sort her out. The boy jabs himself into the front seat, keeps swivelling round to gawp.

I feel very upset, you see, she repeats. *I'm not sure which way's my hotel . . . whatsaname. Down the road away. By the sea.*

Might know the one, the man says.

I been to practice, the kid says. *We hammered them.* He fidgets, tapping his father, bum squawking in the seat. *We taking her to the police?*

Oh, I'm very upset. I'm only in slippers. My hotel is . . . down by sea. You're very kind. Please.

She drunk, Dad?

Mer shrills, *Young man, I'll have you know.*

Then she thinks of what Wes's son yelled at her: clear out of his dad's house, right away, fuck off, clear out. So it's true, then:

she's homeless, she'll end under the *Star*, tied round with dirt and string. But she still straightens, *Young man, I'll have you know young man. Oh, I'm no dero.*

Sobs: *My name . . . Wes said my name's short for the sea.*

But she's lucky, she guesses. The tyres crackle into place. The boy gets out, punts the rugby ball round the gravel as the man walks her into reception. The hotelier's mouth crimps: there's bound to be a telling off coming. Fancy losing a key. But the man puts his hand down hard on the visitor's book and the desk judders. Just enough to sort it. *No need for bother, eh?* He wants shot of her. The man's got weight in his hands, a thumbnail laboured to black like the handle of a tool. He even smells like brick.

He delivers her. She shuffles in, quivers.

He's almost out the room when she says: *A dress wouldn't look any good on you.*

You what?

It's not unholy, you know.

You're wasted.

Wes's son and his wife said, they said. But it wasn't unholy.

Bloke? In a dress?

It looked just right on him. It's what he should've rested in. My Wes. I tried to tell them that. That was all I was coming here to try to say. He was lovely.

You're trashed.

It was right. If you'd seen him. It's how he was most . . . himself.

What are ya? the man sneers. Closes the door on her.

Mer sits on the bowed bed, blinks for a time. Or longer. Lowers herself. Silver scales are on the spread, she can feel them, even with her daft fingers. *Could've cut you down a nice dress of this stuff, Wes,* if it weren't for the tendons, made waves, made gatherings. She dreams him, wedged in his quiet box, narrow limbs garnished with shine, like trimmings of sea. Dreams looking in, the dress, like he likes them, all fluting and gleam, making up for the chill. Making up for finding him, flat in their kitchen, turned that knuckle-bone colour, eyes dug out, has-been. Eyes that won't open. Then stay open, too long, when you blotch them with your thumb and your tears and your talk runs out all lonely.

The slippers gape.

Drop off, one by one.

consent

Let me tell you about consent.

I consented to smile at him. At least, the muscles of my mouth moved for him as much as they did for any customer. He leaned on the counter, sideways, as I rolled the ice cream he ordered, triple-scoop, orange chocolate chip, and he tapped a twenty, folded horizontally, up and down on the metal trim. He was so tall he could look right over the counter, so tall that whichever way I bent his look would be all over my arse or boring right down the groove between my little tits. I tried to pull the apron loop up a bit round my neck, to jam it one side on the sliding glass so it didn't fall down again. But the ice cream was hard that day. All day I had been refilling the metal milkshake tumbler we kept the scoops in with boiling water from out back at the Zip. To roll from the carton he wanted, I had to bend right down, poke my skull into the cabinet, drop my whole weight on the scoop, rock it wrist-wise to get any kind of curl into it. He leaned over and told me he liked how I handled a cone.

I consented to smile again. My face kept moving in the way it had been trained when a twenty kept tapping on the metal counter. My boss had already torn strips off me for not smiling enough at the customers. 'It costs you nothing to smile,' he would say, 'a smile is free.' And anyway, a guy like that, so tall, a grown-up, with a rack of pens in his pocket and a huge coil of keys-to-the-world dangling from his other fist, wouldn't bother with a girl like me, high-school ugly, still in my uniform checks with the logo on a pocket-coated boob, a spit-through blouse that showed up the dimply singlets my mum wouldn't scrap in favour of training bras yet. That was who I was, a singlet kind of girl, a stringy hair criss-crossed with cheap clips, pulled-up socks and bored blue eyes and pinpricks of pus on the chin kind of girl, with a black food-speckled band around my teeth winching them tighter and flatter. So I could smile more.

He held out his hand for the ice cream, his keys now hooked over one big thumb, and I consented to pass it to him instead of propping it up in the white plastic cut-out tray like I always did. I consented to leave my hand trapped under his grip, the hot heads of keys grinding into it, for three seconds, four, while I stared down into the fat cage his fingers made, wondering how to yank my hand out without the cone splitting, the ice cream toppling, the canteen of straws splashing out onto the floor, the boss huffing out from the back and finally axing me. And he laughed and let his fingers ease off a bit, not enough to let go, but enough for me to feel that he didn't even really have to try to keep my dumb hand buzzing with fear in there, the first slick of ice cream dripping, pathetic and sweet, down into my soft, consenting little fist.

He said, *I want you to take the first lick.* And he flickered the folded twenty at me. And he gave a little nudge with the fingers that didn't even have to strain to keep me shackled. He steered the cone like an oozing microphone up to my face and waited, grinning, for me to say nothing.

But even so I want to know what made me lean in and do what he said. I want to know every bit as much as you. I want to know, every step along the way, what it was that made me do the things he wanted: fill my mouth with sticky, chipped cold so the braces froze and stung on my smile, drop my head in his lap and blink at his stench and let his thumb pump the socket at the base of my ponytail until tears belched out of my face. But that came later. That first day he said, *Keep the change.* And I took the scoops out back to the Zip, and I stared as the water fizzed out the way it always did, but I didn't avoid it, just let it splutter out and blister the hand that had lain there inside his. Because in some part of me I'd felt the change, and I didn't want to keep it.

I do know what made me consent to get in his car when he pulled over on my walk home the next week. It's so dumb I almost can't tell you. It's this. There was this guy in my class and I loved him. Don't you laugh when I say love, because this was all the love I could remember for any guy and it still is. I loved his head stacked with surfy curls and the mud that always seemed to be slung up his legs. I loved the way he wrote with black felt on his satchel and painted his fingernails with Twink, and I loved the way he held his asthma pump as if it was a bird or an insect cupped in his hand and the way he made an o-mouth to suck down the vapour once he punched it. I loved the way his thighs went purple in his school shorts in the winter and the way orange Cheezel dust always seemed to be brushed somewhere on his face. I loved the way he would pick up his little sister from primary and they would walk behind me singing or scrapping or, a couple of times, blowing bubbles of dishwash from a plastic pod, and the globes swarmed over me and trembled and popped in my hair. And I loved the way I felt when I lay on my bed after school and wriggled my hand down into my knickers and fluttered the skin until it hummed with a dream of him. I loved the way I could chew on his name in time to the squeeze that hit between my hips.

I consented for the stupidest reason to get in the car when it pulled over then. I wanted to make the guy that I loved, but I'd never have the guts to tell that I loved, notice and be jealous.

You've got the picture about what went on in the car, about what I consented to. I've already let it slip. Down at the place where he always drove me there was a tonne of tame, slimy ducks, shuffling round to see if they could stab a feed from your hand. They had pink clumps of skin over their eyes like tumours and holes in their beaks where some kind of liquid frothed. They flocked round on the grass to me, wobbling and gagging, when I went and sat outside afterward. I'd take little packets in my lunchbox for them, and the sparkle of the paper made them mental. Sometimes he'd be a nice guy after he'd zipped up. He'd mop himself and stroke it through my wrangled hair, laughing. He'd give me a smoke. He'd lean in and run a thumb under my eyes where the make-up I could never get right had oozed off. The first time he said I was beautiful. I do remember hearing that. But while he said it his hand sank my skull till my choking made him flatten my spine with his elbow.

When I choked I would think of those ducks and their eyes almost buried in those scaly red growths and the foam on their beaks and the way he would kick at least one of them every time we pulled up but they never learnt and just came back begging and begging.

So I guess I have to call it consent. But I've been reading about consent lately and it seems to me when they made up the idea they left spaces for way too much pain, too much pressure. There's part of the word that sounds okay and is all about feeling and thinking the same, about two bodies and minds just sharing themselves because, I don't know, they match, they touch, and their skins light up in some kind of agreement. But there's this other side of the word which doesn't sound right to me at all: to yield, it says, to acquiesce to what is done or proposed by another, to comply. There are ways in which that could still hurt. It sounds to me like there's stacks of ways you could get yourself thrashed black and blue under cover of that word. And they could say it that way: *You* get *yourself.*

You get yourself dressed up, for instance, when he calls you that last time. You actually fork out some cash for a dress because he says this time he's going to take you somewhere nice and the idea of not just parking up and scorching your cheek on the steering wheel because he's got hold of your head and bounces it like there's nothing left inside, like it's a ball of bone he could dribble and dribble, the idea of not just getting dealt to like that is like something straight out of a magazine where teenagers hold hands or sit in a convertible with their white teeth flashing out pure public love while they suck from the same vintage Coke and watch the sunset. You spend cash, you spend hours hanging over the sink to get your eyelids tricked out with glitter. You sway the razor up and down over your legs, you jab your lobes with over sixty kinds of studs till you decide on the right ones, lock on the butterflies while staring at the frosted strangeness of your face in the mirror, so fluorescent and tapered and spangled, dusted to adulthood with a can of cheap shimmering atoms. He is right: you are beautiful. And so you stalk, jiggle, stalk, down the front steps towards his car when he finally pulls up and honks.

His car is always so clean. There are no flowers or love songs or shit like that, but it seems that he cleans it just for you. Just so your pulse-points, tapped with your mum's best Poison, smoke with such narcotic prettiness you almost cry.

He smiles. Gear after gear, he smiles. He has a scent also, and it grows with the distance, the miles of light that spurt through the window before the tar seal gives out to stone and then instead of lights there's the anti-lights of long trees croaking and hissing in the black outside. It's a real, thick, out-of-town black. Admit it: you are a little spooked. The car is sleazy on the loose-metal corners, your heart is a fraction off in the straining of your blood. But he smiles. So you smile back. Painted as cutely as you are it feels like the muscles on your face consent a little easier.

You keep on smiling as he pulls up. Oh, it's just like a magazine, a sweet teen movie: he circles round and clips open your door, extends a hand. There's so much meat in that hand, but you forget that, because the car and his keys and his smile are so clean, a whole clean, confident society shines in them. You consent to put your twitching hand into his. So he leads you up a gravel drive to a house you'll never really find your way out of. You smile as the front door opens and the five men inside all smile back at you.

Since when did a smile cost you anything?

It's free.

Step inside.

Now isn't that consent?

Can I put you in my shoes just for a minute? The heels are high and when they're unstrapped and swung at your eye they knock you quite dazzlingly blind. Blood will run down that side of your vision for years with a lightbulb squealing through it. All the faces and the walls are now elastic and come at you in bouts. Can I put you in my head? There's actually the sound of beer tabs spitting because someone has packed for the event. You hear the flop of a chillybin lid: it's a picnic. Can I put you in my hair? It's a leash, tied to so many fists that you feel your scalp split, you see a streak of gelled hair come away in a hand, a gleam of flesh still icing it. Can I put you in my arms? They're stamped on and taped to a pipe in the emptied room. You're hung on the hook of your own bones and scream at the pipe until it howls back at you. Six men laugh, they assemble, they're an organised ring. Would you let me put you in my left eye? Count them: six men, just smashing you calmly, with snarls of confidence, corporate in their bloodied suits. Would you let me put you, just for a minute, right here inside so you go through it with me . . . ?

No, of course not.

Who would consent to that?

Silence, they say, is a kind of consent.

The least you can do then is stay here with me, just sit with me in the silence that comes next.

There are seconds, just a few lovely, numb seconds when I first wake, where I think I am a child, that I must have dozed off and my parents scooped me up and shifted me in the night. Somehow I think, if I lie still and listen, the house will not be totally strange because I'll tune into the trickle of my parents' voices, the murmuring sameness of Mum and Dad, clicks and drones and scuffing as they chat and clear up. They have picked me up, rocked me down some dark hallway, taken off clips that might prick in the night or buttons that dig or beads that might wrap me. They've tucked me in, chuckling lightly, tripping on the room's unfamiliar shapes. We have been somewhere new, on a holiday, we've had a picnic: I remember the flop of the chillybin lid. It's morning and if I listen, even in this strange motel, I will still hear my mother: the toaster will still ching, there'll be the scratch of her buttering, the sound of the seal unwrinkling from the fridge. There is a knot at the top of my head where my child hand can drowse and fiddle: if I just reach up that tuft will be there, that warm hoop of habit, that murky smooth curl and I can weave in my thumb and turn and turn . . .

But in that place, as you know, I am balded and blooded. Pain is a crown and if I move the nerves will spill from it in a gush. Pain is a crown and it will be hard to stand in it, hard to balance, hard to walk under its throb. It will be hard to move down the hall, so hard to carry that red crown, sliding and scraping, trying to find slivers of clothing, find an exit, find home.

Finding instead a mirror, where everything I am has ruptured.

And then, later, in court, as you know, they will crown me again. I will stumble, I'll swerve through those rooms, too, because somehow they'll think this shredded dress is a sash, they'll think that I painted my smile like a gutter to take in the splash of seed and fists, that my pain is a prize, my shame a reward I asked for. I'll stagger again as they crown me, Miss Consent.

So just let the silence go on a bit longer.

Just let me lie here and remember when consent was a word

that still had something in it. Something that sounded like sympathy, that seemed like a sharing, even a kind of compassion. Something that sounded like my parents' voices, their morning exchange of dopey gentleness, lazily pacing and mumbling in the ordinary distance of love.

leaving the body

I have small, clear sightings of her.

I have one as I'm waiting at the airport: curved, in the cup of water I'm holding, the surface of it stretching from the tremor I can't stop in my left hand. It shows me the sliding mechanics of a door which glides on its vast glass withdrawal past my shoulder. The sound is steel cable scraped through ice.

And there she is, her body, caught in that sound.

The steward has left me at arrivals, but it wouldn't matter where he shifted me—my daughter glitters everywhere in this design. All the walls are glass here, the entry halls, the lounges, the long departure tubes: they're all moving panels of tough metal-jointed transparency that float and interlock as if the southern light itself has been engineered, made to rest in stiff decks, flex between these glinting struts. It's due to the mountain, of course; its primacy, its tough, tourist pose, the sharp black disaster of it bursting out the flatland. No one wants to lose a second of that view. So they sketched the whole building around it, made a blueprint for these wide banks of ice, safe cinematic ports where you can line up the ranges, postcard style. I have to sit and watch. I have to watch the branches of dark rock crackle down the peaks. Even in my cup

I have to watch them tower and trickle, like the hanging black tree the human eye really sees before the brain tips it, so we can believe ourselves standing here the right way up.

She is not the right way up when I see her, a dislocated silver twitch in the dial of my cup. She is dug down, my girl, packed into angles, lonely and awkward, her limbs shovelled into the snow. They are still high-tech colours, all her bright death-proof clothes. So I can follow their flashes of fluorescent cutting-edge mesh, scientifically tested to outlast her, resistant to the layers of snow that have reset her bones. They will withstand her. They will stay here, mark her like a series of flags, tiny pinpricks of a conquered map. So I can make out the patches that were her shins, scrape them out of the searing tread of snow. I can grub to the crest of an elbow, find the shortcut to her fingertips, still in their padded bubbles. But all the colours end at the top of her trunk. Because up there the outpost of her dark head is pushed under, sunk into the heavy airless crystal of pure distance. Even so, I move in closer. I'm her mother, it is my job to go. Her head is too deep to read a face, but I look down anyway, stare down at its crushed out-of-focus globe, a dark shape beneath a rink. Or a blurred figure watching you from the vanishing shine at the back of a mirror you would never in your life have chosen to walk towards.

He used to tell her to 'harden up'. She would send me footage online, all that winter of her training, and I would hear him saying it, *Harden up*, a fond but targeted command as he marched through her film. They were scanty updates from basecamp, off-cuts of clip, brief flickers of her downtime she scratched from the official documentary she was making, but I lived on them, set them looping in long feeds of replay, click-dragged her round my dim screen from half a world away. *Harden up*. He was a captain in his sponsored gear, you could see it in the rigidity of his smile, the planting of his clamped boots notched with metal spines. It was a striving body, overstocked with might: she couldn't help but hone the lens in on it, close in on the magnitude of shoulderblade, the attitude packed into torso, compassed in his iris. She spent long, still minutes with the camera on him: sledging his bodyweight into a headwind, staking out a channel in the gale-polished ice, his team behind him stumbling into his footsteps, lesser men, a shaken, straggling troop. You could see he was born to test ground, knock through horizons. You could see the kind of kid he'd once been; gutsy, brutal, all hard games and muddy follow-through, the national brand. 'Become an overcomer', that was a slogan he used and that she repeated, thrived on. That and 'Harden up'. She would laugh back when he told her off, a mate's laugh, taking the ribbing the way she'd been coached, his recruit. But I could feel something else in the way she zeroed in: once, when her long shot tunnelled towards him, the whole plateau spread out on his mask, and when he shoved off his visor, she pulled into the single-minded glitter of his eyes. They looked crafted out of ice. 'This is where he lives,' I heard her whisper at the edge of the film. 'He lives in the zone.' And it was in her voice, the risk she was taking, the zone she was living in.

There is no 'I' in team. Or in love.

My daughter came in and out of focus in the film she sent me, mucking about in the mess hall, nicknaming her crewmates who waved at me sheepishly, shaking their heads at her long-distance gossip to Mum. She tracked herself, babbled bits of narrative as she scanned around her hut, talked me through apparatus, provisions, huddled in her thermals before lights out, sent me exhausted sleep-tight wishes, a diary cam of yawns. Outside, she'd make jokes on the hazardous climate, frolic up and over small stacks of rock, the handheld quavering, bounce jerkily in the spongy cladding of her suit, a big goodbye grin fogging up her goggles, flagging out at me with arm-swings of goofy love. Lined up with her squad, she was a being I did not know, a slogging shape, toughened, featureless, ploughing ahead into hardship, degrees below. It is possible to be both proud and terrified. Sometimes in those months I dug through the remains of her girlhood, crumpled trinkets, seashells gluey with dust, waxy tap shoes she used to clatter endlessly around in, frilled diaries cramped with secrets. I pulled out summer dresses I'd stowed, a lightweight shambles frothing over cartons. They were ghosted with her smell.

She had been an uncertain child; skittish, flimsy, likely to hide. And then the bunkers that she made herself from the furniture—the draped hatches, the cushioned nests, the soft retreats and pegged-out tunnels—became caves, became clambers underground, adventures in black water. She strode out from them, charged with stamina; she'd discovered a need for challenges, a gift for lasting miles. But it was him that she credited. She'd been empowered, transformed, she told me, and I had him to thank. His leadership had made her sturdy, self-reliant, intrepid. 'The world needs people like him,' she said to me. Which is arguably true, which a strong case can be made for.

Except that I write the words 'strong case' and I think of the sled he hauled across the ice, stashed with the instruments and rations they'd need to stay the course, to reach their finish line. A lightweight sleigh: she'd sent me pictures of it, loaded precisely with cargo, a coded pool of plastic-coated stores. She'd sent me photos of herself too, lashed into its harness on practice runs, her face gritted with a wind-burnt smile, her tiny, bold body braced to tow. I think of how it might have been spun around, items capsized, recalculated, set aside in snow. I think of the hollow that might have been made, repacked with my child. But he did not turn back. He had a strong case: he did not use it to bring her home.

He did not even clear it out to retrace his steps, to recover her body.

I think of how she was still alive to listen to it, dragged away through the frozen slush. The man she loved at its prow. Her camera equipment put into his safekeeping.

On my flight here there was a child seated with her family across the aisle from me, who fretted on the takeoff, sobbed in tiny thrashes, gripped at her parents. Her mother tried to distract her with the view out the window, the floating splashes of cloud, the land in dark cut-outs. Then she took the girl's hand and spooled a chain into it, told her it was charmed, a lucky cross, protection, lowering it into her fist with a hush. But it wasn't enough. So her father teased her: if she didn't quieten down the crew would have no choice but to come and shut her away in the overhead compartment. She listened to the warning, curbed her panic into snuffles. When we dropped down through the sloping wake of sky—the fuselage scraped over cloud ledges, buffeted—she stared on, silent, at the line of rattling lockers. I could see it, too: a little girl's body curled obediently into the chilled white bank.

The world does not need people like me. I acknowledge that much. I can see it in the steward's face when he comes back, my walking frame retrieved from the hold of the plane. He is professionally kind but I can see it tires him, this custody. It takes a toll on anyone, to have me in their ward for long.

There are set-backs, just getting out of the chair. The steward tries to winch me up and we do a rickety dance. He makes muddled grunts, tries to lever me back to the wheelchair, but it squeaks askew, off its brakes. He's all flustered niceness, stuck with me in this ugly waltz. I can feel how it embarrasses him, the crooked spectacle we make, so public in the light of the terminal, our spasmodic pageant in the wide arena of seats. And then I am pinned upright at my frame, ready to start the trek out to my taxi. He lingers for a moment, checking, unsure of my vertical. I manage a shanty nod. He smiles queasily, gazing at me: I know it's an appalling project, my walk. But I go on, inching and lunging from my rack. The steward looks away, on behalf of everyone.

My daughter never brought her leader home to meet me.

When I get to the venue, the conference room is just being filled. The audience is bustling, prosperously groomed. My jack-knife in from the taxi, the clanking momentum of my walker are barely noticed: they're networking, practising their salespitched smiles in the over-conditioned air.

This is the end that justified the means: this tour, this circuit of corporate bodies. This is what he's done since the launch of his book: PowerPoints for the business sector, motivating speeches on targets, incentives, the driven, uncompromising optimism of top achievers. Of course, he covers her accident, briefly, her determination not to turn the group from its course, not to deviate from the goals of the expedition: the adversities that strike are opportunities, they distinguish the attitudes of overcomers. It was a code she supported. She followed the principles to the end, never once abandoned the team's objective. She had the heart-muscle of a hero, would not consider jeopardising the higher mission. She weighed the odds, the factors, stayed rational, dispassionate; she did not expect her gender to tip the scales, to plead for special treatment. She had set out into an environment beyond known values, she'd crossed a great distance to put herself beyond limits, beyond the workings of sentiment, the narrow bonds of the norm. There is no 'I' in team. He gives her airtime. He gives her the oxygen she could no longer grasp when he left her at that altitude, fused into her frozen shelf. She was fractured, alone, but she did not go to pieces. Her knife-edge decision had been made, he says, she knew it was touch and go.

But I wonder how she surveyed his face as he did go, I wonder if he paused to touch her, whether she panned his look for pity, that pinprick vision at the centre of his eyes, their blue-white straits. Or whether she just lay there and listened to the hiss and crack of a continent, its endless disinterest.

Tonight it's her photographs that reach the screen first, a drift of her images, outtakes from the store she passed into his preserving hands. They are vast stills, a montage from a cold world, white plains becalmed and killing, cliffs and coasts of blank, inhuman light. It's luminous, this sphere of minus. Its blast comes through the screen at me. I stand in its deserted totality, a white unbreathable vault. The images float on, wrecks and spars of ice. I close my eyes, but they stay, break up beneath the lids.

He mounts the stage against this background. He's dressed for a voyage, his outfit insulated, bodycon, tacked with bright stitching like an outline of robotic muscle. 'Pain,' he begins from his spotlight, 'is just weakness leaving the body.' There is a gust of applause.

My progress is slow, and the aisle is darkened. The audience is riveted, tense with worship. But at some point the grinding treble of my frame starts to cut through his talk. I have taken a name tag from the table in the foyer, although I have written nothing on it except *Mother*, a small word, barely visible on its white face. I feel it, pinned to the spasms of my chest as I jar my frame forward, as I keep on, at my crawl.

My finish line lies nowhere I will ever cross.

They are a condition of my life I don't expect to lift: my sightings of her. There is an 'I' in pain. She's like something tinned. She's so hard you could tap on the crust of her clothing, on her colourless skin. There's a traction like pumice, you could count the knocks of your thumbprint. I unglove her hands, her fingertips glint back at me like stars. There is ice on everything, ice studding her, arcing out from her in fins, ice spiny in the solid wheel of her hair, ice in her ear's white, foetal curl of cartilage.

I think of her pain, in the times when my own returns. I hope she did not last overnight. I hope she slid, numbed and quick, into delirium. I hope she did not linger to feel herself put out, cell by cell, the last of the moisture in her skin fanning out, clustering to itself, crystal at her nerve ends. There is an 'I' in pain. And I hope she did not know it. I only hope the snow took her, whole.

50 ways to meet your lover

3.

Turn left, west, where the voice is telling you. There's nothing here. A zone where they put up the kind of buildings no one needs to walk through the doors of, bleached industrial squares selling things no one wants. But the voice is certain. You're here. You park. This can't be right. You think about backhanding the screen so the useless voice can't repeat itself. But you don't: you can just hear the way your husband would go off. You wait for a while. Decide you may as well scrape up the litter from the floor of the car while you're here. May as well: the whole afternoon feels like a shrug. There's a king bin you can dump it in. So you've got handfuls of slippery till trail, coupons for next to nothing off, plastic wrap from a world of bad choices stuffed in your grip when you catch sight—it's him. It's not. It can't be. Only it is.

It's him. Only.

The voice announces out the open car door that you've arrived at your destination. You should have bashed its budget teeth in when you had the chance.

6.

Your mother calls. She never calls. But she's fizzing. You can't even hear her flicking the pages of her magazines while she's talking. You can't even hear her lighting up. She's not even pausing to poison herself. So this *must* be choice. You wait for the gossip— someone's daughter, no doubt, has dropped a Down's syndrome kid, or embezzled the kindergarten fundraising, or can't fit into anything but polar fleece and crocs because she's *packed* on the pounds. But no: it's your turn. *You've* got her attention. You're better than roll-your-own. You're better than the Emmy spread of best and worst gowns.

She's seen him. She bumped into him at a local do, a reunion, well, it was a funeral really, but everyone had such a beaut time catching up. And she knew he was watching her. She knew it. But he didn't come over for a while. Not until he was properly plastered. There were tears in his eyes. Tears, for real. She's not shitting you. And you'll never believe what he looks like now: he looks *mean*. She'll repeat that, Mean, you would *not* believe. And he told her he'd never stopped loving her daughter. He fell in love with you back then and it had never worn off.

My daughter, she says. He'd loved *my daughter* all these years. And he looked mean, but I tell you, in his eyes there were *tears*.

It's been a long time since you were *my* daughter. It must have made you seem worthwhile. Tears in his mean eyes made you worth calling. She might even spread it, might even hiss it, later, round the ladies' night. You might be the talk of the garden bar.

Whatever, you say. And hang up.

7.

You've got to go because the lever of your wrist is going to give way and splash the phone, the sink you're standing over is going to find your head in it, your mouth stretched in a howl of soapy

Os, your knees unhinged and letting you skid to the lino, taking down a clatter off the bench so you're huddled in a spray of last night's foodscraps, your arse in a puddle and, up in the slack of your lemonfresh disinfected hair, a tiara of crumbs. You're a joke. You're fucking soaking in it.

9.

You are standing in a dusk itchy with flies and stars. There is everything between you. A school picnic. Kids with sauce on their cheeks and tinsel in their hair. Tufts of gladwrap round the paddock. Someone painting faces with oozy stripes that look allergenic and carnival. Someone lashing the ankles of mothers together to gun them three-legged to the crinkle of tape. Pets shitting on the end of their leashes, having clawed off their also-ran ribbons. Kids behind cardboard stalls flogging rubbish they've glued. The smiles on the mothers that bake. The smiles on the mothers whose Tupperware is name-tagged. The smiles.

You want to walk through them all and tug him by the edge of his T-shirt. Over the pitch. Out through the courts, through the posts, to where the field turns to tussock and storm bank and shoelessness and gulf. You are standing in a dusk and that's what you want. You're woozy with the goal of it. You're crooked to the thighs.

But you're rostered on. How could you forget? One of the smiles has to trot over and tell you it's *your turn* on the hotdogs. There's tubs of marge to get to the edges of the bagged bread. There's onions, to give you something to cry about.

11.

People die. People you both know. You hover at the cusp of the ingoing crowd. Everyone has turned slow motion in their good shoes. They bottleneck the aisles. Glass cuts the heat into colours that feel unholy. Everyone is dressed to the point of suffocation. You can't count the degrees of sun reflected on your spine. Your black zipper itches. Your hair wilts out of the fix you sprayed round it, a gauzy radius of triple super-hold. You sweat on the commemorative programme. You try not to smudge the corpse's face.

It's the kind of church where you have to wedge a stool down under your line-up of bad knees and mutter thanks. The litany comes out so half-arsed. It's the kind of church where no one can sing, except the vicar, whose contralto is a shrill joke. He pipes it hard and pious and pitchy so you drop your head as if you're praying. The hymns keep coming so it looks like you and God are tight.

You're not going to look in the coffin. Blow that. Where did it even come from, the idea of parading past the box—from the old days where they needed to double-check you'd carked? You hang back when the queue starts. You pat a tissue at the damp flex of mascara so people will think you're overcome. Not squeamish. At the back of the church someone is juggling a baby. The heat is dialing up. The flowers bulge with scent, looming off the altar. How long does it take to kiss a corpse goodbye anyway. The baby handler is doing a lousy job of shutting it up. The air feels whiney with lilies. You hate that pollen. People file back from rubbernecking death and press against your flanks.

You don't see him until you're saying hallelujah for your club sandwich, giving thanks for the trinity of ham and cucumber and mashed egg with no crusts. Everyone's black clothes are clichéd with sweat, clouded at the impractical armpits. He's flushed too: he's rucking with the collar of his suit, but knocks it off when he spots you. Juts his lats back, his jaw up, the way he used to, tries to look swag as he weaves through the pack of old ladies fussing round the cake. You don't want to smile: you know your gums will be arched with suckers of soft white bread.

But then, you're not dead.

13.

You've learnt to back down from your mother. The guy behind the counter can tell your training is just about to kick in. It's in his face as he goes through the warranty clauses: he's banking on you giving up. And that's what makes you smack both wrists on the bench, your fingernails a tenfold *piss off*. No way, mate. You are not going to stand for it. You want to see the manager.

You wait in the manager's office. The chair they've put you on is munted, so you pulse a little on the plastic seat, a diagonal tock that's out of sync with the minute hand. The lino gives your sandals an unwashed scud. You're not touching the water they've given you. The children framed on the desktop are diving into sunlight only money can buy. You feel ripped off.

You ready your turned back when the door opens. You pick off the fold-back clip on your home-file of docs and get ready to drop them in a splay, an *I mean business* spread, aggressive, on his desk.

When he touches your hair. So you twist to see who it is. His hand goes looking for memory. The air in the room is out of order. Small claims scatter to your ankle-strap. The half-hearted water glass floods. Your scalp goes neon with love.

Lifetime guarantee.

15.

The world is a jigsaw of places you could meet him in. This town is a big dark chunk, a solid edge, its streets interlocking one border of the lonely rented life he's bound to find you in, pretending to trade under your married name, telling your lies. You feel yourself getting backed against it. At night, you look out the window and the street lights click the aimlessness into sequence. In other lives you've slipped past leading, the headlights of his car will pull towards you or away, deciding the direction you'll walk in when

deleted scenes for lovers

you wake, the outline you will chalk into dreams to help your fall. You know what you've got coming.

17.

You're on a jetty. The sea could not be slimier, moving in sucks of green oil through gaps in the boards. Nail heads stick out. Nothing round here is safe. The soles of your feet are good as fish in their grieving. You could paddle on the splinters all day. And why don't you? Take your shoes off or leave them on? Plastic bags wobble past in the foam. The aching of ropes leads down to the water. Everything down there discolours and bloats. The ridges of your mouth don't feel like words will ever split them open again.

He's gone. It should be what's written on all of the hulls that are turning in the harbour. It should be what's written on the concave silk you find when you pick up the bleached scab of a shell. He's gone.

Pace the boards. Your shoes weigh nothing. Testing, testing. Everything down there knows it.

20.

So: reality TV. He's in a gang of contestants, scrounging for clues on an island somewhere. The sun is too good for him. You'd like to kick sand in his face. But you watch his backbone, coming out of scrub. He'll find the idol, he always does. The scramble of his thighs wins every battle, his throat bound in buffs, his torso a tough republic. You map the drip of his sweat, think of swallowing its nutrients. The night vision camera makes you want to slip your thumbs into the phosphorescence of his eyes. The bend of his retinas, his teeth, should be cupped like pearls.

Vote him out first.

23.

It has to be this cheap. There has to be twin lemon polyester bedspreads that smell like burnt hair. There has to be a blue plastic New Testament, chill to the touch in the lino-topped drawer. The blinds have to leave your thumbprints hanging in the dust. By the unit door there has to be a frosted globe of light the glass has busted on, trimmed with the crisp dark joints of roasted insect. You have to stare at it. Wing and thorax, a comical crystal ball of fuzz.

You wait a long time. There has to be time to wait. Or how would you see the detail: the looped pile in the orange carpet, how the ball of your foot can ooze through its swirls. There has to be time to locate the band of hair clustered in the shower grille. It's turning into a crown, bonded with slime. There has to be time to find that. The brown lines parched into the leathery apricot soap. Wire legs on the bouclé chairs. The flex to the fringed lamps thick as tendons. The melted roses on the toaster's plastic tray. How would you feel if you missed any of that?

How would you feel if you couldn't smell your breath in the Arcoroc coffee cup, the fumes of stale remorse damp on your make-up. How would you feel if the vintage TV didn't hiccup through three silver channels, flashes of re-run glitching the water you don't let tip out your pencilled eyes. It's a good theme song for weeping but there's not enough volume. You hover above the bowl to piss. You have to laugh at yourself, squatting upright, your OCD flanks. The blinds have to break up the mirror, seven years of bad luck you only blink at. Your hairdo has to turn orange with the carpark glow. You have to lay down. You decide it's wigs, or maybe the dolls you boxed up back in childhood—yes, the bedspreads smell like wigs.

He has to knock, although he has a key. You have to say no, you've changed your mind. Everything feels like lint; the air on your lipstick, the chain to the faux-panelled door. The ashtrays have to be scallop shells. You can't stand the feel of scallop shells. You can't stand the sound they make on the glass coffee table every time you stub. It gets in your teeth, that sound, that calcified ripple, like tiny bones clicking out of place. It's the sound as you rig your last cigarette, exhaled to the base, in that pink fluted dump. Then open the door to him after all.

Because you're a joke. You have to be a cheap joke, don't you? Everything here has been pointing to it.

24.

Later, he pulls the New Testament out of its bedside cubby. It lies on his abdomen. There's a spiral of hair as dark as all the ex-flies nuked and suspended outside the unit door. The testament breathes there. We have to sin, he says to you. He pulls a preacher's yea-behold hand sign, grinning. Verily, I say unto you. We have to sin. Or Jesus died for nothing.

26.

The woman at the shop has had a gutsful of tourists. Dark brown freckles spurt down her forearms as she grapples with the ice cream scoop. The backs of her hands look like they've been dragged through sand. She's gruff with the mint choc chip—the bastard's iced up.

You've got plenty of time to pick out the change, exact, while she's hacking at the pastel tub. The cone stand makes a graunch as she shoves yours upright—a triple, of course, it bloody had to be. You hold the little stack of coins over her palm, release with a simper. You hear her sling them in the till, huffy, as you flick out through the anti-fly rainbow flaps.

The track there is longer than you thought, and rougher. Your jandals keep skidding on the clay, and you give sudden blushing *Oohs* and off-kilter *Whoopsies,* checking for anyone snickering your way. But it's nice and clear. You gum on the balls of mint.

The heat drips the green down the cone, so you mop up with your tongue.

Your ticker is thudding by the time you reach the stairs. It's steeper than you'd bargained for, a shonky frame of salt-bleached wood. The plastic tread they nailed on the steps has sheared off to poke up in silly black curls from its pins. You suck on the last of your cone to get your hands free. It's beautifully soggy at the ice-creamy base, baggy with sweetness.

Once you've got down, you let your jandals ping you through the scruff of seaweed to the finer white. The rock cathedral is crooked and smells of secrets the earth is keeping. Cool ripples work the distance of minerals up through the strangeness of the roof. The air feels ancient, moulded to your mouth like a song. You slip off your jandals and let your feet mottle the sand. You always thought you'd marry here. Oh well.

There's no sense feeling sorry. It could be worse as you dig your towel out of your kit and flap it open in the sunlight. It could be worse than a gladwrapped package of sandwiches and a flask for one. A little dip in the tide and a paperback romance. You should be careful what you hanker for. There's nothing like getting your haunches settled on your towel with the warmth of the sand humming through to them. You pat on your sunscreen, set up your jandals in a neat couple at the end of the towel, toe-prints in a smutty fan. What more could you ask.

29.

There are no turns to take. Just the grey of a left-handed world driving in through your screen. There are letterboxes. They're not all white, but they look it. The words inside them seem very black when you blink. You blink. He is never in the words. He is never in a letter sent to any number down a road where you are always moving backwards until you reach a house where you still don't stop even though you're at zero.

31.

You don't have a self in a waiting room. You have a name and a vowel sound. They call one and you answer with the other. The two do not seem joined anymore. You are joined to the chair with its blue vinyl grips. You are joined to the steel rings puncturing the curtain. You are joined to the yellow needle stubbed into your wrist with its jack of clouded tubing. When they lie you flat later, you are joined to the keyboard that is wheeled to the ward by a senior troop of do-gooders. The morphine takes no time to climb your bicep and punch across the easy muscle of your heart. The morphine joins you deeper to the song being pumped out of the keyboard, *What a Friend We Have in Jesus.*

Once you used to daydream of accidents you'd have. You thought they would bring him back. He would cross to you and ponder your hair, strewn by emergency. He would not stand to see you suffer. He would make it stop. You would still have mascara on. And if it wasn't him it would be another man. Someone would find you, spritzed with fever, pale and silkily arranged in your tragedy.

When the salvation keyboard has finished, one of the aging singers comes to your bed. She leaves you a flannel with crocheted edges and a tie-on card with a psalm on it. She will visit again tomorrow. It will be the season for you to throw up. The plastic puke container is the size of a Chinese takeout serve and she will hold it although it's not big enough. She will use the flannel to rinse off the pigment of your sick, your pretty lashes dragged away with it.

You will look forward to seeing her.

You will read the psalm and cry.

You will think God looks like a woman with a lukewarm rag who knotted its edges by hand.

You will live for the night-shift dose of morphine uttering its subcutaneous blasphemies.

33.

You're taking off your make-up. Once you used to hate doing this because there was a young girl waiting underneath. Now you hate doing it because there is an old woman. You can't wait to put a fresh coat on.

You try not to look at the still life of your face. If he had chosen you, you would have had a different one. You could have stared at the whole thing, instead of painting in corners. The lines aren't even fine print anymore. You apply shadows, tack around the lips. You strain the skin sideways. Black visors cloak your eyes. You tweeze your brows into broken feathers. Close range, side-on, you eyeball your pores, use a thumbnail to dredge out silver jelly.

All you've done is paint on another face he'll never love.

36.

You're having a pyjama day. That's it, fuck it. It's for mental health. You'll bung your hair in a ponytail where it will wobble around unwashed. You'll boycott bras, or underarm, or breakfast. You'll leave the curtains yanked shut, hotbox the lounge and plug in every crap movie you can think of. Calorie intake will be continuous, sticky and guilt-free. You will let out farts into your flannelette boxers.

You will forget your calendar. You'll forget there's a Trade Me pickup coming. You will freeze at the first door knocks, think if you don't budge they're bound to back off and just go home. But they don't. They head around, hunting for gaps in the curtains. They can hear the white noise of TV. Just your luck that the violins are gearing up to underline a true romantic bit.

So you've got no choice. He starts hailing from the kitchen side, where he can see clear through. What's worse, when you roll your arse off the couch you trip over the manky cat, launch across the lounge with a stumble that's still going by the door handle. He's speechless when the door bunts open. He gives the waistband of his shorts an awkward lift. His work boots are charged with clay up the tread. The print of the cushion on your lazy face must look like a birthmark: you can feel its pins and needles. But turns out he's got a grin to give you. Turns out he's not hard on the eyes. Turns out he doesn't mind his women no frills.

39.

The days are filling with ways he won't meet you. You're still drunk when you wake up. The room is sandbagged with stale clothes, not all of them yours, and everything you touch is an omen. You rake down the blinds to try to bypass the sun but the season is full-scale, the heat won't be blocked. Your tongue is rugged in a bloodless mouth. Small errors blur everything. All the hallways feel like hairpin turns—you get nowhere fast. Outside six birds are picking the kerbside clean. But you can't eat. His face in the back of your memory doesn't help you watch the man in the bed, who turns when you go back to the room, and makes a reach like a shortcut for a better gesture. You lie down under that abbreviation of touch.

41.

You drink on the swings and the piss spreads a sting through your chest. The chains click. There are seagulls everywhere, seed-eyed, strands of fishing line snagged in their feathers and ragged webbed feet. Such mongrel birds. The sea that's supposed to be here for you has backed off for miles. The harbour's full of holes, shallow Os in the flat light, part silver, part shit. They make you blink. Your hips hurt, the bones of them built too wide for the vinyl hanger. You catch a length of hair in the cleats and your scalp pulls up, red hot, at the temple. But it's worth it. Because he leans in and tells you it's a long road, but he knows you're waiting at the end of it for him. Yeah, that's it, you're like his fate. The other girls mean nothing. You're meant to be. So you chug vodka and murmur it into his kiss, as the gulls flog each other for crusts and the mud flicks the sun out.

43.

Just walk in! Great first home! Everything's been straightened, and the realtor's gone with the trick of bread baking, fumed the house with yeasty warmth. But they can't hide the signs of a split. Unfaded frame shapes left on the wallpaper, not a white dress to be seen in the shots still tacked up. Lawyers' cards under the butterfly magnets on the fridge. *Vendors are motivated!* Your husband keeps touching you every room you view—just an index tap on your forearm, out the realtor's gaze, a code for the deal you could score. *Has to be seen to be believed!* You can hear your kids, their racket in the *Quarter-acre section!* You open the bathroom cupboards and one side is wiped clean—though there's shreds of stubble knocked from a shaver left in the corner. So this could be it. Your husband has gone outside to tone the kids down—they've showered the lawn in hoodies and boots and taken to the trampoline. You go to the office, where it's all him, packed into cartons, find yourself flicking up a layer of wrap. The size of the photo you have in your hand is a jigsaw fit for the fade in the living room wall: and the groom is looking straight at you. You go back to the bathroom, lick your finger and dab it in the scurf. Your heart crams with blood. The kids are a circus outside. The realtor's creeping the verandah with its *Wraparound views!* Your husband is walking the narrow hallway and you know from the set of his jawline that he's running figures on *A future in the sun!* You put a hand to the neck of your shirt and use it to scour the collarbone that won't stop leaping, your finger, unforgivable, alive with his roughage.

46.

They send you back to clean Room 617. Someone's complained they lost their wallet—bitch at the office eyeballs you like you're suspect. What the fuck *ever*. Exhibit A: you drag back the trolley, flip her the bird. Crank the key and the smog of sealed room hits you. You're well into the off-season. The only couples that book in now are up to nothing good. They need to get well off the map. You rark through all the likely spots, yank back curtains, the shadows in the sou'east of the wardrobe. Everything stinks of emptiness. Everything's holding this chill of cheap carpet and sweat, base-rate rooms only used for a fuck. Pastels, no extras, the scent of dripping taps, but the splendour of skin gone to shine in endless wrangling—rooms that get to stage the epic dirty things no marriage does. Or so you reckon. But you can't find a wallet, no matter how you dredge the corners. Until you've got down on your gut, aimed your head in the dark channel under the Super King. You need to get back up, ram the handle of the mop back in the gap to swish the billfold free. Then you squat there, turning the clear plastic flaps, your body stiff in its budget uniform, viewing the faces of him and his kids, a line-up of birthdays and mugshots of travel, his wife with her middle-class strings of fob chain dangled from the shoulder she's got tensed with the fucking Taj Mahal in the background.

49.

In the left-hand corner there's the edge of his board, the scuffle of wax up its curve gone murky with toeholds. You remember that. Behind him the bed, you know, will be riveted with sand. His T-shirt will be greasy, and you'll be pitiful, tapping the print on his diaphragm where the logo for a car yard leads nowhere near his heart. The room will smell like mosquitoes, a high-pitched smell so full of summer you scratch and pant. Your feet will be bare, but still reek of jandals, the nub of wet rubber haltering your toes. You'll pull off your singlet, but still have a bib of sunburn, dribbled with freckles, like scraps of a better girl's tan. You'll try to kiss him until your teeth ache. You'll let him buckle your legs and slide you back on the lino. You'll want to get that ugly 70s print tattooed in black fins on your back—go on, let him walk on you. There's a spider plant dangled from his mum's macramé which hangs there like a brown beaded spine. Your mouth is branded Lion Red. The windows are scaly—the whole town looks like salt. But there isn't a town out there anyway, only a spit, a flatline horizon, kids dropping like gulls off the one-lane bridge, a distance of pines carved off at the stumps, trucks low-gearing out to the exit you're too young and thick to take. You'll take it later. Maybe you will. Freehand now, you're just all over his skin. He's sour and the low tick of veins are in your mouth, one real deep thump where your lip meets cock base, a spaz of hair that tastes of togs. There's ants, single file, where he's left a sandwich, stubbed in tinfoil, a collection of shot glasses, flags he scored for some shit at school. For being first, for being beautiful. You get up and study the shape of the photo that no one ever takes, the shadows of it fluid on his outstretched trunk, the fused light waiting in the blue pools of his hand. You walk out the memory and pass it to me. I add it to the album of moments I never got to frame before he changed his mind and kicked me out the room like the easy lay I was.

49.

Write a story. Place him at the right-hand edge of the sentence, crouched. Use a shadow, running the length of his shoulder, to signal his intent to turn. Lay a comma on the brink of his hipline, a suspended pause of dark. Space your fingers on the keys: they are the roots of his hair. Pray he never gets closer than the page.

the turn

You know you'll get the hit of a million cigarettes. A mile off, still, you can smell it on him. It's bad light out the back of his place, but it's a smoker's shout he aims at you, a rough greeting to guide you round the stockpiles of junk in the dim shop, until you get to him. *Howzit mate?* He knocks his forehead back, expecting a bloke, then maybe you come into tighter focus, out of the shed-front of square-on sun and edging round the dump of bung machines with some tilt to your hips or something, so then you get his toked-up grin. All tobacco molars up back—but that can't block the eyes, which are bad-news blue and playing up whatever sun they've got. To the max. And smoke. Smoke round him, like you haven't wanted for years. To huff it hard down into you. Drag on it fully and hold it, chocker, in your gut.

'You the pick up, eh?'

And he knows. Knows full well his eyes give him leeway. His stare gets more than an innings down on your hips. Then climbs up, in no hurry. And Jesus, you've hardly put a thought into how you look, heading over here, last minute, giving your husband all kinds of lip on the phone for thinking he could just send you round to do his shit jobs, *It's not as if it's* work, *even*, you'd spit into the sink as the teeth got maybe a once-over, still freaking at him down the phone, *it's a* half-*arsed hobby, it's for losers,* what kind of loser packs the house out with random munted stuff that he flogs off for fuck-all and thinks he's like some shrewd top fucking dealer. Trade Me is for wankers. So you've hardly yanked a comb through your hair, you just balled it up the back of your skull as you were stamping down the drive, and punched some clip up through it that you grubbed out the glovebox, still ranting. Still going off into the air in the empty car, because when you told your husband you'd got the *hospital* to visit, remember, he'd tried to use it, he'd tried to get into it, gentle and whiny, *No you don't have to babe, you know you don't have to,* but you just launch, you just cut him off, *I told you we are not fucking talking about that.* And now you are standing in a wrecker's to pick up some junk he's bid on, with way too much sunlight up your back and sweat fanning out your T-shirt pits. And there is a stare coming at you from this guy that makes you think back to a line you used at high school, *Take a picture why don't you, it'll last longer,* and you can feel the load of your hair slipping out its shonky grip. Some afterthought of scrapping it out with your husband, like sadness, getting loose on your scalp.

You dizzy bitch.

It's the motion, though, this guy's look going through you, and how it gets lodged somewhere, spinal. And you can't even be sure when you last got scoped like this, so you go hunting for a memory of some point when you used to move sleek and cool through a pub or a backyard at parties because you knew there were eyes on you, there were looks aimed low. But all you come up with is sadness again. And your husband had said when you were clashing, *It's years, babe, I don't think you look in the mirror anymore, you do know it's been years, eh?* And now it's like all the ribs in your chest don't fit, won't flex to let you shrug it off. They're gridlocked. So you stare off instead at the hunks of machine the guy's got stashed round the shed, and it's true, they all look in better shape than you. All this shit is at least good for something. You are the write-off. Nothing in you worth storing up, reusing. There's no yard for you.

'Heat fucking with you, eh? Need a cold one?'

Place is a maze of parts. There are propellers, paddles, in the heap out left. There are windshields, tie-downs, drums. You stare around the shed, the lean-tos tacked onto its tin sides, tubs of bolt, racks of tools. Tanks, straps. You try target your stare, like you're fully running inventory, like you've got an eye for a good deal, weighing up. Like your head's not stocked with tears.

But blink. And Christ, now there's an output of wet. At least you manage to turn your back, partly, to get, if nothing else, a shoulderblade between him and you. Pathetic. Just make out it's the sun in your eyes, or maybe a dose of fumes, and palm off the slip down the left side of your face. Try make the blank side mutter back, *Yeah, fucking heat, it's like, how many fucking degrees can it get.* But that's not what comes out.

There's nothing but the sound you make. The groan of it. Unglued. Like words got stuck in muscle, and pulled out of shape there.

Then there's like, a ricochet, like your noise knocked loose some bit of metal. Listen to it. Some thin piece of rig or trim drops down in the distance, tingles, through its high pile.

And if he's fazed by you he doesn't make much show. He sticks with the heat line.

'Takes it out of you, eh. Cranked up the aircon, but it hardly makes a diff. Mate, I know you from somewhere, eh? Nah? Nah, I reckon I've spotted you. Somewhere round. Anyway. You wanna rollie?'

Yes. You do. You just need to get a grip, on a single word.

He is onto it, but. Goes for his pouch, down the right-hand of his overalls, loose-fingered, low-key. Like it's no biggie. Like he gets people bawling in here every day maybe.

You get into some trance, tracking his fingertips. It's the

routine of rolling that always left you calm, just to watch it, the small motor hush of the moves. Feeding out the dry weed. Flick of dirty thumbs up the paper. And tongue-tip, barely off the lower lip, lazing and flat, a wide, easy run. Just watching it, you go quiet to your fingerprints.

He holds it out to you.

'Answer for everything, eh?'

You can nod. Just enough, not to tip more useless wet off the edge of your eyes. And then before you get closer, take the smoke, you can tilt your head back as if it's all about sorting out your hairclip, keeping your manky fringe scrunched clear of the lighter.

Then you let your mouth open, lean in, line up your face with the wrecker's dirty hand.

Take a jaw full of who you once were.

Drop way back in that smell.

Watch the rafters, up there, dark beams buckled with metal, your head arced in thin sheets of smoke.

You quit years ago, but it's not like you remember what for— it's not like you want to breathe these days in any deeper. Yeah, how's that for a trip?—you gave it up to keep your lungs clean, and now you spend most days trying not to breathe your own life in. Don't want to inhale the facts. Any of it. As though if you keep your ribs good and still they might not pick up too much trace of the life you're stuck living, it might not get right under your skin, might not stick. It's not a well thought-out programme. Just a way to cope. Adrift, sideways. Without looking at the state of things, head on. Like the way you watched the land back away from you on the drive over here, or like driving over to the hospital, most days, only half-awake. Black hills in the rearview, pulling easy out from your gaze. Flatland outside, wired into lines, floods of smooth field moving in reverse, miles you can let leak past you. You could just keep your head half-afloat there, with the coast cruising off to black in a backward haze. No counter to the wheel, no pull, just your hands laid open on the circle, ten and two, like the shape of some emptied-out prayer, loose-palmed. Coasting out to a vacant horizon. And why would you bother, why would you shift your look back to the road? Eyes front, there is fuck-all oncoming. Life is not exactly going anywhere. Not likely to change now. Not for you.

Either way, not for your bro.

Which is not good. It's the smoke. The smoke has brought him back with it, up from way-back, from far out of his state in the hospital, from somewhere you've got a memory of him living, your brother, the two of you teens, hanging out on the rear bench that summer day when your dad got married again, little mongrel know-it-alls that you and him were, in the good gear they made you wear, scowling at everyone except each other, ignoring the pastor and keeping up this mean-as swap of sneers throughout the service. And then your bro actually lights up. He actually goes and lights up while they're maybe two-thirds through the love and obey and whatever. And passes it, grinning, like a total bastard to you. And fuck it tastes so good, it tastes like you've got someone on your side forever, no matter that your mum's a goner, and your dad's up there getting hitched to a cheap cow you can't stand, who he hooked up with before your mum was even cold. And her kids are like everywhere, quarter of your age, expecting to have their sticky fucking hands held, expecting to be part of the team, like they've got rights to you and your dad just because everyone's got shiny wedding clothes the same gross colour, like this new family will just get matched up, all one unit of tight shoes and photoshopped smiles. But not your bro and you. You are way out. You are buzzing on the pisstake you keep going through the whole wedding deal. And now you've got your faces down here in the chapel, down where there's like fold-down prayer steps you're meant to kneel down on and blah blah suckful praise, and instead you've got the smoke moving, in and out the radius of your two faces, yours and his, him and you. Where it's easy to see who belongs to whose family, because your face is a trade-off for his one, scrub this Maybelline rubbish off it, dig that nasty halo of flowers out your hair, and you're as good as twins, with smiles of one a switch for the smoked-out laughter hissing up the mouth of the other. With your eyes popping and your ribs humping, your lips jammed in a line, trying not to cough. And the thing that caps it off is: he's got to go up and sign the licence. There's a photographer up there waiting and everything, all rigged up to take the shot. And you hold your hand out to snatch the smoke off him before he goes, but he sends you this *Nah, mate, have a jack at this* look. And he swags up the aisle with it in his fingers. And he puts it down—no shit—he props it in the flowers on the table where they're waiting to sign. He actually balances it, super careful, right on one green meaty megabucks leaf. And it smokes away, this fizzle rising up in the total tense-as quiet of the church. Then he sits down to scribble, and gets up straight-faced, and picks his fag back out the flowers, says *Sweet*, and takes a slow stroll to his seat with a nice load of ash getting dropped on the church fucking carpet as he takes his laidback time.

Let it drift through your teeth, the smoke. Haul it in, heat up the ridges at the back of your throat. Look square at him.

'All good?' the wrecker says.

'Course.' Because that's where you are. Way out from that day. Waiting, to get the deal done, in a yard.

'Can never remember what I was stressing about. Once I got my head wrapped round one of these.'

'True.'

'Too true. All that shit on the box to put you off. All that *Ka mate koe i te kai hikareti*. Big whoop. Take more than that. The way I see it. It's worth every poisonous minute.'

Those are the words that make you grin back at him. Then glance off. At towbars, struts. Outboard winched up in the centre, chained. You don't have to look far to see yourself in mirrors, wings and rears. At all angles. The whole place reeks, but it's somehow good to swallow, in with the smoke, the heavy solvent stink of metal, a tank water taste to it, some brew like sour fuel and old leaves. A faint ache of diesel where the roof of your mouth backs down into throat.

'Pays to keep a few spares, eh. Ha.'

And maybe it's the word *pay*, but you get on with it, dig out the wedge of cash in your jeans.

'Should be the total. Least that's what my husband said.'

'Beauty.'

'He was planning to pick up, but got caught at work. You might want to check. I took off in a bit of a rush and just grabbed it. Think it's all there, but.'

'No worries. You didn't bring someone to help put their back into it?'

'Just me.'

'Right. That might be the catch, eh.'

'Sorry, mate. I didn't know. Tell you the truth, I can't say I actually know what I'm here to pick up. He could've bid on anything. For all I know.'

'Ha. That right?'

'Sad to say. Yeah. Don't know what half the crap he drags home is. Just know my house is packed with it. Can't get in the spare room. It's coming down the bloody hallway now.'

'Sell you something off any old shit-pile then, eh? Ha.'

'You could try.'

'Nah. Wouldn't do it to you, love.'

'Yeah, right.'

'Nah. Not you. Special terms of trade. For sheilas. Of a certain type.'

'Fucking come off it.'

'Ha. Nah, come on. Thing is, right, it'll be a pure bastard to shift. Just between us, I don't reckon you'd be up to the thing. No offence. But not too sure your bloke was really thinking it through.'

'That'd be right.'

'That so.'

Try not to nod too hard.

'Needs his head read, eh. You don't mind me saying. Expecting a little thing like you to take the weight. Fuck me. The damn thing'd flatten you. If you can hang on, but, I'll see if I can jack a mate up. To give us a hand. Got a mate lives right up back, next property. Young guy. Bit of a munter, but do anything for you. Should be sweet as. No reason you got to shoot off?'

'S'pose not.'

'Said you were in a rush, but.'

'I thought I was.'

'Things change.'

'I probably . . . just wanted a reason to let him have it. My husband.'

'Fair enough. Gets like that, eh.'

'Some days. You want to just. I don't know. Have it out.'

'Sounds like wedded bliss, eh. Know it well.'

And there's smoke moving in and out of all of it, you and him talking. And something on the end of his sentences, this seedy twitch like he knows what's coming. Or could be. If he plays his cards right. He's banking on his eyes, on you reading how the glint is dialling up in them, bits of sky building in his iris.

'So. Nothing to lose then, eh.'

Which suits him. Far as you can see.

And you say, 'I'm meant to get to hospital. For a visit. Someone there I got to go see.'

'That so. Well, look. We can sort this later then. If you've got a mate not doing too good.'

'No it's . . . It's not like they're good. But it's not changing.'

'Sounds rough.'

'So it doesn't matter what time I go. It's the same deal. Whatever day I make it. They don't know. They don't change.'

'That's a bugger.'

'It is what it is.'

'True. You go there a lot, maybe that's where I seen you. I go in sometimes. On jobs and shit.'

'Oh, yeah.'

'When they get issues up the boiler room. I fix the burners and stuff. You wouldn't believe the system they got up there. Fucking ages old. Got to make shit up to keep it running, out of this lot. I've had to go up and put in all kinds of parts, scavenged from this heap. You wouldn't credit. And I don't want to even think what they burn off in there.'

Which moves you away. Which is too real, the dark outline of what he's telling you. And he must pick it up. He rucks in his pocket, flicks you his stash and says, 'Anyway. Roll yourself one while you wait. I'll get on the blower, get my mate fixed up. He'll give us a lift. Shouldn't be too much of a hold-up.'

You're not fit to talk. So you take up what slack you can by scuffing round the shop. Making out you've got an eye for what's down in the far bins. The shadows there are colossal. Jacks, off-cuts. The walls held up by whole dunes of machine. The guy's got a foxhole of semi-office space, cleared just barely out the iron banks, a flimsy retaining wall of file cabs, a greasy roller desk, a bulb on a pull-chain. And you can hear him: turns out his mate is up back, should be down before you know it. You just drift on, take shortcuts through the high slopes of junk. You hardly know what any of it is, what it's worth keeping for. All of it steep, tough, without meaning, so far without meaning, that you feel your mind black out around the edges of it. Or could just be your eyes, still playing up. The leakage is getting a habit. But what's the diff. And anyway, it's not like you'd know the meaning if you looked under the hood into an engine that was running, where the charge was good. It's all the same to you, the bands of dark plug, the pistons punching life into the geared-up coils. You wouldn't know the difference between a working slab of engine and a heap of unhooked junk. And you think you could tell him this, maybe, the wrecker. This is the problem: how do you tell?

Tell anyone, might take some weight off it. But it's not the kind of thought you can let last.

Because thoughts like that are an easy track to memory, just the place you don't need to go. *You don't know the fucking diff,* same as your bro always said, looking up at you from the car he's working on, nights when it's like the two of you in a club, your hangout the half-lit shed down back and what's in the front house all wrong since your dad got hitched. So the two of you hunch on your crates and only lever off an elbow to light up and stare at the bad joke of your dad's silhouette in the lounge playing dumbarse baby games with all those new kids he's taken on, so what else would you do, the two of yous, but gang up and sulk in the garage, your bro banging shit out the panels of rando cars that he picks up from all places. The neighbourhood, the town even, knows to tip their mongrel wagons out back of his shed and yell *Good fucking luck to you mate,* so you spend your nights shaking your head at the next sorry dumper he's dug in under the chassis of, telling him *Fuck, bro, what goes through your skull,* but his voice underground in the grille is full of love, he tells you what a dream ride he'll make of the heap, he'll tell you *Nah, you wait, she'll come up a beauty, she's just got a bit of brain damage, that's all,* and reach his hand out to you, wait for you to drop the answer into it, in the shape of the next tool, the right bolt or hinge. And you don't have a clue, do you, wouldn't know what the fuck to pass him. So all's you get's a follow-up shot of laughter, the next round of pisstake. But you don't mind. Not so much. Because it warms the shed, it warms your sternum, and the way your life's in outbuildings now means this is all you've got to warm it, you and your bro is all, this greasy kingdom, where it's okay that the wheels are off everything, okay that you crouch out here basically muttering nothing to each other round a series of wrecks, it's like the whole place says *No loss, whatever,* it says *So what* if you've got to hang round in here, numb while your dad clowns round with a houseful of new kids, *big deal,* there's the music of your bro unbelting a panel that's been puckered like cloth, there's the orchestral tingle of tools biffed on the concrete, there's the feel that some shit does mend, at least enough to flog a few more miles out of it. There's the sense of something bonded and thick, watching his hands climb round the dark compound, the mess under the hood. And if your dad comes out to tell you again, *You two need to buck your ideas up*, to give you a piece of his mind on the subject of two stubborn youths refusing to live under the perfectly good roof he's provided for them, then you two can just stare back at him with your *what-the-fuck-would-you-know* gaze like it's trained on him through cross-hairs. You're so like twins in the grimy light that hangs from the one bad garage bulb, you know it freaks him out, your one face recurring in the shallows. You smirk at each other when he gets to his last flustered blink. He'll say, *Ah fuck yas then*, and stamp back to the house. And you will laugh, although it's not a laugh that reaches deep. It doesn't fill you. It's not like the fill you get from the nights when you spend so long out back you just crawl into the trailer your bro crashes in, you're so tired and lagered you can't be fucked taking the few dark steps that would get you to the house, you just slump in the metal box that he's made his, a covered junk trailer propped one end, with a hole in the roof that's been knocked through ragged with stars and a bucket to lash on to try pick off the rain, which flickers in anyway, when it wants to, and sets off the flaky smell of rust which—you're so sick—you love to suck into your nostrils and feel prickle there. It's all like comfort, you two uprooted kids slung in the trailer with the babble of rain scumming the bucket and the sting of rusted metal sour and chafing up the back of each calm breath. And sure, there's guys by now, there's guys that turn up and cramp round the wreck with only half an eye on anything to do with the mechanics of it, that spend their night shooting the shit with your bro and walking wide outlines round your presence, keeping their eyes in check when they pass you brews, not puzzling on your wrists or where your tits hint out from beneath your T-shirt, busting out these drum lines on the leg of their jeans to signal how laidback they are when you slink past. But you know, so you twist, and let a shank of hair scrape them, let this solo finger leave a trace on the cold one you hold out, make them jump, drop a stray touch, but it's not enough; you play them, vague as, you leave them no proof, and your brother knows too, he's onto you, and he raises his eyebrows at you, and there's that smirk again. And he says, one night, when you're banked up against him kipping in the trailer and the slurp of rain is silvering your sleeping bags anyway, screw whatever the dumbfuck bucket is supposed to achieve, he just says, *You may as well put one out their misery.* And you love the way he slurs *may as well.* You tease him, *Marzel, nice prodrunkenunciation dude.* But you may as well. And you wait. Then the one he suggests is your husband. It's that simple. Tag, and he's it. Your husband is one minute this kid shrugging in the wraparound haze of your late-night sessions, then next he's the one whose lap you arrive in, loose-limbed and woozy like it took you getting dieseled to do it. To weave across the concrete and trip against blank parts and topple, making like you're aimless, like your nuzzle is an accident, just a mishap, like something relaxes, there's a half-cut slip and you loop yourself around him just by chance, just by freak. It happens. You shelter in his grab, and that's where it stops.

And you stop, now, in the wrecker's, and you think of what your husband might be doing. You think of the burden of black hulks he's hoarding in your house, the rooms he's stocked with mongrel parts, and how the whole time he might be trying to trade you back there. To the place where things got put back together, in your past. Except there is no show. Because it was always your brother who fixed everything.

So it's a breather when the wrecker's mate brakes up hard outside, a full speed park-up with the radio on max that sends out a rip of dust and static. The noise goes on, a rash of echoes on the tin, relayed on your spine.

'Fucking tear up my drive, why don't you,' the wrecker yells out. 'You manus. What are ya? Here's me trying to make out to my customer, who's fucking of the fairer sex in case you haven't clocked on, that you are a fully fucking reliable source of helpful muscle. Not a total munter with too many muscles in your head. Or rocks more like.'

But the mate has no comeback. It's clear enough from the wrecker's hassle that there's a working pattern of pisstake between them and that most days they'd rark each other well up, take a crack big time, knock each other back. But the way they would give-and-take most days has gone flat, one-sided. The young guy doesn't toe it. His face is shut down, looks thick with what he can't start saying.

Instead he shoves a page across at his mate.

And *mate* is all that gets said at first, when the wrecker reads it. 'Mate. *Mate,* you're fucking kidding me. *Mate.*'

'You can do it, eh? If it's gotta be done, I'd fucking rather you.'

'Nah, mate. I don't have the rig. That's the full-on deal. The compactor. And they tie all that side of things up, the legal side. And even if I did, mate, I don't reckon I'd have the fucking heart to. Couldn't do it to you.'

'You could tow it back here, but.'

'Mate. You won't want that, eh. It's like, you know I'd do it for you. But you should think that through. It won't be fucking pretty. She'll be totalled. Don't reckon you'd want to put yourself through.'

'Fucking got to bring her home.'

'I don't know. I'd fucking mull over that one, mate. You only just got this letter, eh.'

'Fucking sticking out the mailbox when I come down just now.'

'So, mate, yeah. I'd be thinking that one through.'

'They sold the last one off. On Trade Me.'

'Yeah, but. You won't want to be doing that.'

'Know how many bids?'

'Couldn't fucking stand to look.'

'Got a stack, the way I heard.'

'Yeah, probably. But that was the first one. In the bloody news and all. So the price was up.'

'Went to some charity. So they fucking say. Yeah, right.'

'Mate.'

Which is when you catch on. You remember the clip, the first car they seized, some boy racer done for a backlog of charges. The law could take the lot now, crush it. You watched it on the newsreel. The lid of the unit wedged down. A smooth hydraulic stomp. The windshields fizzling. The panels giving up. Hardly much more than a crumple. Until the car was pressed, eased off the bed with a forklift. The woman who had put through the legislation climbed on the flat hood, posed with the order to destroy, in stilettos. It was level as a tombstone, the size of a hospital bed.

'Fuck this,' the kid says. 'I'm shooting out back. I'm taking her up for her last burnouts. You keen?'

The bloke looks flustered.

'I owe it to her,' the young guy says. 'Before they wipe her out. She deserves it.' His vocals get loose in the high shed's acoustic.

The older man's considering, but frowning your way. He's going to come down on the side of: he's busy, he's tied up, he can't turn a cash job away. But you've done it before thinking. You've stepped up.

'I'm in. You can take me up too.'

Which feels like the moment when you were in the wagon with your brother, way back, when the seconds just came at you, terminal, their shape already locked into a countdown you couldn't decide to rev out of, or brake, or swerve down a different track, because you don't plan out the way time detonates, it just explodes into sudden being through you, it was always going to be, this machinery of seconds where every way you thought your lives would take you, you and your bro, where everything looked clear, splits wide, roars into the open. You and the vehicle that hits you go slamming over the known edge of all your lives, take all the corners you were ever going to turn down and pour over all of them at once. Except there's not a scratch on you. You get out of the car and there's not a mark. This happens. Everything folds up. Everything rolls and up-ends and crushes. And you climb out, you wander along the brink of it. And sure, your skull is ringing, your head is playing a pitch you never hear again. But you are upright. When nothing else is. You are untouched. Except for how your skin is very lightly smoking.

They put you in the front. They don't want to at first, the kid and the wrecker, but they let up when you won't shift, when you won't veer from it, however they try to talk you round. They've got good reasons, but nothing feels valid or immovable. You know what you're meant to do. You don't tell them that, though. You make like you're into it, big time, like you're so fucking buzzed. And the glare is a factor, coming down at you from some high-up east pane. It's a half-arsed window but it picks up a good catch of sun, which you can't afford to let in your eyes. Not after already proving they're prone to run. But maybe it helps you play it up. And maybe the wrecker is thinking he could do worse. Of an afternoon, in the back of beyond. Where there's not such a range to choose from. You're not exactly export quality. But you'll stand up. He could just about take you round the block. So maybe that's what gets you in the front seat, despite the kid's best *Nah,* mate, *fuck*off.

The three of you in the car go nowhere to start with. Then the kid heel-toes it, full throttle and hard brake at once. The tyres scour in place, pumping out rounds of gravel behind them. The noise goes like nitro through your mind. But then he lets up. And fats it. You're roads out, it seems like no time, a mix of routes, metal and seal, taken wild. You wrap a hand up along the window frame. The wrecker in the back leans through and primes the radio, picks up a bunch of static and flags it, hits the off. No one says a thing. And after all, the kid's in mourning. This is his girl and he's got to put her down. He's got to give her up, forfeit the keys and just leave her there, let them shut her body down, turned from this honey you're moving in, with the only live air you seem to have breathed in days streaming in through her windows, and curves of torque sweeping gold dust out the back of her into an iron box, into a narrow slab. He handles her like he'd rather write all of you off. He rakes the gears and swings the corners out. Stones teem off the side, and she grinds up a pack of turf on the shoulder. He's rigid, doesn't flinch, got one arm pinioned to the wheel. You don't like the range of his eye, it's dead on, with a pinpoint on nothing like he can't be much fucked keeping track of the details rushing through the screen, the swim of trees up the sideline, the sudden black weight of the animals bending in their bleached-out paddocks.

But the wrecker knows how to tone him down. He hunches in from the back, not fazed, no speed in his moves. Just an offering.

'Here, mate. Seems like you need one of these.' And he's rolled one for you too, passes them over, smooth. Sits back, lights his, doesn't say much. Until.

'You can put her in the yard yourself, if that's what you want.' He inhales, waits, follows up. Louder, to get it over the engine. 'But if you're going to waste her, I'd rather there was no one inside at the time, eh.'

That's all. Exhale.

You wouldn't know the kid's heard, for could be a K, or even further. Then you feel a give in the air, just a notch, taken out of the momentum. Your gut relaxes a fraction, you can feel your torso lift slightly out its tough cramp back into the framework of the seat. Just an easing. So even the smoke moves looser in the car, so all your breathing's got more space to work with, and the smoke can stretch out. It's better than anyone saying anything. No one watches the needle. It's just a feel, a lowering, and when it gears down again, it's good round the back of your neck, that velocity letting go, that levelling. So your heartbeat isn't saying there's something hard coming at the end of it for certain, some final wall waiting that you've got no choice now but to hit.

It's the kid who seems to take the most impact then, from the deceleration, the quietening. Like the grip that he's got on the steering is suddenly slackened, and the wane opens up his chest. This sob comes out his body. He's suddenly aiming off-road and whether it's the braking or the contact with the bank that pulls her up when you jolt to a stop, the car and the kid both end on an angle, the car lodged up on a slope so you've got the apex, you look down on both of them, the kid keeled into his door, the wrecker tipped back at the low point. It's not going over, nowhere near, it's cant but not fatal. But you brace anyway, back to your door, knee on your seat, watching them.

'Reckon I might be having to drop the price I charge your husband,' the wrecker says to you. 'Let the buyer fucking beware doesn't really cover this.'

You laugh. But the kid is all shoulders, shunted in to his door panel, head away, bawling.

'Mate,' the wrecker goes on to the boy. 'Way I see this, you want to think it through. You want to take her out for a last burn, you've got to head where they can't spot you. You go taking her out on seal and they clock you, you're only making it a fuckload worse for yourself. I know there's fuck-all traffic ever round here. But you know how fucking keen they are, you know they got a whole unit on yous. You tell me where your head's at, and we can still go up and let her loose one last time. But that's all we're here for. We didn't sign up for this eh. And same thing goes, you decide you just want to flag it. Fair enough, you just turn around here and head for home. We're good to go. Nothing wrong with sending her off in one piece, mate. You could take her in so clean, so fine you make them fucking cry. That's what I'd do. Drive her in shining. So you just chill. Then let us know. We'll hang out here and have a smoko on it.'

And it's possible to just rest, even with the kid facing out, shuddering, in his state. It's best to leave him: it's clear in his ribs, in the grate of his breathing, he wants to work it out for himself. Is what you think. But then the shock hits. The kid turns and looks at you instead.

He says, 'I know you. You're always at the hospital. They made me do a work programme down there. Community work, you know, I got stuck on a team. I was in that bunch, building the garden. Round the side with the benches in, so smokers can go out. I seen you sitting there. Not smoking, but I seen you. You sit there ages. Fucking like a statue, eh. One of the guys on the group cracked this joke about how we'd have to dig round you, concrete you in. And the warden told us all to shut the fuck up. Told me who you were. He made a point of telling me. He said, he thought it might help wake me up. He told me about your brother. He told me to go in and take myself a good look at him. Because that's what I'd end up like. On machines. With someone sitting outside, day after day the way you do. And I'd never know they'd been.'

'Did you go in?'

'Shit,' says the wrecker.

'That's right, mate,' says the kid. 'You remember, eh. You were there, you were working some of that time, down the boiler room.'

'Fuck me,' the wrecker rubs his hand round the side of his head. 'I said I had a feeling I'd seen you. I didn't know that was you, but. Fuck, you look like him.'

'You went in too? You both went? Into his room. My brother's room.'

'Like the kid says. The warden took us. Thought it would straighten the little fucker out.'

'Did a good job. Obviously. Yeah, thanks. That makes it *all* fucking worth it.'

'Nah, nah. It shook us up. I know it looks like it didn't make a difference. But, it hit home. Fuck. You couldn't look at him and not feel sorry for him.'

'You reckon? There's plenty of people if you want to fucking know. Plenty of people can look at him and not feel sorry, not feel fucking anything. People nick his clothes, did you know that? Time after time, his clothes go missing. Fuck, it could have been you for all I'd know. I bring his clothes in, because he's going to get up isn't he, he's going to wake up and need gear. I actually iron them, I iron his black jeans and his Tool T-shirt and I put them in a plastic bag, I put his high-tops in and I leave them waiting in the locker by his bed for when he wants them. Because he will. And people pinch them. So don't tell me they feel anything. Plenty of them feel nothing at all. Half the staff at the fucking hospital. I'll tell you what they want him for now. They want him for spare parts. They've run this stack of tests on him. And they come in to show me all their readings. They reckon it all points to the fact there's nothing left. He's gone. That's what they try and keep telling me. It's just the machines that are doing it. But I don't fucking see it. Or I don't want to. So they run the tests again. Because they're so keen, by this stage. To get him out of there. They're so keen to ship him off that their hands fucking shake when they try get me to sign. They've even got the papers ready. Far as they're concerned it's all good to go. I just give them use of what he's got left. My brother. You know what they call it. A harvest. They call it an organ harvest. And they tell me how he'd help people. And I don't give a shit. They're not touching him. And I don't give a shit if he helped you either. He's not fucking spare parts. And that's it. And I don't see how he could be some big example to you, anyway. Because *I* put him there. It was me. *I* turned the corner, straight into oncoming. *I* looked and *I* thought the way was clear. And then it was over. It wasn't even anything to do with him. And the thing that tops it off is, he was the pissed one. I wouldn't let him put his tanked-up self behind the wheel. I took his keys off him, he was so dieseled. I had a go at him because he'd been at it all bloody night, I gave him an earful about what a loser he lived like, always taking off loaded, I shoved him in the front seat. Then I wrote him off. So it's not like I even get to sit here and tell you, learn your fucking lesson or something. I don't get to say it's fucking boy racers like you. I'd fucking like to, because you know you're a pack of total dicks. You don't even fucking think. And it's true, you will end up wiping someone out. You're bound to. And you don't stop to even give a shit, when you've got a choice. I'd like to sit here and tear fucking strips off you. But I can't. Because the sick thing is, it's people like me, too. People that aren't tipping oil on the roads and driving pissed to bits or running mental fucking risks just for kicks. Just people who think they look both fucking ways. And nothing's coming. And then they pull out. And it is.'

And then no one can find a thing to say. There's an age of it, just sitting there, the pack of you, on your lean. Waiting to have something to do or talk about, that gets the feel of pain out of mid-air between you. The long grass ticking at the chassis. The distant, thin trace of the fencelines trying to rule the wild off where they can, tipped over into the dark that hangs between hills, like so many broken ladders. Just stare out the car and try follow their threads. There's a gust of shadow, a black run goes over the field like a season just spilled past. And the three of you, motionless, nothing to say for yourselves, just watching, until the sun floods back on high. Just the glare and the heat banking up in the cab means you're going to have to get forward, get out somehow on the road from here.

The wrecker says, 'The thing of it, I mean, the only way you can look at it is, an accident. It's just pure accident, right? What else is there. And like they say, accidents happen. Could be to anyone, too.'

And the move you make back is both a yes and a no. Because you're always in this skid of thoughts up in your head, where it's *yes* there was nothing but the lurch of the car into a groove you could never pull free of, the two of you swallowed by the turn of the day, and the reap of the wheel you could not have seen coming. But it's *no* also, the spiral goes back the other way, so you know there's a moment when it all leads to you, to a point where it vanishes into a split-second blindspot at the back of your head, where you made a call, a decision that only you took. There was a window. There must have been. A brief flash of instants that looked wide and open and straight, where you watched and you judged and you gauged. And it was you who chose to act. And then the window was gone, already shattered by his body being driven through it.

So you say, 'That's the thing. It seemed to me, at the time, like it was a choice. I made it, and I moved out, on what looked like a clear-cut choice. And then the accident was just . . . waiting. Waiting there behind it. So how am I supposed to know this choice will be different. I can weigh it all up, I can look at it from all sides. I hold onto their papers and I try. I do. But how do I *know*. That the worst outcome of all isn't just waiting there. Right in behind it. Right there in behind what looks like a clear-cut answer.'

And you give up now because there's this massive gap in language, there's a hole cut right through the thing. Like there's nothing in between the fucking small talk, the bits of *Yeah, for real bro?* and *Cheers, fucking fine, mate* which are all you've got to trade. All you've got's these spare parts of used-up talk, bits of munted word, secondhand to start, nothing to get what you need across. And if you found the real words, who'd fucking trade them. Reach out a fist and say, here, here's a free handful of the heavy bits, make one fucked-up story of me out of that mess, if you can. It's a trip round a wrecker's, to even start talking through a life. A tour round a yard of burnt-out parts.

And even the wrecker's gone silent.

But the kid says, 'Well, what the fuck would I know. But it's not like you'd want them to take that kind of choice off you. I'm not saying, I mean fuck, I *know* it's not anything like it is with me and the car and everything, but you have to think how fucked it would be if they went and took that choice off you, like they just got to make it for you. Ah, look, I'm not fucking saying it right, eh? But you get what I mean. It's like what it comes down to. There's this choice and it's fucked up, but only you could be the one to make it.'

And it shouldn't be so easy to slide into memory. But that's where you've slid, looking over at this kid like he could be your brother, like he's just pulled the stunt your brother used to, skidding off the road-edge just to wake you when you'd dropped quiet in the passenger seat, when it was just the two of you covering those last long miles to see your mother, who was on her way out, not going easy, so you'd get in the car and have nothing to say, hunch into your seat and just try to black out through Ks, knees up against the door rattle, head on the rough sling of seatbelt that reeked of BO and turps. But he wasn't having that, he'd sled off to the side to bring you back round. He couldn't take the head space of a trip to visit Mum with you napping, couldn't take the boredom or the looming of it, so he'd let you get under, just, he'd leave you till your doze was half on, then he'd choke it, he'd jolt you back to front and centre freaking, piss himself laughing while the rear tyres cast round in rubble. *Catch a few zzzzz's there sis?*

Yeah whatever, you'll *fucking catch it,* you slap sideways, good backhand to his ribs.

Fuck that, he says. *Back to me sis, eyes front.* Then he drags a sound over his throat, like he's snoring. *Time enough to sleep when you're dead.*

Brings you round cold. But you still don't talk about your mum, don't talk about the low-lit end of her ward, or the colour her skin's turning, or the dripping sound effects of her machines. You talk about stuff that makes that go away, just bits of random shit, just noise and scrap and stupid jokes-not-even, that cancel out the ticking feed of her drip. Then still, you need to stop on any drive you take to visit her, need to kick clear of the state that builds up in the cab, need to stand road-edge and breathe again, you and him, nothing for it but to pit stop, take a slash, or just let the munter car cool off, let the honeycomb radiator sizzle halfway into sky, because the shitbox car is *giving up the ghost,* too. Nothing for it but the two of you shrugging and passing each other those *rest-area* grins, that empty-handed *yeah-it-fucking-sucks-so-what's-your-point* smile you both got a way with. Or maybe, on the best day, he pulls over by the good hole he knows down the bridge, strips off and bolts down the clay, and goes bombing, straight in, whack, so the whole valley echoes with the flop of him, his trunk shocking water all sides into the glade of dark quiet. And you don't skulk too long, hover a bit in the shade, then make a grab for his gear and tear off with it, that dash, the roll of stones rivering under your jandals and wet ferns grating your slithering shins, with him bawling out of the pool at you, *Oh yeah, good one*, starkers, yelping and floundering, *good one*, but still laughing with you, laughing, laughing.

'I didn't take his clothes in, the last time,' you say into the car now. 'I never took them in. The last time they got nicked. I got a new set ready, good to go. But I left them. They're sitting there in plastic, at home, and I've left them there for days.'

Which gets nothing back, from the wrecker or the kid. You don't expect it. Not a nod or a phrase. Just a null. Then the sound of the wrecker smudging some dark into place on the paper, thumbing the tube into shape with a slow exhale. Sealing it off with a fine pact of spit.

'So, where the fuck are we then? Going or staying. Or what.'

Then 'You wanna take her?' this kid looks at you and says. 'You. Go on. You should take her. Last turn. Your turn. You take her.'

So that's how it happens. Takes a bit for the kid to crank the car out its lean, but then you're standing by the driver's door looking down at him saying 'Go on then, shove over, eh.' And once you've got the course back he's coaching you, the road coasting past in horizontals of dust, bursts of laidback haze he's teaching you to skim up from the margins, with short outs of brake, scuds of wheel. Just semi, just a trial of it, because you've got to get out to the quarry, got to get off-road to the east, the arena of the old works gouged miles deep into dirt, the hillside trucked out in wide hacks. But you pick up the rev and the rein-in as you go, give it a burst, the wrecker and the kid yelling help, howling cheers at you. And it's not so far to the place where you can lose it, not far to the scoured-out wake that the quarry left curbed in clay, an undertow of earth mowed into bands of drag and, when you take a few passes with the kid calling the cues, you carve it and the two men hoot, but you feel it coming, the wider track, the big one, the swerve that takes out time itself.

Then it's come. And what happens is you spiral into memories, you brake and wing out on the missed arc of his life, you pivot through his lost flash-forward of scenes like an oil spill of images your mind keeps spinning through, and light sprays out and out but there's nothing you can grip. There's just the burn of a kaleidoscope of scenes he never got to, fragments of a life he couldn't live, like you've swung the car against the tide of the world, against the body of time and where it's moving, the direction of your bloodstream pumped back against the panels, the skid of sound up through your throat, the echo of his, your scream the outbreak of the shout he never got to lift. His darkness levered open on your spine. And your brain ignites with him, he sparks off and shots of him splash traction sideways, a future cut away in random skids where he doesn't get to live on in his radiance, he smashes with it into the hard face of unending heat, and it is not God he feels, it is metal, it is zero, it's the wild machine of living slammed into freefall, and he's not driving in the seconds that split around him, no one's driving it, it flies into pain, it flies into questions, it flies into atoms. That go out like light whiplashed silent on the halo of every place you touch his body and turn cold with a need to end its hurt.

And when you stop the last of him is in you. There's an updraft, like smoke. It settles. And then you know what to do.

local sluts in your area

She has three car accidents in two weeks. After each of them, she climbs from the wreck and walks off down the road. It's simple. The white lines lead her, hydraulic. The clouds feel close to the side of her head. She walks in their corridor. People who have pulled up to the scene try to follow her, use her elbow to steer her back. They prop her shoulders with jackets, step in her way, speak heavily into her face. It's the shock, they say. To listen to them she has to blink. Their words are loud in the red beneath her lids, but when she opens her eyes their voices dissolve again. Up in the silence of her hairline she finds she can dig out seeds of fresh glass, guide them into the open and watch them tip off the pad of her finger onto the curb. A truck bores past and she can watch it flatten the grass in silver spasms. She's surprised to learn later that the three different men who were driving are all still alive.

Her mother's latest boyfriend turns up to stay. He stands in the doorway of her room like a cliché. He has half a finger missing on his left hand, and he plays the joke of tucking the stump in his pocket and pulling the lack of it out, pop, like a non-rabbit out a hat. It's a small, neat room—easy to back her into. There are posters on the wall of men who don't make her gag. Cross-legged, she is sitting on her bed and knitting a halter, a stringy work of summer on oversized needles that sweat. He pulls it again, his trick. She should giggle at this: the air beyond his knuckle strange with emptiness, the bulb battered flat. She should ask what happened, she should blush as she squirms. But she doesn't. The jump makes the needles skid, the tips swerve out the next knot. Her mother's boyfriend laughs as she watches holes rush in sequence through the guts of her top. When he goes out to smoke later he leans on the power box outside her window and she hears his jandal squeaking on the side that reads voltage.

Her mother gets called in sometimes to play. Short notice, with a sound guy who shrugs at the set-up and says, Close enough. The leads are left sloppy on the stage. Her mother still fits into her dresses but not her skin. When she sings she is wet eyes and cartilage. Under her feet there is electrical tape peeling in pseudo-crosses all over the carpet, multicoloured as weeds. She sounds like a woman with bills overdue.

Out in the green room she listens to her mother's voice, off from the first bar by a minor third. The sound guy rubs his hand a matter of degrees from her cunt. Her legs are her mother's, he says. The spitting image. Someone has biroed into the 70s wallpaper, asking bands to stop pissing in the corner.

Her mother loads the melody wrong. The back of the sound guy's neck looks like snakeskin. Diagonals of nylon lantern dip on their wire out the high grid window. Give me a reason, her mother is singing, with her body in the clutch of a red dress it won't recover from. Everyone buying their drinks looks at the back wall. Her mother is not what was advertised. It's the word love that's bad news. The word love makes her cave in around the neck and she does a move stage-left which looks like sidestroke.

On a reef of posters she waits for the punchline of the sound guy's thumb. These last-minute nights of off-pitch sadness are all that her mother has got.

She gets a second job cleaning the school. There's the drone of the teachers backing out the carpark. Everything feels like glue. Clods of bog paper have been fired, wet, at the lino ceiling of the boys' loo, and she has to use a ladder to pick off the baked white nests.

In the old classroom that used to be hers, the children have made fake self-portraits. Butterflied metal pegs their too-big heads and their too-pink skins to a washline. They stiffen over the sink and watch her, teeth in a neat box, eyelashes winging out like splinters. When she roughs the mop past they make a grey paint-buckled sound, like a photocopy of thunder.

When she has finished with the polisher she sits on the carpet corner where she used to have mat-time, the teacher squatting on a cut-down chair, the pages of a story sucking over in glossy airless flops. There used to be a melt of corduroy cushions, brown and pummelled in a heap the kids could lie on—she can still smell them if she lets herself, nuzzle the musty sound of the word *snooze*. She nearly does. Before it drops out the sun goes the colour of her long-ago paintings, wide-angle, done by hand. The truth is she should get on with her job but she stalls and watches the sunlight weather her shins, in shapes like pages there's no time left to turn. She isn't hired to daydream. She's old enough to know now not to put her head down, let tears roll off it into a dull corduroy knoll.

Hanging over the stink of the warped bins, she shoos away a veil of drowsing flies.

Sometimes she reads about disasters to a woman in a unit. The aging care used to be by the sea, until waterfront prices. Then they moved it to a road out by the sewage plant. The unit is yellow and the woman was once her neighbour for a couple of years. She was little when, up between their houses, there was a flush of geraniums, a sketch of fence gone crooked under them, wire in a slack silver hint through their juicy sprawl. She never loved those flowers: the climb between sections was grazed with their fibres and their compost sweetness. The rattly shelves inside were what she visited. The old woman let her tiptoe the china figurines through their icing of dust. The stories had all turned the colour of apple-core.

The old woman cannot talk anymore. The unit is alarmed and there is a doping effect to its four tight walls. Time and muscles around the eyes go into the woman's painstaking stare, until the room seems to blink with her, drawn into the force of the skin contracting round her iris. As a tiny girl she once survived an earthquake, used to cluck out tales, bathtubs coasting along main-street, the glittery widescreen death of parched fish flipping in mile after mile of cancelled sea. She likes to have the illustrated horrors turned over for her. She can't narrate them anymore, but catalogues them with swoops of swollen blue knuckle. The book on the earthquake is heavy and the plastic gatefold digs into the knee the girl is using to lever the story's dead weight—she gives the old woman a kiss before she leaves, and tastes Deep Heat and urine and lavender. She tries to find a channel so the woman has a reason to keep her eyes open but on TV there are only other rooms with nurses.

The three live men all look the same, although she met them different places in the two weeks she crashed. She works out back at the pub in her other job and after closing she turns up at parties, the cars she's stepped into to get there a blur to her, a revving emptiness, a sequence of flashes of head-lit letterboxes, hotel fronts, near-miss trees if she closes her eyes. Which she is learning not to. She stands in rooms and is handed glasses and does the dance of laying her head back, technical, the sway of liquid lapped headlong off the rim, while her hips, rocked opposite, sip at the outskirts of the beat. She likes this, for long seconds, laughs at the coma she feels coming on, drops shots back into the laugh, goes barefoot, rotors with the song, cyclones her hair. The rain is purple, if she lurches long enough. She's lead guitar, she's make-believe. She laughs at how easy a dance knocks pain off-camera, a drink tips the past out of shot. She is growing up. Then she trips and the glass of a side table turns to crimson tokens in her hand. Everything's cut. Until she wakes up with her vision cornered in a whining, vinyl wedge. A man she does not remember pumps her lower body. She watches his blank shape, jockeying. She smells the blood before she lifts it, groping the handles of a car door she can't smudge free. It runs down the hand that she squirms at the window, her wrist filling with ladders of it.

Their latest house used to be a butcher shop and when they move in there are still display trimmings, edging the glass front and the doors that open right on the pavement. The risk is, anyone could walk off the street, but they have to watch TV with the swing doors propped to ease air in, so every sunset there's the thrum of plastic grass with model animals clipped into its fringe, stock before they're sirloin. When it gets dark, the passing cars stretch a silhouette of high blades up the wallpaper, the plastic beasts looming in a blurred parade of limbs. Close-up to the shop front she can still make out the choice cuts promoted in the shaved red paint.

Out back there is the old chiller. It can be clamped shut from the inside. She stocks it with boxes of stuff that wouldn't jam into her room with its flimsy narrow walls. She goes to visit them, liking the noise of the door as it seals, bolted and emphatic. She even unpacks some things she hasn't seen in a while. Her dolls all end up smelling like homekill.

Her mother is a memory of good looks gone to tan and sinew. But she likes her camera, a Kodak that feeds out instant shots. She keeps it in the kitchen, on the shelf with the pills, so it's at hand whenever a new man arrives. The fridge is a collage of headshots. The girl hates the gallery but likes the moist, mechanical buzz the camera makes, the oblong blank ejected with a squeak from its lip. She likes to stare down at the black shine of panel and sense the photo coming round, like an image in a coma, hints of movement flicking in its skin.

She is wasted when one of the three men offers her a ride. She only remembers one face and one voice, but the rides are all taking her in the same direction. He comes into the toilet when she's cleaning up after the guy she's just let fuck her out back. The party is winding down, someone hurling, someone tossing empties into a blue plastic sack. He's heard from the last guy. They have a system, a way to pass round girls. He kneels by the bog, burrows into her legs, and his fingers pick out the stepping-stone freckles of her jaw, walk over the bridge of her nose. Freckles, he murmurs, are such a fucking shame. She doesn't need a mirror to know she's mapped. There's one gone slushy, a dark stretch of sunkiss, under her right eye, just waiting for his thumb.

A.M., her mother takes an angle on the table, the kitchen window diagonal to her jaw. Her ankles spread wider than the chair legs, like she's bearing down. Her cami dangles from strings that are no longer lace, and talk juts her collarbones. But she wants to talk. She wants to talk to her girl when she's lost. Counter clockwise: that's how she stubs her cigarette. Baby, baby come. Talk to your mother.

There is a watch, too wide on her wrist, a bangle that her baby has never known how to read. There's no numbers on its face, just gold slits spaced round the cut-price oval like they're supposed to mean something. There's no waterfront through her windows. The forecast is a view of walls. North of her mother's face there will be smoke in a layer that semaphores for days.

If it's a good morning, she will leave her door open so you can hear a man's breath coming from her sheets. So you can hear that the house has weight, fresh obligation, a ribcage you can't shift. She will let you soak that in for a second, the good news of that phlegm melodic. Then she'll pucker a grin round her cigarette, twitch the place she pencils on her eyebrows to nod at you. She's won.

After the first crash she goes to visit the boy who used to be her best friend. He's lying on an orange beanbag watching re-runs he's taped off TV. High school has taught him that she's worth nothing but he lets her touch the back of his hand while he mouths the lines. Through the window there's the primary-coloured mini-golf course his parents own, the slant spaceships and chipped windmills. All their moving toy-town parts keen in the light that goes fibrous on the green plastic putts. She watches children squeal at a distance and pelt the balls too hard, the failed shots tocking off concrete hairpins. They used to play for hours there, back when he would be seen with her. She tries to nudge her fingertips in through the curb of his fist. He's shirtless, so she stares at his breastbone, the span of hard trunk that looks like shelter. They are crashing cars on the show he's taped and he can't be bothered with her.

When he won't talk she wanders to the inside garden, a paved rectangle at the centre of the house. In the inside garden there is bamboo and a plastic kiddy-pool, not blown up. It's a squashed carousel of smiling animals baked flat in the shaft of sun, and when she tries to peel it off the tiles, she feels the sound of its slow bleached suck, like a plaster hauled too soon off a cut.

He calls her in later. From his bedroom she can hear the milling of the novelties on their synthetic lawn. The race cars on his drapes are red with a trail of cartoon getaway. She watches them as she stoops, puts her face in the hip-height muzzle of his hands as instructed.

Friends don't let friends drink their come and walk home alone after an accident: she keeps forgetting they are not friends anymore.

She takes the bus to see her father. He works in a kiosk at a mall, grinding keys into shape and sticking the soles on shoes with yellow jelly. There are spiders for sale in bubbled plaques, dark fur globes with fans of jointed leg. There is a spin-stand of padlocks and tikis. He lets her fiddle with an army knife while she waits for him to take his smoko. She likes the torque of the tiny components, the neat pull it takes to make all those miniature fatalities unfurl.

He pulls the metal grille down and takes her for a Happy Meal. He doesn't seem to know that she's outgrown the toys. Or maybe it's just cheapest. She asks if she can move in with him. His mutter moves his shoulders. He's in-between, he's, you know, at loose ends, got stuff coming good, could be something big lined up. She cleans the burger out the bumps in her gums, rolls her mouth to rescue her lipstick, nods. They go back to the shop. He groups shoes behind the fort like Mondays are busy. He's got a laptop behind the counter open to a page that says *Local Sluts in Your Area*. She gives him a waterproof smile, tells him yeah, no worries, she's taking off.

Her lipstick is *Longstaying Afterparty*. In the bus home she smiles again, smooths on the next coat over the Happy Meal pith.

When they are best friends, they walk back from school across the mangroves to drink milk, do homework to cartoons in a huddle. She hitches her sundress into her gruts to wade the channel, and he pokes around to dislodge shells, flipping them into the upturned pouch of his T-shirt. But one day they come across a tub someone has capsized where the mudflats fill. It's claw-foot, so they lever it over with bodyweight thrown into the base, legs gouging at the slop. When it rocks free there are creatures underneath it, tiny fused skeletons of kittens someone has trapped. The harbour is very wide and dark around their breathing. They scramble into the mush to drag it back.

No one hauls the tub out. It stays in the causeway, nudged

adrift sometimes by a storm tide. Which is why she can walk out
to sit on it after her second crash, listening under her body for the
echoes, cool hoops of incoming flood.

The nurses call to say she can visit the body. She takes the camera
in with her. A terrible lull has come into the room with the old
woman's closed eyes, as if the walls can't focus. They have tucked
a hibiscus into the puzzle of her hands and the lines of her face
have run clear. The skin says something she wants to aim the
lens at, something as definite and ghostly as chalk. The silence is
airless and the cicadas that mar it seem to sing directly to the lens.
She sits on the candlewick spread and stares down into the photo
to see if she's pinned it there. The thing that swims into focus is
heavy, a smear gaining gravity as its outline sharpens. In the end
it is the face in the frame that convinces her the old woman will
not move again, that nothing is tingling under the arch of the
fingers, waiting in the crumpled lips. Nothing is tapping pollen
onto the sheet in tiny imperceptible quakes.

The first crash is too small, the next crash is too big, but the third
one feels just right. The white lines after the third one lead out to
the dump, where all the pointless heaps are roped off. She's not
wearing shoes but it doesn't matter. Her white feet pick through
the patterns of breakage. When she looks up the gulls are in
reverse. It's afterhours and no one in overalls mans the shed.
Some canal has opened in her neck—there's a pulse in her nape
the size of a knuckle. The sunlight is holding still and there's a
ute on the outskirts where the fridges are hulked, someone with
a shottie taking out the spray of seagulls. She freezes for a while
to watch the cull. Then she sits. Aimless, she watches the stroke
of her fingers through the pile of splintered things, the hull of
something, a kennel, a quilt, an easel. It's a jigsaw of rot with no
one's sadness attached: she shrugs and feels herself fit in. She
doesn't understand this made-to-measure driftwood, kicked out

of lives where people must know what they need. She blinks at the stencil of wasted sunlight piercing the splits in her hand—just her own fingers seem strange today, that the end of her arm should be broken into five moving pieces, letting light through them like bone stranded inside a star.

the names in the garden

I do the flowers. I've always done them. They asked me not to this time, they took me aside and they told me, but I still had the key, so I let myself in. I lay them out on the bench like I've always done. I go by feel, I've never known the names. So I lay them all out. To look at which ones can take the weight, and which will have to drape. There are some that can stand for days, and some can only trail. Some are tough, but then the limp ones could be where the beauty is. But you work that into it. That all comes in to how you see it. They're out on the sink and you take a long look and you can see where the backbone is, and where there's just threads. Or whispers, I don't know. Bits that catch the light, that's what I'm trying to get at. It just comes to me, when I take a slow look at them, spread that way. The centre stands out, the bloom that takes the eye right down into it, the place that needs to be the heart which all the rest weave round. There's always one you don't notice in the cutting, that rises out when you take them all in. Even if it takes me a while to find it, I stay calm and just keep watch. And then you see it lift itself out from the rest, and the others just nest in around it where they need to, or link at the base and spray.

So I'd had to let myself in. And the talk with the pastor had been hard, about how they didn't want me to go on doing it. And so I made a mess of it. When I wanted to show them. I wanted to do something that would make them stop and hold their breath. And for that young couple, something they could join their hands by on the day and we could look up from the pews and it would be like the front wall poured with flowers and the whole church could feel white spilling all round from what I'd made. I thought I would. I had the key, and I told myself, I'll do what I always do, and I'll lay them in the good light out the back and if I watch them long enough they'll fall into shape. I thought I would see, glowing there right on the sink, the core of the thing. I could pick out the soul of it. But I hadn't been let in to the gardens. The people that usually let me come round and do the cutting had said no. The pastor had told me. He said people were uncomfortable. The families.

I said, *But nothing was proven.*

And he said, *But as things stand, it looks bad.* So I asked if I could just take the ones near the gates. I wouldn't even go in. They wouldn't even have to see me—though they always used to wave at me when I did the cutting, they used to send their little ones out to help me pick and to carry, and they used to chatter away. But the pastor said no, that a clean break was best now for everybody. The families entrusted him to make it clear to me. And then I said I would just kneel down by the fence, where there's even lovely heads that poke out through the bars and I could snip them off and no one would even know I'd been. And when he got short with me I said, *My husband never sets foot. He's never even in the same street. It's only me in the gardens.* I said, *Please. It's only ever me.*

But he made it clear I couldn't go in. Not even near. It was what they all wanted. It had been decided. All those gardens, where they used to let me in to take anything I needed. All those blooms and the green and the little girls dancing out to keep me company while I moved the fronds and leant down deep to cut low through the stems.

And so when I laid them out I couldn't see it: the one to give the centre, the shape. I did what I always do. But it wouldn't come to me. I took down the bowls and the traps and the oasis, and I stared at them too. It was very quiet, except for the long line of humming that comes off the new light. It makes that back room very bright and, true, it's a good light for doing the flowers in, but it does get up under the lids of your eyes, a white line of it that feels like grit. After a while, it seems to press right round the back of them, the buzz of it. So you blink and blink. And the bowls don't help, either. They have some beautiful vases, my church. So heavy. Like offerings. Some of them you have to pick up and hold like children, the colour of pearls. There's one I like that's got some finish on it, running down its sides like oil, only white, white oil with a kind of silver clearness that gives you the shivers. Or at least it does me. Like freezing silk to touch. But then it's a chore to pick up. It's a beauty, but a dead weight, and it slips. Or at least, I get full of the fear that it will and my heartbeat gets into my hands and makes them dizzy. And once it's packed out then I have to get help in to do the lifting onto the altar. With all the weight of the flowers wired in, it's too much for an old body like me. I don't have a chance of raising it up.

So I don't know what I was thinking, letting myself in, trying to change what they thought of me. It's just that I'd always done the flowers. So it didn't seem like it could be the end. I hadn't thought it through, but then I never need to think the flowers through. They just come to me, where they should be, and whether they should push up into crooked knots or they should hang down like a net, and whether they want to drift out and touch lightly as froth or they want to shoot and be twisted. They've always joined for me, in my eye, before I even started to touch them. And I thought for a moment that a flash did come, of how to work it, like the ripples of a star if you were too close to it, like its glory would make you weep but also had a sting to it. But then it went out. Just out, like the dark in its place in my head had always been there. A cold black I couldn't shift was just waiting in my head behind all the beautiful things I used to see. Then I found that I couldn't keep myself steady. There wasn't any calm left.

And I made a mess when I stopped looking and I started to handle them. Because I don't know the names in the garden where I've always gone, but I know them all by feel. And it was hard to find anything, when they said I couldn't come. I had no sense of where to go. I had to go creeping all over town, and it didn't seem like anything good was growing. Not where I could get to it, not without asking. And the way the pastor had made it sound to me, everyone felt the same, and I wouldn't be wanted even outside the gardens, even strangers would know when they looked at me, they would have heard the stories. Only he said the *news*, not the stories. As if it had turned into truth already. When it hadn't. I saw that news too. I stood by our letterbox on the day it came and opened the page and it was like the sun went out, and the words had shadows that rushed right through our front yard and I knew when I turned around they'd be all over our house and they'd be there too when I looked down our street. The thick ugly words they use in their headlines, moving down the street like weeds. I think I said that to the pastor, even. I said, *I knew those stories were spreading like weeds. But I didn't think they would get into the church.* But he said he had a duty, he said the feelings of the decent community would be with the poor little girl. So I walked around after that looking for blooms and I couldn't bring myself to ask, even when I saw what I needed, not if it meant I had to look at doors opening and decent people staring down into my face and thinking ugly things of me. So I wasn't left with much. And when I found something that gave me some hope it was down in the gully on the river-end of our street, where I've always shrunk from going. I've never had to go there because the gardens were open to me. But now, being shut out, it seemed like the only thing I could do was go down into that gulf. So I made myself cross over. And the fence into it had been broken. And the trees were thick and cramped me, and the smell soaked into my clothes. And the cold feel got deeper. And the dirt plugged up my shoes and they weren't even dry when I let myself into church later, so I walked it in with me, the smell of that swamp. It was steep down, so everything felt tipped on a slant. I wasn't dressed for it and I tore something I'd kept nice for years. And I had a hard time not slumping right into the muck. But I did find flowers there. I'd always known that I would. I'd just never looked.

So I let myself in. And I still had hope, that I'd see something shine up into my eyes when I looked at them. They hadn't looked in such a poor state on their bank. They'd looked hardy enough, quite stubby, and they had a rich leaf and a sprinkle of gold in the head. But I could see from the start when I let myself in, that something had happened to them. I don't know when. They were lovely, but you could see that the light had leaked out. There were breaks all through them, and juice came out the crushes in their stalks. The damage was done. It must have been moving them. I didn't notice. I wasn't ready to give up, though. And I thought I could anchor them, and make them prop each other up, I thought I could stake them so they didn't give way. So I started to wire them. But the wire seemed to mash right through the stems, and all I had were tangles of wet. I kept sweeping through them and trying to find one more I could brace. Then the next one turned to waste. And all I had made was a pile of shreds. And my hands were stained with the white sap that leached out of them.

I knew then that this was the end. It was that slimy milk that came off the plants. You couldn't scour it off. It stained. I just wanted all the foul things gone. I started to push the whole mob of flowers down the bin. They were useless. But I couldn't take the sickly feel of them sliding down my fingers. It showed up in the creases of my hands like it did on the stems, the glint of it sticking in the bruises. And then somehow I started thinking of the day when I married my husband and of how we'd been standing in a halo of stiff white flowers and it was lovely but then he couldn't get the ring to fit. And everyone was looking and he was annoyed and had to get hold of my wrist and push and push and I watched the skin of my finger lift up in red bands, and it stung and I bit down under my veil until it slid.

But then I came round. It wasn't clean out back of church, in the good light. The flowers had bled and bled. And I just wanted all the good things kept away from them. Their wet and their stink. And that's when it happened. Because I was in a rush. I wanted all the offerings back in their place again; the vessels, the vases with their skin like pearl. I wanted the bowls stowed away again, heavy and holy. I wanted to know that at least I'd kept sacred things safe. And the roar of the bowl blowing open seemed to pound through my ears when I never even felt the sides slip. Everything seemed to go backwards through my wet hands, and my eyes were a shatter of sharp white when I don't know if I ever really watched its body smashing open at my feet.

But if I did, I left the mess. I don't know how, I just left it. And I don't know how I got home, but once I got there I knew that he was gone. I did check. I walked through all the rooms, looking for a sign of what he'd left, and what he'd taken. And nothing had changed. He hadn't touched a single thing. But you could feel that he was gone. He'd just moved out, after all these years, and hadn't paid anything for all the time he'd stayed here, like a bad tenant leaving in the night.

So I went outside to the shed where I knew my husband would be. To tell him God was gone. But of course, he was gone as well. Although he had left me to clean up. And they made more headlines out of him too. Perhaps he thought he'd put a stop to that. He could kill the words off along with him. But the words go on and on. The black weeds, there's no end to them. They're like the things they've been bringing up out of that gully, terrible dark arrangements that don't have names. And now there's no place for me, I can't keep them back with white flowers.

I never went back to the church to clean up my mess. But then, neither did God.

.22

Her hair was wet but she hadn't tried too hard. Green eyes, yes, but with nothing special done to them, and damp hair. Bland and lank, uncombed. You wouldn't have called it any colour much. The pictures you see now were taken earlier: the woman I met didn't seem like a blond, and it wasn't a model body to me, just tired, and needed meat on it. Collarbones, I remember those: too high under her yellow T-shirt. Her elbows were thin for the plastic table where she leaned, blue and scuffed at the tip. When she swallowed, the lines in her neck were too thick and . . . off-looking, now. At the time I just thought she could have taken a bit more pride.

Most women have tidied their houses, too. But there wasn't much she could do with this place. I don't know what the landlord was thinking, laying the carpet down where he did. It went right under the sink and the cooker, grey, raised patterns that looked like clouds. Looped horizon of fat and drainage by this stage, like you'd expect. I felt sorry for her. I knelt down to tie up my shoelace at one point and under my palm I could feel the smelt in the pile. It put me off: that gluey deep-fried scent. I drove past the place a couple of nights back, and slumps of the coated stuff were on the lawn where they'd hauled it out. There's more than that will need stripping out of that house. But somebody bought it so they must believe that all things can be scoured.

The same clouds were sour on the table where I put down my folder, lifted the questionnaire out. Her collarbone, now I think of it, was where she rested her fingers while she answered. Only the mid-three—the thumb and the little one twitched to each side. Her nails were grime-lined. The cup that she gave me had the feel of being washed up last in sullied water. He wasn't home yet, but I had to ask her set of questions out of his earshot anyway. So I thought we should just start.

I asked her how long she had known him. She took her hand down from the yellow shirt-band and looked at it, straightening her fingers to count. Her mouth moved for years, and she closed one fist to keep place, and turned to the uncurled hand. The tally made her blink slow. 'Since we were kids,' she said. 'You don't think of the numbers, do you? I mean, you don't often count.' Then she smiled—when she did you could see that picture they keep reprinting. Something was left of that face. But a split-second trace was all I could say got to me. And when she spoke, the words worked down to the base of her narrow lower teeth, and the state of them put the smile out of your mind.

'And how would you describe your marriage?' The clouded table was well off-kilter—it tipped then. The jerk was quick but enough to make the tea slurp. We both stared at the diagonal splash. I was fussy about my folder, because it was from my wife, real leather and a gift. She'd got my name embedded in the front and on the spine there were metal initials. So she could see it flustered me. The rag she snatched from the back of the taps was not what I would have used. But she was trying. She swabbed the wet from my pen. I said, 'Perhaps we had better get on.'

'In one word?' she said.

'Oh? No, I see. However you like. Describe it in as many words as you need.' I pointed down at the form. 'There's quite a large outline. That's fine. As many fit in the box.'

There was skittering from the other room. But I didn't see the kids then. I only heard the low noise from the TV they must have been scuffling in front of. You could hear cogs turn in the cartoon, some pranking animals caught in a bust-up, the silly chimes when one takes a fall, the sound of limbs scratching air in a panic. She folded one arm across her abdomen, and said, 'Fair.'

I left my pen waiting at the end of the word, and looked down at the form, not at her, to see if there was more.

She went on. 'Ordinary. Solid. You know. We've . . . got each other. And that's . . . lasted.'

Looking back you always know what you're looking for. That's what people forget. But you don't know when you're at the table, and there's a kids' cartoon playing in the next room, near mute, but with all the explosions and howls which those funny figures pull, murder set to music, the kids' hijinks in front of it, muffled and slap-dash. And the tea in the cup she's passed you is turning in whatever afternoon sun can strain through the blinds, 3 pm through the film of winter which has soaked up the fat of the kitchen light. And at that moment, something dislodges on the fire, and thuds down to ember the tiles, and she rushes to bridge it back up with the tongs, and opens the handle beside the hearth and it turns out it's not a chute but a double-sided cubby, which serves the living room as well, so a kid's face pokes through the gap above the wood pile, looking like a stray severed head which got wedged in the stack. Or it does when I think of it now, knowing what I know about the end in that cubby, the terrible occupancy of it, the little things backed up in there with no way out.

My dreams are heavy-handed. I answer my own form, nights I lie awake, I take my words down and watch them in each box, wondering how I could have missed what hers meant or hid.

But at the time, I just laughed. The little head had its tongue waggled out, its eyeballs crossed and quivered. Skinny, she looked like a kid herself—I thought she bobbed forward to tousle the crown, give the shocked face a kiss.

We were chuckling when his ute pulled in. I like to keep a proper tone, so I was more wary of cutting my own smile back than watching when hers quit. I hadn't finished her section, and it had to be done without him in the room, so I made the handshake firm. He didn't seem bothered. He went out to offload gear from the bed, so the rest of her questions we took through the scrabble and thump of lumber off the ute and to the outshed.

Her yes and no responses were standard. We got through them steady and swift. I try to see how she looked when she said them, now, if she let something slip in her hands or her head. A flinch in her throat at *No*, he never suffered anxiety, a crick in her wrist to *No*, no history of aggression. But I'm almost sure there was nothing. You've probably seen the form—they printed it by her picture, a tidy simple list. She was very still, her fingertips balanced on her neckline again, but light, not fixed. Sometimes the thumb stretched stiff, but her voice was neutral. The sound of him outside didn't shake it. Iron scraped the drive, the shed door was belted with a chain but I didn't spot a tremor. We signed him off, tick by tick.

'Do you consider him safe around firearms?' I could hear him lighting up on the back steps then, using the concrete to torque off the heels of his boots, the laces levered wide. By rights, he shouldn't have been in hearing range. But I let it stand. We were so close to done.

'Yes.'

'And why do you hold this view?'

It's never an easy question. The ends of her hair were drying now, lifting ratty around her neck, the broke strands in a halo while the wet hung close. No one ever answers quick. There was a noise like a bottle rolled off the last step, and he yelled out, 'All good.' Then the boy raced into the kitchen, pulled a long panicking sock-skid hairpin, and paddled his hands down the hall to make the door.

She said, 'Because he follows rules. He's very aware of rules. He always follows them. And he makes sure others do.'

You've seen her other answers, no doubt. And his. He was calm, got everything right. I liked him. He was relaxed: he peeled off his work socks while we were talking, and he buffed at a toe where the nail had ruptured, gone black. But he was respectful, and looked at the notes I was taking like he cared for the way I was filling out the page, word for word and streamlined. She never looked at what I wrote. And afterwards he led me to inspect the gun cabinet, bolted into the hallway cupboard, braced to the hot water cylinder with heavy straps. There were clothes in a ruck on the shelves, bibs and fleece that had seen whiter days, and a sprawl of grey delicates I could've done without. But his end of it was regulation. The job was sturdy, it fitted all the specs. You could see he had an eye for finishing.

When he walked me out, she was sitting in the sunroom on the side of the house. It was a strange old arrangement, not much more than a glass case, narrow and crookedly tacked. There was nothing in it except for the chair she was on, a bare one with red-tipped metal legs that reminded me of school. The glass was banded by battens at chest height, and over it the line of her look must have been at both kids who'd now shot out. The girl was bouncing on a blue trailer. I did think of safety, but she was too small to make it tip. When I went over to her there was an apple core and two white feathers lodged in a splinter of the bed. It's odd what you think of. The boy was pedalling a moulded motorbike that was in a bad way, yellow plastic sun-struck just about white. He was hooning with the red handles, rickety. He rammed it through the potholes with bloody-minded gumboots. The trailer rumbled but the girl's feet couldn't make it seesaw. I just thought they were lively kids.

She watched while I shook his hand.

Over at the letterbox there was a green balloon tied onto the nib of the flap. It was half let-down, from a birthday way back, gone darkened and slack. Its wobble on the loose string in the wind is another thing I see that makes me queasy now. But it didn't then.

I did go over to say goodbye to her, thank her for her cooperation. The strip of sunroom had a chill and on the concrete her bare feet were flat. For something to say I admired the tight plait I'd noticed in the little girl's hair—it was complex, the scalp primed hard through the cross-hairs.

'Yeah,' she said. 'It takes me hours. If I can keep her quiet for long enough.'

It was an afterthought when I asked her if I could pop back in to use the bathroom—I had miles before my last stop of the day and the call of nature crossed my mind. She nodded, 'First on the right.' There was carpet in there, too, an orange from the 70s, a brown corona round the pedestal, gone vile. The toddler's plastic step in the corner was a green hippopotamus, grinning and unclean with stickered teeth. I was less than impressed, and scrubbed my hands on hot. When I came out she was standing in the hallway. At a loose end. Awkward, it's true, when I think back. But I was wagging my hands in the air: the towel on the wonky rail did not bear thinking about. And neither of us said a thing.

Like I told you, I drove past the place the other day. When you look back you know everything is evidence. But the new owners must have had permission, now the case is done, to tear the fittings out the house. There were huddles of the wall-to-wall, rotted, the blinds in a sleazy fan, buckled and fly-blown. Nothing was left of the sunroom of course—but that doesn't stop me sitting with her. In the silence I go on marking the page, like she'll speak up, leaving dark bullet points. Her fingernails move on the thick bone skirting her throat, or she stares at them, counting down. I ask her questions, and her look at me is dead-eyed, waiting for the glass to jackknife. People don't ask for help. That's the lesson. They don't believe it's there to be asked for. What's coming is loaded in the dark outside.

the longest drink in town

'Them bitches yours?'

The boy stares at the bloke behind the service station counter. There's a bird-shape of grease wiped up the guy's boob, a drying crow of thumbprints over the car logo. The bloke gives a hoot you can hear snot and tar in, and twitches his head out the shop window.

'Them over there in the carpark. Them bitches, carrying on.' The guy stops to belch, then jolts his head again. 'They got something to do with you?'

The front of the shop is glass, dirt-frosted. Through the grit Jeremy sees the shapes of his mother and stepmother. Fumes rise from the metal stems that customers slot into their car tanks. The women are distant and heat-bent, but everyone can see the scrap. Movements that are jokes of rage, squawking elbows, high heels stabbing the tarmac. Christ, a chick fight. Pitchy, hissed little bits of their voices drift across the forecourt. The boy sees people shrug, cough out chuckles or scorn, hunch back over their filling wagons.

'Things you see when you don't have a gun, eh boy?'

Jeremy watches the man add another wing-mark of stain across the guy-tit, which is clear and plump under the cheap uniform. He feels the snicker, general and mean, waiting in the torsos of those queuing behind him. They're mostly cockies and truckers, all bashed-up boots and rock-shapes of muscle they rub while waiting, but there's the odd nana, tracksuit smelling like the kitchen junk drawer, rancid butter and gladwrap and biscuit and fag.

They're all as bad as each other and want a bit of goss.

'What's their deal then, eh? Why they going at it?'

Jeremy stares at the guy. He wants to tell the nosey prick to rack off, but instead he mutters, 'It wasn't supposed to be her, my stepmother, coming to pick us up. It says on the rules. For visitation. It's meant to be Dad. But . . . she turned up instead. And she's in a new van. And Mum's old heap of a munted Holden hasn't even got a rego or warrant.'

The razors are on the counter, cardboard wrapped. Jeremy shoves them over the glass top, watching them knock his Coke can. The red can tips a bit, shudders in circles, croaks. It bothers the boy when things move slow motion like this. Like . . . this: the spiral of asterisks on his Coke can, empty wet prickles which swell up and burst in your eye, but then don't tell you anything. Not anything.

The man bleeps the razorblades over the barcode gap. Jeremy knows the kind of crack that's coming: his little-boy lips are like meaty petals, spit-tender and far too fucken pink. There's only fronds of hair around them, and a big rut up to his nose as waxy as a kid's arse. Fucken tear-drop shaped.

He's gonna start spluttering. Fuck, fuck. He's gonna get going, big bubba, big sook. No, he's not. Not for this wank, no way.

'You wanna watch you don't put someone's eye out with that stubble, mate.' The man apes a serious bloke-to-bloke nudge of the head, his fat eyebrows lifting.

'You wanna shave that growth back regular, before it gets dangerous.' He cracks up at himself, his tit-crow flapping up and down at his comic timing.

The boy drops coins, picks up the razors and punches out through the customers. He hears them behind him, hacking up smokers' applause in the hot, packed shop.

*

Madeline lies in the van, half-awake by the baby. The baby is in its plastic cocoon in the back, the blankets tucked into a little ditch for its head, knots of yellow fluff. Madeline pokes at the big woolly halo, supposed to hold its wobbly neck, its no-bones neck which makes Madeline think of the worms they catch in Tip Top containers, although even the worms seem to know how to make some sense out of their sleazing bodies when the baby just lolls, its worm-pink wrinkles going nowhere. You could put the baby, Madeline thinks, in an ice cream container of dirt, too; you could snap on the lid and listen to the air squeak out and forget to punch holes in. The baby would just lie there, jelly and hopeless, not even trying to nose down into the soil.

The baby is less than a worm. The baby is even less than a maggot. Madeline has seen maggots, too, their curly little pipes all noisy on a hot dead sheep she'd found after dogs got into the next-door paddock.

Madeline is half-asleep. The baby is half her sister, half not. The car is as hot as a dead sheep or an ice cream box someone forgot to stab the knife in. Things come up when she's half-asleep that just don't seem to make sense to Madeline.

But Madeline is not as stupid as the baby. Madeline can wrestle on the sticky seat. She humps around and lets out her arms and legs like tentacles from her body. The van seems empty, but Madeline doesn't wake to find out why, where her mother, her brother, have gone, why the baby is left there. She dreams of wriggling down into dark pulp, finding coolness with tiny threads of herself.

*

'Screwing. You ever thought about that?'

She's leaning against the high wire fence, the skin of her back pushed hard into its diamonds. He's hanging just down from her, leaning too, watching: her freckles are cold sand or raw sugar, one or two darker, dirtier tips. Damon focuses through the grid: how many freckles are caught in each section? She thrusts with one sandal, raises her pelvis, her bare shoulders cut even deeper into the fence; when she lets her body thud back on the wire he can hear all its hooks singing. Not gonna take any notice of their mothers, over the carpark, red-faced and wild. Just gonna hang here listening to this, her body moving on a rack of sound.

His stepsister's body. They went and made her his *sister*. Just when he could *taste* her. Jody, Jody: he writes it at home on his desk and her name almost *looks* like *body*, like body pulled long and warm, blurred, untied. Or body with his own long warmth pushed into it.

'Because screwing is all it's about, you know. All *this*.' She flicks her hand across the carpark, at their jerking mothers. There is the sound of a hand, beating flat on the bonnet of her mother's tin-can car, then a handful of gravel sprayed across the van. Men have strayed out of the service station and pub across the road to watch the women scrap. Spurts of laughter come out as they wallop their T-shirts and frisk each other. Jody and Damon watch them, a coarse hairy mime, with mocked-up girly grunts.

'Shove—the FUCK—OFF!' Jody suddenly screeches across the carpark.

The men look ready to split her in two for a minute, then one of them jostles his mate. They turn and slouch back to the bar and the shop, although the angriest turns with a final finger, fixed and vicious, his teeth bit into his sneer. Like he means it.

'Well, fuck them,' Jody whispers.

'I can't believe you did that,' he says.

'Why not?'

'You'll get your fucken head ripped off. That's why. Dumb *as*.'

'You think they'd notice?' They take a look at their mothers. Pathetic.

'Nup.'

'You think they'd notice *anything* we went and did? *Anything*?'

Damon looks at her, his head, like hers, rolling on the fence. And her face is close and, suddenly, full of everything he wants there. Everything he wants, staring right back into him, hitting his throat and his gut.

'You ever wonder why they think it's worth all this? Screwing, I mean. Why it's such a big deal?'

He swallows. It's the only answer he can give. He thinks about it every day, about how her father must think about his mother the way he thinks and thinks about her, Damon and Jody and his mum and her dad getting mixed into a wild knot of tongues and cocks. Which he can't climb out of. And he wakes up sick with. And goes back to sleep bucking and wanting more.

'You wanna find out?'

Everything under his jaw is suddenly water, voice, guts, bones. She lets her face run closer, closer, her hair sliding in the ridges of the fence. The wire smells like diesel, and her face in its freckles looks like it's wearing a mask of wet dust.

*

Ruth hits the van window with Barbie's head. Madeline isn't waking up. Ruth tries again, a stab with Barbie's ice skates. Madeline stays asleep, fat-rag-bodied on the back seat, but her legs twitch up into her dress. Ruth presses her face to the window, lets her nose bulge, her mouth fart, a puffy wet ring.

She stares at Madeline. Madeline reminds Ruth of the long-skirt dolly at home, the double dolly, the one you tip up and instead of a set of white legs a grinning black head pops out.

Ruth has never liked the black doll side: her side of the skirt looks cheap, like a tea towel, and scratches. The white doll side was always her favourite, classy pink with glitter lace on it and a little plastic tiara glued to her big flop of yellow hair. But lately Ruth lets the black doll stay out. Even with her bald head in a red snot rag. Even with her evil eyes with white fish shapes supposed to be tears sewn into them.

Ruth leaves her mouth on the glass, doodling and slimy. Behind her she hears her mother, hooting. It's not like her mother to be scrapping like this, but lately her mother's voice is not like it was: words crack open in it now that she never used to say, never. There's no kiss goodnight left in it, no once-upon-a-time sound; it's not a voice you want to lean back against, fall asleep on, its warm throat hushing and muttering. It's a voice that *shits* and *fucks* and makes doors slam and dishes break and dinners burn and cars turn hard and pull fast into nowhere, into stones. It chases Jeremy down the hall, it runs to its room and stabs and sings there. You hear it on the phone to your dad, like the cord is pulled round it, tighter and tighter. And it shoves her stepmother, now, shoves and trips her. And Ruth doesn't know if she really cares. About either of them.

There's a triangle of van window that pushes in. Ruth wriggles her arm in, waves it over Madeline. She can't get a poke, but the dress hem shifts, a toe showing up beneath it, one dirty bud. She pulls her arm back out, nudges Barbie through and digs at the kid with the doll's ice skate, the thin blade folding over on her boot.

Madeline must be pretending. Shitty kid. Stuff her. Who needs her to play. You're always getting stuck with her. Only knows baby-talk shitty games, anyway. Should push the window back up and choke her. Should hook the van to fill up and snuff her like Mum cried to Dad on the phone that she would try.

Ruth spreads her lips on the window, fluffs lightly, then blows, hard. The blow balloons her face, and she feels air running the bone above her teeth. The second blow squeals. The third is so hard that her top teeth chip down at the window, and when Ruth puts in her fingertip one front tooth is juicy and creaking.

*

Damon and Jody wedge through the fence. It's a tight fit, but okay if they go easy, creeping through the high gate wrapped with chain. They hear their mothers, the rattle of stones, the argument coming in seizures.

'What the fuck are they on about now?' Damon is through and he puts back a hand to hold the gate-slit wide as she's shunting. He can't look straight at her hips or the warp of her tits as she's sliding past his fingers. He looks back to the women. They're figures in a silent movie, their tragedy spiky and sped-up.

'Dunno. Your mum pulling up in that dirty new van is what I reckon did it. Mum was already ropeable about her crap car by then. Jeremy had climbed in the car when we left, and told her off because she didn't have the rego up to date. You shoulda heard her go off: *It's a sticker, Jeremy, and there's no bloody money left to dress up the car in fucking little stickers. I can't go forking out wads of the weekly food budget just for stickers.*'

'Oh,' he says. Her stomach is close to his thumb-joint. He watches her push through a notch, the skin between singlet and jeans contracting. Her belly button is a white loop, rounded and fragile as an eyelid.

'Jeremy gets all his tackle in a tangle when things aren't legit. He's such a square. Mum just lost it at him. Then, what do you know, here comes your mum, grinning down over the wheel of a shiny new van.' She's working her crutch past the gate pole, tender jolts. 'God, this thing's gonna tear me a new box.'

Christ, he can't think about that. He'll explode. He tries to get back to the conversation, back from the sight of her little box rocking under denim. He knows what it'll be like in there: he's got there on one other girl, just lately, outside a mate's party, got fingers into that warm socket. But he was still thinking of Jody. And felt like a true dog, his fingers rough and awkward in some other girl, her staggering on them, half-drunk and knocking the brick wall with clucking noises. And when his fingers clumped, thicker, he heard a licking sound coming up through the wet. Jody, god, Jody.

'I didn't want to move in there anyway,' he says. 'I mean, it didn't seem like your dad should be able to get back in the house. And get you out. Plus we had our own place.'

'She couldn't pay. The mortgage and that. But he could. So he told her he'd buy her out. Mum just needed the money.' She's through, panting. They watch each other. When she squints, a horseshoe of darker freckles forms under one eye.

'I can't follow it.' All he knows is he now sleeps in her old bedroom, and goes mad thinking of her there.

'You think I fucken can?'

They shrug at each other. She turns and walks towards the first house, a demo-home, the paint sharp, the plants all shining pots of flax and claws. She prowls, focused, rattles the doorknob, runs her fingers up aluminium frames. Nothing opens.

'You know how to break in?' she asks him.

'Nup. Why would I?'

'With your mother? Thought you'd be a natural at home-breaks.'

'Get fucked, will ya.' But he thinks: Don't be angry, don't be angry, please god, Jody, god, *don't*.

'Why we're here isn't it?' she says. 'To get fucked.' But with the sneer she stretches out a hand to touch his T-shirt, the cracked plastic Goofy on his gut—why to christ had he worn *that*? She rubs, rubs the dumb Disney grin between breastbone and bellybutton. Damon feels the logo stick and peel with her finger's rhythm. When she stops, he looks around the empty lot, picks a stone out a big plant tub, strips off his shirt and wraps the rock, then swings it, clean through a side window.

*

Round the back of the service station, Jeremy kicks the bog door. The glass rattles, already part-broken, cut into rows of stars like the ones on the coke can he crushes and biffs. He puts his head to the panel, watches his leg swell in the reflection, almost man-size. But the real leg is puny, too much little-boy bone down the foot end, although muscle grows in a hunk up the top, a wedge of it, secret.

He kicks again. Course, they'd keep the fucken thing locked, wouldn't they? Look at the poncy sign: *Customers Only (Please Inquire for Key). General Restroom Located over Road in Rest Area.* Well, there's no fucken *resting* there anymore, he thinks, not with his mother and stepmother shrieking like hos. Serve the damn place right if you just unzipped and took a slash anyway. Looks like people have been, too: there's a galaxy of mildew in the green brick wall. Jeremy drops his forehead on that now, kicks again. This time his school shoe makes for the wall base. A chunk of sound, rubbery. A throb up through his toe-nerves. It heats and widens, buzzing along the bone.

He wants that. He wants to get in, somewhere quiet, and hurt himself. It's the way it's so ordinary that makes it worse. The way everyone shrugs, and says, *Yeah, you get that.* It's ordinary, your mum and dad splitting: you can't say you've got all this pain just from that, big deal. *Yeah, tell someone who gives a shit. BFD. Hey, Jeremy, what colour are your eyes, sooka-bubba red?*

You got to do something *not* ordinary, something not normal, just to match it.

Jeremy found it, the thing that matches the pain. He found it by accident, dragging his dad's stuff out the bathroom cupboard when his mum was too freaked out to start the packing. There'd been a box of porno shoved in the back. The cardboard was soft with fungus, the pages sucking on each other with slime. A troop of pink limbs split open as Jeremy thumbed at the corners and pulled them back. The mounds were all hairier than his mother's, shots taken right in at flushed, rambling lips. The women all looked like they'd taken a tackle, but they looked rowdy and animal as well, skidding on shiny floors and tabletops, chucked down but daring whoever was looming above them to dig the boot in again. The pictures were taken like it was your bulk above them, you that they snarled at and begged. Their nipples and slits were all lassoed with red and black lace. The lace reminded Jeremy of veins.

He'd kept on cleaning the closet. It smelt like the brown coast of make-up that always went streaky round his mother's face, her neck a sorrowful white below it, the blue traces in there, a deep bloody crop. Such a weakling. It had seemed, when he pulled out his dad's stash of razors, like something meant to be.

When Jeremy fitted one into his leg, he didn't know who or what he was cutting. Everyone, on every side, just got cut, in his head, as he lowered it in. He rocked it one way, then lifted, turned, watched right angles of plasma rising. And the main point was: *he* was doing the cutting, not his father, or his mother. And the other main point was: afterwards there was a wound to match the pain.

A little crusty crucifix. All showy and useless. When he walked off to school in the morning, he could feel it glittering under his shorts.

The visits make it worse. He needs a whole rail of crosses then. He normally starts on the morning he has to go, sets up a boundary line, straight and gristly round his thigh, where no can see it but he can hoard it, a secret, squatting on the low C block seats, the dark meat pulling along his leg, nervy and crystal. But today got all messed up because it was swimming sports, and he had to strip off for freestyle and butterfly. No chance of laying down fresh work: even the band of white scars was barely covered, kept flickering, suspicious, as he took his mark. But the dive is his best bit, his moment: he's a competitor, he leaves the pool-edge like a bullet of bone, and Jeremy knows that no one sees anything but a hero, a star, head boy. *Well-adjusted, a confident, focused all-rounder*, says his school report; no one is checking for blade tracks around his thigh. His home life is *ordinary*.

He needs it now. He's got to get it in, somehow, to help him get through the visit. It's a line he needs: he can't cross to their side without something there, between him and them. In the beginning, he'd said that he wouldn't go, that his dad could just stick it, could keep his new kids. He wasn't going to fucken visit, just so his dad could show round his school report, slap on his shoulder and talk about pride and achievement and rising to *challenges*. But his dad went all legal, and courts got roped in, and Mum had no money to fight with him. Jeremy needs to feel the razor seesaw into the meat. It's a fence, but it's also a tally. He needs to see the blood, keeping score.

*

The stones on the window are tender, a sprinkle. Madeline sees them through a pleat of light: she's not going to really open her eyes until Ruth has gone away. Go away, bugger off, she thinks. But Ruth keeps tapping and groping at her, the rod of dolly's leg dug hard in her cheek. Madeline knows the only reason Ruth's kept hanging around so long, squeaking and poking, is she can *see* her sleep is fake, her little sloppy breaths and twitches a put-on, shamming. But she keeps playing, dead and baby. She doesn't want to play with Ruth. Ruth is born bad and plays mean anyway. *A mean streak*, Madeline's mother says, always shakes her head, *both those little madams*. Madeline thinks Jody's mostly nice, but she can imagine the streak in Ruth, a long black cable up Ruth's body, that splits in two inside her head and sparks in her dark eyes when she goes nasty, her neck and cheeks all red-patched and crackling with badness.

Last time she visited, she'd been the meanest of all. She'd done mean things with the dollies. Madeline's dollies and Ruth's dollies, all mixed up and pushed into Barbie's pink bed, and Action Man, who she'd pinched off her big brother Jeremy, ordering them to do sick, sick deeds. Giving them telling-offs, tying them up with elastics, Action Man's hand going scooping under their fairy costumes, plastic and whipping, and making Maddy feel gross. And then she'd taken the baby dolly and made Barbie carry it up to her balcony: up on the top yellow floor of the highrise, Barbie had laughed and thrown off the kid. Ruth had even made squelching sounds, to show how the baby would splat open.

When Madeline cried that she'd tell her mother, Ruth had just said, *She'll know that you liked it. She'll shut you right up in your room because she'll know that you liked it. All the way through.*

So Madeline tries to freeze, tries not to jump at the shots of gravel. Until something louder clips the van window, something crunchy in a wet mass of sound.

There is a red smear on the window. Madeline climbs up and sees Ruth behind it, a few steps back. Ruth's face floats through the red sponge left on the glass. Her front teeth fork and she has a hand up like a crib below them, cupping the blood. But the blood will not be cupped and drips down, wriggling, over her school pinafore.

Ruth is alone in the carpark, her hand full of worms.

Their mothers have moved away, haven't seen. Madeline looks around for them, spots them over by the toilets. They're grabbing at each other's hands, scrabbling apart, then making a cradle, their joined bodies thudding into the block wall, until someone wrestles out, and the other one comes for them again.

'Try nga rip ovva rings.' Ruth has come to the van door, lets her mouth run as she opens it.

Madeline shakes her head, big-eyed: she doesn't get it.

Ruth makes a gulp, her thumb on the bent tooth as if she's afraid it'll go down her throat.

'Vey're trying ta rip ovv each uvver's rings.' Blood gets stuck: the words sound gurgly, stringy. Madeline is busting to get a good look at the tooth. She likes the dental nurse's because she likes the pictures: one cartoon tooth looks yellow and twisted, the other is plump and shiny, marching along with its brush on its shoulder like a gun. That's the way she imagines herself, compared to Ruth. Ruth is the yucky tooth, Madeline's the good one, a little Colgate soldier. She smiles.

'Mum only got one lev', she sol' da uvvers,' says Ruth.

'They fighting over rings? She sold her rings?'

'Yub. Bud she keep her wedding ring. Your mum yelling ad her to ged it ovv.'

'What you do to your face? Did they hit you? With a stone?'

'Nub.'

'Shouldn't we tell?'

'Vey don' care.'

'But . . .'

'Look ad em. Vey don' care.'

Madeline looks down at her own rings, her treasures, sweating on her stubby hand. She has six plastic gems and one ring of paper she coloured in today with hearts and taped on. She's learnt to draw hearts just this week and she's drawn a parade of them everywhere, shivery, slow, tongue-out curves. Her mother says she presses too hard, but she likes the way the paper goes furry. She secretly liked the way today's hearts got heavy and hairy and blotched through the page, leaving stamps all over the lawyer-papers her mother had ready, about the visiting rights. The hazy pink slops had made her mum angry; she'd snatched them up, flapping the pages at Madeline's face. Madeline sulked, didn't care: her mother should have told her hearts were this easy, just two wormy things curled together, heads and tails. Anyone could make one, a dumb shape like that: her mother was too busy with the baby.

'What about the others?'

'Vey all gone.'

Madeline looks around for her brother. She did draw hearts on Damon's homework, and he slapped her with the plastic-wrapped book, leaving a sting all over her titty. But she didn't think he'd be angry enough to leave her. Just to leave her here.

Or the baby.

She looks at Ruth's face.

It's funny how different teeth can make you look: when Damon got braces they'd made his whole face look white and slimy and kind of caged. The things clipped onto his teeth looked like tiny sticks of dynamite: it worried Madeline, seeing her brother with those shiny dark things strapped under his face. But Madeline had heard her new daddy yelling through the telephone because his old wife said that Jeremy needed braces too, but she couldn't pay for them. *There's a limit,* her new daddy barked through the phone, *There is just a limit to it,* and even when he'd smacked the phone back on the wall, three times, he stood there saying it. Madeline thinks *the limit* could be the name for the wire round Damon's teeth, but she also thinks it could be the name for the mean streak that Ruth shares with her old daddy.

'Is that your baby tooth?' she asks Ruth. 'Or the big one.'

Ruth says, 'Yub. Big one.' She makes a guzzle and Maddy thinks of the slurp you're not supposed to do when you suck to the end of the milkshake you're only allowed to get when the other kids come, from the corner dairy in the super-tall giraffe cup. That's the only good thing about visitation, that you get to hold onto your very own money all the way down to the dairy till the queen's head is burning hot, to pick your own flavour and guts yourself with that sticky froth. That's spoiled now, though, looking at Ruth. Now the whole thought of the fluffy milk feels yucky, even the giraffe she loves. Madeline doesn't like to think of Ruth's blood at the same time as that giraffe grinning at you, the *knock knock* sound of the empty cup, waxy and crushed. *The Longest Drink in Town.*

*

It's not easy, the mix of slither and balance you need to get up through that frame. You know you're going to get cut: let's face it, you're climbing a square of knives, it'll slice you somewhere. But you push off, try to strain up with just your fingers, try not to let your palm skid down, hope the dumb soles on your school shoes are really as tough as the advert says, with that big hulking teen hero slamming down his lightning-charged lace-ups like they're supernaturally cool.

You think so hard about your feet and hands that it's your dopey head you scrape. You feel it, a rake of needles through your scalp. You jump so hard at the shock you knock your head up and feel the glass get thicker, go deeper.

You give up, want to get it over with now, throw yourself through the final gap. Another nick on the spine, but nothing much. You land in splinters but manage not to drive your hands down into them.

Straighten up. Done. Damon, you're a legend, he thinks. Damon, you *are* the man.

He puts his hand through the spikes of hair gel to the stinging. No chips, just some thin fresh streaks of blood. He feels his eyebrow taking the first long trickle, steering it down his face. He's hit with a vision—sharp, electric—of opening the door to Jody, pulling her through it, brutal and no-questions-asked, into a grappling kiss. One of those kisses, slow mo and animal, you see on the movies, a snap-kiss like an attack. He wants to grab her like that: necks rotating, mouths chaotic. He wants the kiss that his blood runs into, raw against her mouth.

But that's about as true as the cosmic cool of school shoes. He can't sell the image to himself very long. He hasn't got the voltage, hasn't got the ball sack. He blinks the picture off, finds his way down the hall to let her in.

What he does, when he sees Jody's face, is shake. He feels his gut start trembling. *Oh, you're a legend all right, Damon.* She angles past him, wanders the hall with one finger tracing the wallpaper. He walks behind her, drinking in the sound of her finger, feeling the hiss slip through his trunk.

They go to the kitchen, out of habit, as if there was something there for them. The room is like the rest of the bald house, plasticised, in eggshell shades. It smells astringent, and when he flips through the cupboards they chill his hands. They have the texture of the cast he once had coating his broken arm: he thinks the whole house is like that, fibrous and chemical, a cast of a house, of a model family.

Jody's buttocks rock up, slide across the kitchen bench. She watches him flick open, drop the cheap cupboards. Slap.

'Hungry?' she says.

'Hey,' he says. 'Teenage boy. Always hungry.' The grin he gives her is quirky, shot with nerves.

She says, 'Yeah, some guys from my school went over to yours for some sports gig. They told me all about you.' The last words are stretched, a tease, a trail. She purrs. But there's something stagey in her voice too, a kind of bluff, a quaver.

She goes on: 'They had a whole lot to tell me, actually. About the exploits of my *step*brother. They said you've got the weirdest rep ever. For swallowing things. For money. They said you'll chew up and knock back almost anything for cash. They saw you doing it. You're like a freak in a ring somewhere. Taking bets.'

'Yeah. So?' She's toying, she's playing, he should tell her to rack off, but her sweet, sleazy voice gets him a hard one.

'So,' she blows out, 'don't you think a girl's got a right to know what's been in that mouth? Considering?'

He grunts, kicks at the drawer between her dangling sandals. Turn your back on the smart bitch, he thinks, shove her like you used to when you were kids. When things got solved by a Chinese burn or a horsebite. Sting her with a good game of slaps.

'I'm waiting.' She sing-songs it, light and nasty.

'I'd love to smack you one,' he says.

'You'd love to eat me, you mean. And I wouldn't even have to pay you.'

And there goes his tough stance, flattened. If there is a chance of her skin coming close enough to sniff, he's folding. He's in the bag.

'What do you want to know, then?'

'A goldfish? A butterfly? What the fuck else?'

'A pack of smokes. A can of cat food. Not much else.'

'Christ. Why the hell would you do that?'

'I don't know.'

'Well, neither do I. Jesus. That is *putrid*. That is just the sickest, *sickest* thing.'

He feels it then, standing in the kitchen, the memory of butterfly wings, a kind of spiny, flexing light in his mouth, a membrane rapid and delicate. Terrible watery twitches of tube and ribbon before his jaw can end it, before he can show round his gross metal grin to the crowd, lick it with victory. Everyone else looks queasier than he does: he jabs out his hand for the strips of cash.

'They do it on TV,' he manages.

'For like, fifty *thousand*. *Rancid*.'

'Get bent. I don't know why I smashed in here.'

'It's not like you need the money, even. You're the one with all of it now. She hasn't seen any of it yet, my mum. He owes Mum money. Big time. Oh yeah, didn't you know he's paid up piss all on the house you're living in. And she's been selling stuff, you know. Selling shit, even rings and old books Nana gave her. Stuff she cries over. Stuff she would've given to me. He's a bastard. He eats people up. That's what he eats. Chews them up, spits them out. Doesn't even taste us going down, doesn't even feel us hit the sides, his kids. Is that what you're learning? Is that what you're trying to prove?'

'Who the fuck knows?' is all he can croak out. He can't eyeball her, shuffles backward. 'You fucken tell me who knows. You fucken tell me who.'

He feels like he's going to cry, feels whole sobs backing up in his chest, great clouds of bawl. His Adam's apple sucks up and down in his neck, tries to push the howl back like a piston. He can taste salt. His eyes prickle but the skin on his tears holds tight.

And then he sees her nudge down from the bench. She doesn't move in that slutty way, sly, but gives the jump of a kid. It's cute. And when she gets close her drizzle of freckles is even cuter. She looks like she's only just noticed the blood, dips the pad of her finger into it.

Her bitching is over. Now she mutters, leaning into him, whispers things she'll let him do. But she makes them sound okay: she makes it sound like she thinks them, wants them too, his clumsy dreams, no longer dirty or bullying, but okay because she's greedy too. Her arms ply, her mouth fits, her pelvis grazes him. And oh, that apex of warm, hollowed out bone. Tell her it's love. Tell her it's no-joke big-deal love, too late and forever.

Tears go slack, come loose from his hot eyes.

She wipes them into a meek, nuzzling kiss.

It all speeds up, awkward, beautiful.

At the last minute she marks the way with two fingers split open, a long V, *fuck you* or *peace*. He slides—can't *believe* it— slides through the middle, and there's a cold silver ring on one finger that grazes his penis. There are ridges in there like the roof of his own mouth. That tighten as his cry jerks across it.

*

In the workshop, posters are stuck up with slanted scraps of tape, mostly women leaning on hoods toying with long, gleaming cylinders, nozzles of oil. When Jeremy hears the shout, he turns—there's a real young guy, a mechanic or something, up on a workbench kicking at tools, his overalls shucked to his waist. The sleeves are tied but not tight enough: his hips have started to slip through the dirty noose.

'Any of these get you hard, mate? You hear me?' He bangs his hand on the posters above his platform: there's a chick shackled in the biggest one, slippery yellow-skinned, wearing silver car-guts round the good bits. The car parts that cuff her are so clean they pick up the glint of want in her teeth, pure hate in her eye.

'One a these babies. You want one?' the guy says again. His fingers fan on the yellow abdomen, stroke it. Fresh grease shines on her; the poster gives a spasm.

'What'ya taking them down for?'

The guy looks down, shoves a couple of things with his boot, shafts and axles. 'You want the key for the shitter, mate? Come back and I'll give you the story. About to knock off.'

He jumps off the bench, pulls a key looped over a nail on the other wall.

'Here you go, bro.' He has an angled grin, fleshy in his soiled face. 'Go shake hands with the unemployed,' he says.

When Jeremy gets back, the guy is peeling the last of the smutty posters down. He rolls them, puts the funnel to his eye, makes the offer one last time. Jeremy, shy and grim in the guy's dirty scope, gives a scuff at the concrete in place of a headshake.

'Sure?'

'Nup.'

'Suit yourself.'

The mechanic sticks the posters into a crack in the giant metal bin, drives them down with a screech between chunks and coils. He struts to the edge of the shop, pulls the remains of his overalls down off his shorts, working himself up through them with butts and skips. His shorts are hacked-off jeans, already filthy.

'Sweet,' he breathes. 'I plan to get shit-faced. Wanna join me? Only got ten steps to go.'

'The pub?'

'Nah, the church, dopey.'

'You were gonna tell me. You know. Why you taken all the posters down.'

'Yeah, all right. Over a beer, but. Fucken depressing.'

The mechanic stuffs his gear into a washing machine, the basin chocker with other mulchy shapes. Jeremy stares: it's strange, homely, the way he shuffles the gear around in the drum for balance, drizzles long streams of white grain from the hand he holds high above the tub.

'Mate,' the mechanic says, bumping the lid down, snapping the black buttons. 'You all right?'

Jeremy gets out a nod. But he can feel the new bleed flex under his clothing, more of it than most days. He moves and the wound lets out a warm, heavy slurp. Back in the brick bog he's tried to keep the slices tidy, stared at the raised glass stars on the door, tried to nick himself in easy clusters, scratch the skin in parallels. But some kind of vertigo has hit him, over his own skin. He stares down, dazzled by the radii of cuts. His hand is an engine. He says, 'Daddy,' then drops the razor harder to try and cut himself clear of the word.

But it's the mechanic's voice now, loud and hollow in the present, in the black garage.

'Snap back, kid. You look a bloody world away.'

The mechanic lets out a jab-cross, knuckles lax and friendly, into Jeremy's ribs.

'Let's go get trolleyed, eh?'

Jeremy follows him.

Alongside him outside the workshop, Jeremy tries to copy his walk, its slouch and scuff. The lope is not easy, loose but with a threat somewhere in the muscle, a mark of how quick he could snap, strike, lunge into a fight. But he doesn't: he rocks to a halt outside the pub, grinning, his fists giving little pumps inside his pockets as he sways.

'Got any pingers, mate?'

Jeremy watches the guy, the sinew flickering in his arms and throat. The guy looks away, a rogue, cunning and lazy, rolls back and forth on his thick boots. He lets out a giggle, relaxed, looks back at Jeremy.

'Whatever, mate,' he says. 'Thought you could shout me in here, while I tell you the story. I'm skint, that's all. No biggy.'

Jeremy pats around in his pockets for cash. There's a few shrivelled notes, a couple of coins. He rakes it out with his fingers, awkward. The pack of razors flips out too.

Perhaps there is too much in the kid's face. Or a flinch, a wincing. He's too young to curb it. The mechanic is fast. He punches the kid away, playing, then weaves down and scrapes the pack up from the gravel. The razors lie, box open and wet, in his hand and he stares back at the boy.

'Mate,' he says.

For a few seconds Jeremy prides himself on saying nothing. Then he feels his body glide downward anyway, his head arriving at the end with a thud. Back in the toilets he couldn't cut deep enough: it was getting more and more like that these days, getting to the stage he'd need an artery, he'd need an amputation. But now, as the impact ploughs up the side of his head, the fix he couldn't cut to comes on. Finally. He must look gutless, lying down here like a little bitch, but he doesn't much care. He lies there, feeling the pressure released from his brain, as if a black balloon has popped.

*

Ruth does not look like her streak is switched on today. Her mean black eyes are not fizzing, her skin not blotched. She's not scrappy, not stirring things up, she doesn't look sneaky. She's sitting in the gravel, smudging her legs around. All loosey-goosey, like she's run out of trouble.

It makes Madeline feel a bit in charge. She tries to think good grown-up thoughts just like a mum. She wishes she had her nurse's equipment: the tubes you can switch on to hear a pretend heart bumping, the plastic needle that sucks up and down on pink syrup.

'Well, we need to get you cleaned up then. Don't we.'

She uses a there-there voice. It comes out ladylike, fake and sing-y: she's pleased with it. It makes her bold enough to pick up Ruth's hand, fiddle finger in through finger. She gets their little fists knitted up, bobs them up and down for comfort.

'Come on,' she says. 'Creek's down there. I can wash up your face. I'll be very gentle. Very extra.'

There is extra traffic now. The way they walk, the cars get thicker, louder. Some faces screw up in the car windows, wonder, even go a bit slow. But the two girls get to the creek, squat and then bum-heel down the bank. It's only a trickle, a drain, not really and truly a creek. Empty packets blob and crinkle there, dirty fish shifting with slimy whispers.

Madeline has seen a movie where a woman rips a hunk off her skirt to tie down the blood that's squirting off a cowboy. She tries. It doesn't work. Her mother sewed up the edges too good. So she gets Ruth to lie down right by the water, bunches her sundress and kneels beside her. She dips the skirt, first in the furry water, then dabs it on the face. She keeps it light, a drizzle, watching the pulp thin, become wings under it.

'Out of one to ten, how would you say your pain?' she questions in the sweet voice.

Ruth drops her head back and forth, grunts up at her.

'I heard a real nurse say that once. Once when the baby might not have got borned. Or got borned too quick and little, or somethink. You know, how the lambs in the next-door paddock come whooshing out too soon, when they're not supposed. Your dad had to take us in. Fast. It was night. I remember what the nurse sayed. But I don't remember my mum's number.'

Madeline lets the skirt paddle. It flowers, squirms: beads of green hair come loose from the stones as the skirt grows over them. Madeline's knees slip a little in the water-fuzz as she hunches, closer to the mouth.

'You got a number?'

'Ngub.'

'Nup.' Madeline looks back into the water, thinks a bit more about that night. The colour of her mother's neck, grinding and puffing above her fat body with the baby in. The balloon they blew up on her arm, like a floatie to help you pop up when you couldn't swim. But they only blew up one black ring, and Madeline pestered the nurse about it. *You need two to keep her up really*, she bugged her, but the nurse had shushed and steered her away. Madeline sat in the waiting room then, pushing the tangled toys round the basket. There was nothing whole to play with, just parts of things, sucked-on heads, and cracked-off wheels, a dog with its eyes chewed out and a caterpillar snapped down the middle of its plastic bubbles. Loads of stuff that was supposed to move by itself but didn't anymore, like the people in the beds. Then a priest had come in, and crouched by a woman, and told her that her husband was dead. He'd hunched down, guarding the words, made them low and private, like he could shut out the listening kid, but Madeline had stared back at him, watching his hands pat-pat the ugly old woman. Madeline liked to think of death, that the baby she didn't want might simply fall out—but she would have liked her mum to have two rings, so she could be certain her mum would bob up and stay splashing above the dead baby. With two blown-up rings she could just lie back, angel-shaped, while her belly emptied the baby and its pool.

'Nup, nup,' she chants again. She picks at her paper pinky ring then. She doesn't know why but she wants it off, rubs hard, turns its tape-shine into a dirt-red string. She shakes it into the creek, watches it turn, swing in the murk, drop softly.

'You want to go for a walk, now you're cleaned up?' she asks.

Ruth has pulled, curled herself up. She looks garden gnome-like, gross and perky. She's stopped trying to talk, but makes snot-coughs and burbles from the back of her throat.

The two girls skid up the bank, hook, slip, and roll themselves up to the darkening roadside.

They stand for a minute, unsure, thin. Loud stripes of white traffic pass them.

Then Madeline points. 'Down this way is where Damon told me those kids threw the rock down.'

She lets her foot stroke, stroke at the gravel. She shivers a little, feels the sound of the black grit flexing and mixing in her skin.

'You know? The ones that hit that lady and got put in jail. You want to go and see that?'

Ruth's throat snuffles, she swings at Barbie.

'Anyway, I don't reckon there is one,' Madeline says as they walk. 'You know. A pain number.'

*

'That hurt still?'

'Nup.'

'What about . . . when you're at it? Sticking yourself. That hurt?'

'Nup.'

'So you're one of them cutters?'

'It works.'

'How's that?'

'Dunno. Just does.'

'So does suicide, mate.'

'Fuck off.'

'Fuck nothing, you mongrel. I mopped you up. I'll dump you back there if you give me any shit, right?'

Jeremy stares at the young guy, harder. In patches it's a bit of a girl's face, close-up like this, but the rest is lean enough to make it to manhood. When he smiles there's a ditch right down the tough muscle of his cheek, a trench that grease has gotten into and deepened. But the cheekbone above is maybe too pretty for a bloke.

'So what's your story?' the mechanic says.

'There isn't one.'

'Fucking must be.'

'Nup.'

'Well I'd need a fucken good story to go carving myself up like the Sunday bloody roast.'

'Yeah, well. Your parent's splitting isn't a story anymore, is it? Not a big enough deal. To count.'

'Maybe.'

'Families are history.'

'You reckon.'

'You know any fucken long-term husbands and wives?'

'I actually do, mate.'

The mechanic squats down by Jeremy. The kid's leg was a sight; it knocked him, maybe not so much the gashing but the blood that got everywhere. But he feels better now he's got the kid back here to the workshop. To him it's a clanging black heaven of junk. It's paradise, it's shelter: he loves the shadows of lurking parts, loves just to hang out here handling the muzzles and casings. He drinks in the fume and glug of oils, loves his slithering hands as he works his fingers into barrel and chamber. He lives to hear it, the little click when he's jointed something, rod to breech. It kind of helped to look at the kid's leg like that, sheared wires, a leaky connection.

He says, 'You want to know why I was up there taking those posters down. I'll tell you, mate. The boss, out back here, couldn't cope with them up anymore. His wife just got out of surgery, you see. Had both of her breasts off. No shit, I mean they took both of the babies right off, as well as all the gland things that hang on and that. But doctors told him that's probably not going to be enough. They reckon it's shot all over the place, little pin-pricks of it, the cancer. So the last thing he can face seeing when he comes in here is these posters, he reckons. Says they're not just tits to him anymore. Ha.'

The mechanic gets up from his squat, stretches. Jeremy watches from the spot he's hunched in, a booth amongst the junk. There's a rail around the workshop bench and the guy spreads his hands

213

wide and hangs back from it, knees bent, like he's limbering up before a swim race. He levers his weight and scoots his hands in, claps hard, no grip for a second. Then he lunges, as if the floor's liquid and he's about to slash in backwards for butterfly stroke.

His grip hits the bar with a bang, last minute. The bench quakes. He laughs.

'Boss is always on at me to pack that in, too. Says I'll have the whole fucking thing down one day.'

He pushes off from the bench, stalks round, knocks some parts with a lonely shrug. A bolt takes off and rolls across the concrete with a dull jangle.

'Think they were primo myself, the posters. So were his wife's tits. Ha. But there you go. I suppose I can see his point. I dunno.' He looks at Jeremy. 'You see his point, kid?'

Jeremy looks down at his leg. Red is drooling all over the rag already, although the mechanic yanked it round tight. If he moves too suddenly he feels like he's travelling behind himself, dragged off-side, catching back up with his own whereabouts with a shudder. There's a cold spot of pure black waiting just out from his neck: he won't turn that way in case he drops into it.

'You think we should be getting you somewhere? Emergency or something?'

'Nup.'

The mechanic crouches again.

'The boss says his wife isn't coping with hospital. Just lies there and cries, he says. I was going to go in for a visit. She was pretty tidy. Before she got crook, you know, she wasn't so hard on the eyes. For an old chick. She's always been a bit of a sweetheart to me, actually. If she was a few years younger I'd have hooked right in. But the boss said, Don't bother going in to the hospital, said I wouldn't be able to take it. Probably right.'

He goes on, 'S'pose so, eh. If there's one place you want to keep out of it's a fucking depressing dump like that. While you got the choice, eh. While you're in one piece and got the choice.'

He licks the hard cracked pad of his thumb and stamps it on the concrete to dab up a thin metal shaving.

'Apart from this, mate,' he nods at Jeremy's leg, 'you stand a shot at staying in one piece.'

Jeremy doesn't speak until he's sure he can stay out the dead patch of cold by his throat. It's long as his own shadow now, an outline of frozen air hanging there like a body bag, and if he slips aside and fills it he doesn't think he'll get back out.

When he thinks it's safe and the workshop is still around him, he says, 'It's not the same way it was. It's not like . . . a choice now. It used to feel like choosing, like keeping . . . some kind of control on things. It did use to work. But it doesn't now. Not like it did.'

'Must be time to pack it up.'

'I tried. One time.'

He even tried to read up about it, like the A student they all thought he was. He got online and googled for cutting. *Tools commonly used*, it said: *Diamond blades, drill bits, fingernails, front teeth, broken glass.* He thought it sounded like poetry. Then he scrolled up and saw he'd hit the wrong page anyway. *Cutting is the separation of an object into two portions, through the application of force or stress*, it said. *It only occurs when the total stress generated exceeds the strength of the object cut.*

He'd wondered for a moment if that's what he was doing: it was like he couldn't see his parents, in two, apart, in his head, couldn't keep the idea, or the sight of them separate there, couldn't stand the thought of them in two places and bits. As far as he, his brain and his body, was concerned, he still looked at them as one thing that couldn't be split. Trying to see them in two was like trying to look at himself in halves, slit open.

Perhaps he was just trying to get that straight. He needed to face it, to get the fact of their separation, once and for all, *into* him. The force it took had to be *acutely directed*, the article said. That was the *simplest applicable equation*.

*

They dangle Barbie, just by her ice skates, upside down in between the bars of the bridge. There are not enough rocks: they must have gotten cleaned up after the bad kids biffed down the big chunk. After they swish off any little bitty stones they can find, Maddy takes the clips out of her hair and flings them up too. Going over, they swing and sparkle, zig-zag like butterflies. When they hit, in a series of pretty spatters, the wheels flick and suck them. The girls press their heads as far as they'll fit through the struts, stare down and watch them jump, shiny bugs, until they're crushed. Lastly Madeline slips her rings off, wiggling them up her chubby fingers. She counts some over into Ruth's blooded hand. Then they keep counting when they drop them. They both know they're wishing something they don't tell. They chant the numbers like a bad spell, baby voodoo. Some rings drip, some rush. It's not enough, just not. Damon, the pig, has always told Maddy she throws like a pussy little girl. But Madeline thinks that maybe her arm doesn't belong to a girl anymore. Really and truly, a girl's arm wouldn't ache so bad to have a rock in it.

Ruth is the same. Speckling her neck skin and up behind her black eyes, you can see the mean is switched back on again.

'You liked vat game,' she says. 'Ve one we played.'

Maddy's legs are thin enough to slip through the edge of the bridge. She skids her bottom in, threads through her legs and lets them sway, pretending they're ribbon or rope, playing dead or dolly. She looks at her knees, with their scrubbed white circles of skin, and doesn't answer.

Ruth, bigger, shuffles in, curling side-on. She scratches her face with a sleeve, a track of snotty-blood brushed up her cheek. Her grin glints with sorrow and pulp. She has no-good plans, but Maddy can tell she got them out of sadness. That's what sad can do, Maddy knows it now: mix with mean so you can't feel which is which. Ruth is like that black doll she sometimes brings on visits, those stitched-on fish in the shiny eyeballs which are meant to be tears but end up looking evil. Maddy's legs, poked through the bars, have gone so cold she can hardly feel them hanging, and Ruth snuggles close-in with her red face puffing. The thought of that flip-flop double-headed doll makes Maddy feel yuck.

'We could break her ub before we drob her. But maybe she drob bedder ad once,' Ruth says. She humps as much of her shoulder as she can get out over the drop.

Madeline reaches through to grip the other skate. Legs split wide, Barbie capsizes, faceless under her skirt. The bulk of her plastic hair hisses.

They miss, and she only bounces a bit, jiggles on the road. When a car hits her it doesn't even make a nice crack. Just a sort of crinkle.

It's disappointing, so disappointing. It makes Maddy feel a bit like crying, the sort of cry she gets shut in her room for at home, a non-stop stamping cry, coughing and squelchy. Until she sees Ruth put her fingers up, in through the dappled slime of her lips. The piece of tooth waves up and down for a little, then lifts away with the tiniest wet click. It's just a triangle but it glitters the brightest, and the car whose screen it taps on does give a small skidding twitch.

But no one notices them. That's what it's like for the grown-ups, Maddy decides. Little accidents, little hurts happen all the time, but no one notices them.

'We should go back. To the baby,' Madeline says, after they watch for a while. Her voice is so ladylike in the cooling air she can hardly believe her luck.

*

Damon scrapes out through the gate first, then grabs it to haul it open for Jody.

But Jody has dropped back, unmoving. Steps away, she's his stepsister again.

217

His grasp lets go. The pipe flaps away from his hand with a metallic twinge. He stares at her. All the angles of the way she stands—neck, hip, ankle—chill him, so he calls out nothing, just listens to the long fence hum. The aftertaste of wire replaces her along his skin.

'You think it's worth it?' she says. 'You think, what we've done is . . . worth? Them. Everything they've done. Cancels it. Would you . . . do anything for it? Actually forgive them? Like it could cancel out all this. Just.'

'I don't know.'

'Just.'

'Well, maybe.'

She's even more distant now, talking down at stones.

But she's also at the fence, hooks her fingers through it. Her voice is flat. He doesn't understand how her face can get so pale, pull away beneath its spatter of freckles like there's nothing going on under their dust.

He only says, 'Jody.'

'Mum's always begging down the phone to him. You know that? She still *begs*. I bet he laughs when he gets off the phone to her. That right? I bet he tells you all a joke about how pitiful she is. I wish I was there with you, listening to him crack his joke. That's how terrible being on her side, listening to her, is: I'd rather be there, with him, taking the piss. She thinks we don't hear her, whining on in her room. She snivels on forever. She breaks me up. I bet you all laugh, over there, in *her* house. I bet he hangs up on her, and tells you the story. Round the fucking dinner table, all of you, I bet he makes you laugh and laugh about how she still loves him. Sometimes when I hear her weeping that into the phone, *I love you, oh, but I still love you*, I just want to beat her with it. I want to take the phone and bash her face in.'

He looks at her. There's some pulse gunning in his head. Words jar his mouth, so he bites down, tries cutting through the struggle of them. Like clamping your jaw on the shiver of a butterfly: he's tempted to pull back his lips, show her what a mess he's making. What a mess he is. He wants to say something, no reason why, about last summer, last summer when she played at his place, when they were kids enough to still say *played* (*Hey, wanna play over at my place?* which was always okay because their mums were such good mates so the kids always thumped in and out each other's homes, groped under gladwrap in whichever fridge had the leftovers, slumped with their tangle of gaming wires on either couch), and he crawled underneath the trampoline (last summer, was it?) and lay spreadeagled, face-up, daring her, betting she couldn't make a jump so wild she'd actually hit him. And then he'd nearly shat himself watching the black mat strain and ricochet, hearing the springs churn, smelling the plasticised air puff at him as she drove it down with the bony missiles of her bare feet. Then she went for a spinal slam, hair thrashing and legs kicked up to reload with sky. Or she rolled and bellied it, and he lay freaked beneath the bang of her flat guts, the hard pegs of her elbows, knees, the dig of her small tits he couldn't close his eyes against. In between each launch towards him, she pedalled and boogied, scampering in light, chucking hair into the sky. When she slowed it was on her hips, her backside dabbing up and down towards him. Then she'd curled on her side, her hair in a flag so he couldn't see the face above him. 'You didn't move,' she whispered. So he'd reached up and tickled the shape in the hammock, half-play, half-gamble. She'd turned on her front, staring down through the black mesh and he'd moved on, breathing deeper, to make deeper stabs, then less deep. His dirty blunt fingers had crackled.

He wants to get his fist through the fence now, get to the freckles, wake her up under them. She's gotten buried in there. He needs to get his hands through, rock her face in them, shake the colour and sound of her back out.

It's not the face that had hovered above him that day (Why can't he say, just start, lost summer, last summer?), let him brush it through the dark elastic, dip his fingers into the black pool that stretched across the mouth, not the face that nuzzled the friction of his thumbnails. That day, that day, she'd hung there forever and sometimes she'd slid her face aside into the hood of her hair, hidden her breath in its scratchy static. But then his mum had wandered out back humping a basket of gear for the line, looked over and called out, *Stop that.* Jody had murmured down, *Don't, don't stop, Damon,* but his mum had snapped again, *Cut that out, cut that out right now, you two.* So he'd stopped and wormed himself out from under the tramp and gone over to help his mother. Because the shape of the baby was there in his mum, already, a delicate watery bump he'd seen her tying under her old wraparound. And he didn't know yet whose it was, just loved it, for some dumb reason, loved to think of its tiny little see-through limbs reaching out from its chrysalis body, to think of it somersaulting, slow motion, star-like there in the dim warm of his pretty mum.

'The only reason Dad really left us is because of that stupid baby,' Jody says. 'If it wasn't for your mum and her baby he wouldn't have gone. Not for good, anyway.'

It's all in the way she cuts off what she's said and sticks her fingers to the side of her head, as if she'd like to strike clean through there, make a stab in for the words, put a stop to the thoughts.

He says, 'You . . . '

'You don't know . . . '

'You think if you have a baby . . . '

'Don't . . . '

'He might come back home again.'

'I'm not her.'

'You think that might bring him back.'

'I'm not weak enough to want him back. I'm *not her.*'

The fence echoes, wiring the screech along its length.

'If I have a baby,' she finally says, 'and it's yours, then you'll be its uncle as well as its dad. That's choice, eh? That's priceless.

And what about the other baby? That'll be . . . I can't get my head around it. Some kind of double aunt?'

He finds himself staring at stones and thinking how it felt when his mother let him cup her stomach, the morning he found her in the bathroom when she was wrapping her old skirt around the baby's rise. She'd told him he could rest his hand there, wanting him to feel the quickening, the secret shiver. When he shook his head, she'd smiled at him and said, 'Oh, I wish you could. It feels just like a butterfly.'

He wants to be sick, and starts to do it. But as he bends he catches Jody's look. He turns, drinks the acid back down.

Across the carpark there is no one. No vehicles. No van, no car. Just marks where they were.

*

The baby cannot even count to ten.

Maddy, in the waiting room, kicks her legs from the big chair and practises counting from ten, down, backwards. Sometimes the backwardness gets so hard she has to blink her eyes up into red hearts and use her teeth to stop her tongue wriggling off without her. But she loves the inside out, falling-slowly sound of it. That's what it sounds like to her, as she listens. The words fall humming wrong-way-round out her head, through her speaking, and keep falling slow, slow. It is very bright in the waiting room, the whole square whited-out with buzzing tubes of brightness. But Maddy can almost see the numbers, splotches dropping all around the white air as she chants.

The baby cannot even count. Before they took Maddy out of its room, she saw that. That's what the machine said. Even with a big machine helping it, the baby is so dumb it can't count.

The nurse that brought Maddy in here can't count too. She said it would only be a little while, chatted cutely to Maddy for a bit, then parked her here beside the tubs of gluggy flowers and the toy basket. But the toys here are broken too, just like the box in the other hospital. 'They're all bust,' she told the nurse. But the nurse only chirped, 'Well, see what you can make from them then.' When she left, Maddy tipped up the whole bin and walked on them, feeling little snaps beneath her bare feet. Then she jumped on the big chair and see-sawed, swinging her feet so the sting of meanness trickled up and down.

Maggot toys, noisy and bust, like the sheep. Sucky dog-got toys. Can't move, like the people. All the people, too dumb to count backwards out their tip-top rooms. Their buzzy white rooms, waiting, waiting, for someone to stab air in.

They've all gone off to other rooms: her mum with the baby, Ruth's mum with Ruth, and Damon with the mechanic who helped to drive them here. Everyone has gone off, to get the broke bits fixed up. But Maddy doesn't care. And ha ha, to Ruth's dad, anyway, ha ha to him, so there, running in like he did, with a face like when she showed him round the next door's paddock, with the sheep-the-dog-got-to lying everywhere, so he didn't know which noisy one to go to first. He doesn't know which one to go to here, either. He doesn't know which room comes first. Ha ha to him. She doesn't care. The nurse said, 'What's your name then, little girl?' and she said, 'Maddy' but it came out inside-backwards, mean plus sad, meany, saddy equals Maddy. She doesn't care. She can count. She hopes the priest is coming.

She is going to tell the priest that she found the pain number. The way she did it was to screw up her eyes till red spun. The way she did it was to turn her mind inside out and push the numbers through her red tears like black fish, little black fish swimming backwards, backwards, into the zero of real pain which is also, always, a pool of cracked toys, hearts, worms, where tied-up flowers drink the dirty waiting room light.

And it's only there she'll ever remember her hand on the window. Backwards. Forwards. Tipping in, or out, the longest drink of air.

*

The mechanic hangs out. He's into the machines in Jeremy's room. Scuffs round, checking them, while Jeremy's getting seen to. Wouldn't mind having them to bits, when the nurse's back is turned, taking a crack at their workings. One of them, clipped onto the kid's finger, goes on the blink.

'Oh, near enough,' tuts the nurse. She charts the reading anyway, gives the mechanic a grin, sideways. Strokes of fresh lippy nicked and shiny on a cream front tooth. Come to think of it, he wouldn't mind a quick crack at her. Not too shabby.

'Not going to tell me off, are you?' she smirks.

'Not even if he carks it.' The mechanic's got a rude-as look on his mug, big front teeth in his pretty bottom lip, eyebrows flashing, hunched. Jeremy starts to cry.

'Oh, mate. Mate. Get a grip. Not like I'd *mean* it.'

The nurse scrunches a laugh through her nose, trades a grin with the kid too, unwinds a bit of tubing, gives his collarbone a coy pat-pat. 'Come on. You're not critical, sweetie.'

'Wouldn't a been funny if you weren't well out the worst, now, would it?'

The kid shakes his head, but the whole thing's full of tears, loaded with them. Heavy, chocker tears, pulling down his eyeballs, sucking them back into his big wet baby skull. *What colour are your eyes, Jeremy, sooka-bubba red?* Tears go on crowding his mouth.

'It . . . hurts,' he manages.

'So you wanna avoid it in the future then, eh? Genius.'

From the door, the nurse leans back for a second. 'Doc'll be in for the stitch-up in a bit. It *will* hurt. But I've got a good one for pain,' she says. 'You want to get your mate here to sit, and just tap your head. All it takes. Just a little tap. You wait. Make's all the difference.'

'Yeah, cheers. Good one. Tapping his head. Fuck me,' blurts

223

the mechanic, rubbing his own head, pop-eyed, cheeky. 'You're a legend.'

But when the doctor gloves up, gets busy, he sees the point to it, mounts a boot solid as he can on the wonky plastic chair, crouches up by the kid.

Jeremy feels the finger come down—drip, thud—into bony sweat. Rough-cut, soft, it drops, levers, drops. Into memory, somehow, too, like the clocking sound is in a backyard somewhere, kids snuck out into scraps of daylight saved up after chugging down dinner, *You've got five minutes, and counting, before bed all you kids*, chucking round a ball through the muffle of far-off traffic, sparrow and sitcom song, the sloppy soak and sink clack of dish-time, baths sloshing with bubbly toddlers, and Dad on his first beer-and-smoke maybe wandering out sometimes for a quick round of lazy perfect lobs, one-handed, the hefty curve of muscle on his forearm, hardly bothered but beautiful, beautiful, thick with promise, the pitch loose, tall, smoothly sloping through the air, thrown so gentle, familiar, strong, on target. At you.

The author gratefully acknowledges the assistance of Creative New Zealand for the award of the 2010 Louis Johnson New Writer's Bursary. Thanks are also due to the editors of the journals and anthologies where some of these stories have previously appeared.

The novella *The Longest Drink in Town* was released by Pania Press in 2015; 'scenes of a long-term nature' won the international Bridport Short Story Prize 2014 and was published in *The Bridport Anthology 2014*; '.22' appeared in *JAAM 33* and 'local sluts in your area' in *JAAM 32*; '50 ways to meet your lover' appeared in *Sport 43*; '7 images you can't use' was published in *The Harlequin*; 'the wait' was published in *Landfall 227* and 'leaving the body' appeared in *Landfall 226* after being shortlisted for the *Sunday Star-Times* Short Story Competition; 'note left on a window' was published in *The Six Pack Two* after winning a New Zealand Book Month Award, and was also selected for *The Penguin Book of Contemporary New Zealand Short Stories*; 'the names in the garden' appeared in *takahē 81*; 'how to leave your family' was published in the anthologies *Orange Roughy* and *Milk & Ink*; 'consent' was published in *Landfall 214* and also selected for *Some Other Country: New Zealand's Best Short Stories*; and 'short for the sea' was the featured fiction in *takahē 69*.